ONCE UPON A ZOMBIE

BOOK ONE: THE COLOR OF FEAR

BILLY PHILLIPS
&
JENNY NISSENSON

Praise for Once Upon a Zombie

"A gripping and involving story . . . This wise and witty take on a famous classic will delight both zombie fans and lovers of Lewis Carroll's imagination and humor."

—Jenny Woolf, author of *The Mystery of Lewis Carroll*

". . . a compassionate and humorous novel . . . written with gusto and sensitivity . . ."

—Jack Zipes, Professor of Comparative Literature Guggenheim and Fulbright Fellow

". . . an intriguing and original story, and one that's bound to appeal to fans of popular fairytale characters. There's a lot to like here: a modern, fun, and engaging voice . . ."

—Children's Book Review

ONCE UPON A ZOMBIE

BOOK ONE: THE COLOR OF FEAR

BILLY PHILLIPS
&
JENNY NISSENSON

THE TOON STUDIO PRESS

Beverly Hills

THE TOON STUDIO PRESS
Beverly Hills, CA

No part of this publication may be reproduced, or stored in a retrieval system, or transmitted in any form or by any means, electronic, mechanical,
photocopying, recording, or otherwise, without written permission of the
publisher. For information regarding permissions, write to Toon Studio
Publishing, Attention: Permissions Department, 141 S. La Peer, Beverly
Hills, CA 90211

"She's Not There" by Rod Argent, by permission of Marquis Music Co. Ltd.

Cover design by Hyun Min Lee, Hl Design
Book interior by Morgana Gallaway

This book is a work of fiction. Names, characters, places, and incidents
either are products of the authors' imagination or are used fictitiously.
Any resemblance to actual events or locales or persons, living or dead, is
entirely coincidental.

For Marianne

ACKNOWLEDGEMENT

Special acknowledgment to Michael Tabb who gave me the inspiration to finally write my first book of fiction. Michael, thanks for your generous spirit, integrity, and love of craft which deeply inspired me, and for suggesting that I set this first book in Wonderland with two sisters in the "starring" role! You are an immense talent with an immense heart along with a magnetic personality to match! Thank you!

Land of Oz

Neverland

Enchanted Forest

Wonderland

Zeno's Forest

Camelot

THE KINGDOMS

The following story is based upon actual

fictitious events that took place in

various graveyards around the world.

PROLOGUE

SIGHTINGS!

THE FIRST SIGHTING TOOK PLACE AT THE KIRRIEMUIR CEMETERY IN Angus, Scotland, on an otherwise unremarkable Tuesday evening.

A second sighting occurred about two weeks later, on the other side of the Atlantic—in Glendale, California, at the Forest Lawn Cemetery.

Only a few days later, a third sighting was reported at a graveyard in Berlin, Germany.

The sightings were reported on Twitter and Facebook by various witnesses who warned of peculiar occurrences taking place in their local graveyards. Some reports concerned mysterious lights seeping out of graves. Others involved an actual moving body.

Immediately following the fourth sighting—only forty-eight hours after the third—video footage began showing up on YouTube.

This was also the first time the word *zombie* was used. Apparently one of the dead and buried had become undead and unburied at the Cemetery of the Holy Doors in Florence, Italy.

The video, though dark and shaky, showed what appeared to be a body climbing up out of a gravesite and moving about the headstones by the pale light of the moon.

Most people figured the sightings were pranks. Especially when a groundskeeper at one of the graveyards reported finding clusters of what appeared to be some type of exotic chickpeas scattered on the lawns.

A few small, local newspapers, however, did report that some local cemeteries where sightings had occurred were beefing up their security.

The sightings began to gain traction when unexplainable-news.com picked up the story. Readers were intrigued.

But not one of these reporters or any one of the website's readers had figured out that these bizarre events were not happening in arbitrary cities or at random graveyards.

A definite pattern was forming.

There was one individual, though, who was following the goings-on with compelling curiosity. One person knew exactly what was happening.

And why.

Should you Google the Kirriemuir Cemetery in Scotland and should you dig deep enough to discover the identities of the souls resting there, you'd find that J. M. Barrie, the famous writer of *Peter Pan*, is coffined and consigned to that old graveyard on a hill.

The burial ground in Berlin—the St. Matthäus Kirchhof Cemetery—happens to be the resting place of the Brothers Grimm. And Forest Lawn Cemetery in sunny Glendale, California, is the eternal home to L. Frank Baum, author of *The Wonderful Wizard of Oz*. The Gothic-style Cemetery of the Holy Doors in Florence, Italy, is the keeper of the bones of Carlo Collodi, the man who brought Pinocchio to life well over a century ago.

Most kids—and most adults, for that matter—associate these writers with enchanting stories of princes and princesses, puppets and pirates, and fairies and godmothers. Most don't know that these revered authors also spun bloodcurdling tales about ghouls and ghosts and witches and phantoms and a whole other world that lies beyond the grave!

This brings us back to our most unusual and anonymous friend, who clearly sees and understands the terrible danger that lurks in extraordinary places unseen by the human eye, a danger that was prompting the living dead to rise up from the grave in search of the one person who just might be able to prevent the unthinkable.

Our friend is also looking for this one person right now, at this very moment.

She comes in colors everywhere;
She combs her hair
She's like a rainbow

—"She's a Rainbow," The Rolling Stones

CHAPTER ONE

CAITLIN FLETCHER WENT NUMB WITH FEAR WHEN HER NEXT BREATH didn't come.

I'm not breathing!

Her muscles went taut, like a tightrope.

She couldn't catch a lungful of air *automatically*, like normal people do.

She had to *think* about it.

She had to *consciously* inhale and *willfully* exhale because her body was no longer breathing on its own. It was as if someone had jabbed a long needle through the wall of her chest and shot her lungs up with Novocain, paralyzing them. Or the part of her brain that regulated involuntary breathing had been switched off.

She began obsessively picking at a fingernail until it bled.

Her legs trembled.

What if I forget to breathe?

She started breathing faster and faster. Soon she was sucking air like a vacuum cleaner.

She became light-headed. The room spun. Brutal panic set in. She was wild-eyed. Manic. Verging on a total freak-out.

Caitlin Fletcher then dumped the contents of her brown paper lunch bag onto the dresser in her bedroom.

Container with scoop of tuna on a bed of lettuce. Bunch of red grapes. Apple-pumpkin muffin. Skittles. Energy bar. More Skittles.

She placed the empty bag securely over her mouth and nose.

And she breathed.

Inhale.

Exhale.

The paper bag was supposed to relieve these wretched, god-awful symptoms, at least according to Google.

Inhale.

Exhale.

Her heart rate had to be clocking 120.

Inhale.

Exhale.

And then—

Caitlin was so involved with her bag, breathing, and beating heart that she failed to notice that her eleven-year-old sister, Natalie, had just wandered into the bedroom. Natalie calmly and casually climbed out onto the tenth-story window ledge of their new split-level London flat on Royal Street.

Inhale.

Exhale.

Caitlin caught a glimpse of herself in the mirror. She was mortified. Staring back was one fourteen-year-old, inflated-brown-bag-wearing girl with thick, black-rimmed glasses and a tumble of waist-long, cinnamon-colored hair—though the hair was actually quite lovely.

Suddenly the whole episode seemed totally ridiculous to her.

Then again, when you're reasonably certain you're dying—or worse, going crazy—you're no longer concerned how blatantly absurd you might look. You'll do anything to free yourself from irrational, indefinable, and suffocating fear.

Caitlin slowly lowered the bag from her face.

The bouts of oxygen deprivation had gotten worse lately.

Some were even as bad as that very first one, the *incident*, which she loathed remembering.

She knew her current crisis had triggered this latest attack. She was having major anxiety over the possibility of having major anxiety. All because of—

The masquerade ball.

Tonight.

On Halloween.

At her brand-new, hoity-toity high school.

In a new country.

On her birthday.

My birthday!

The Kingshire American School in London was supposed to put on the most "epic" event of the entire school year; the annual All Hallows Eve Masquerade Ball. Each year, loads of kids from other schools tried to crash this fabled bash.

Some tried making fake IDs to sneak in. Others tried to bribe their way in. She had heard that last year, a few kids traveled all the way from Manchester and offered the bouncer at the entrance fifty pounds to let them pass. But the bouncer was seventy-three-year-old Mrs. Sliwinski, the social studies teacher. She refused the payoff and gave those bribers the swift boot.

Caitlin had a hunch about why the masquerade ball was so popular: for one magical night of the year, kids didn't have to be something they downright disliked.

Themselves.

They were free to be someone else, which is what most of them secretly longed for every day.

For Caitlin, thoughts of attending the major happening—or worse, *not* attending—had flat-out overwhelmed her.

Dodge the masquerade ball?

She'd blow a grand opportunity to make new friends at the biggest social event of the year. It would be doubly hard to break into any of those cliques that had been forming since the start of the school year. The uppity kids at Kingshire might label her a loner, a loser, and a liability. No one remotely normal or cool or popular would consider befriending her. She hadn't been any of those things at her old school.

Attend the ball?

Difficulty breathing. Potential panic. Or worse: a strong compulsion to flee a crowded auditorium.

No. Caitlin couldn't risk it. Not after what had happened at the last Halloween dance she had attended. Too painful.

Thoroughly humiliating. She had hoped all that panic stuff would've disappeared once she, her father, and her sister moved to London from New York.

It hadn't.

And then there was her absolute most dreadful fear. The very reason why she was ready to ditch the ball, ruin her social life, and wreck her reputation at her new school.

Dancing.

Inhale.

Exhale.

There was just no way Caitlin could or would dance in front of other human beings. Never. Ever. Not after the *incident.*

And because she was also the new kid at Kingshire, it would guarantee curious stares at the very least. How could she possibly dance and enjoy it while imagining everyone gawking at her, judging her looks, scrutinizing her dance moves, and critiquing her rhythm and coordination? A thousand probing eyes crawling over her body like buzzing beetles? Ugh!

At her old school, no one focused that degree of unwelcome attention upon her. All the kids had known one another since childhood. They'd played tag on the playground during elementary school. Then they'd spun bottles, binged on frozen yogurt and went to movies together through middle school. But here she was enrolled in a brand-new high school where she didn't know a single soul.

And suppose she did show up but turned down any requests she got to dance? By the next morning, she'd be christened the official wallflower of Kingshire. By lunch, she'd be cast out and consigned to a corner of the cafeteria to eat her lunch solo for all eternity.

And that was the best-case scenario. Suppose no one asked her to dance? Or, worse, she had no one to talk to and couldn't think of a way to join a conversation? Oh God. She imagined standing all alone at a school dance, looking awkward, feeling like a misfit and being forced to fake texting on her phone so she wouldn't look like the lonesome loser of London.

Caitlin was totally conflicted. These were uncharted waters for her. She had been well known and well respected at her old school. It was publicly funded, so most kids didn't really care what your dad did for a living.

The Kingshire American School in London, on the other hand, was privately funded by benefactors such as the Sullivan Family. They were in investment banking. Other bigwigs and dignitaries from the US and abroad, who preferred an American curriculum, sentenced their kids to Kingshire. Rock stars too. And famous athletes. Even Brits grooming their sons and daughters to become international citizens of the world enrolled their kids here.

When Caitlin's dad had requested a temporary transfer to the UK, his company agreed to cover the costs for Kingshire so that his children's US education wouldn't be interrupted.

Ya, right. History class would continue uninterrupted while Caitlin's social life would suffer a severely spasmodic disruption. She and her superclose friends back home were always secure enough to dress themselves in whatever fashions they wanted. There had been no stress over worrying about whether the wrong outfit or fashion label would make you feel unbearably out of place—or get you shunned at school.

When you walked the hallways at Kingshire, eyes skimmed over you like bar-code scanners at Macy's or Harrods, calculating the cost of your outfit.

That's because the kids judged you according to the three Ls:

Label.

Looks.

Legacy.

If your clothes bore the right label, if you were considered attractive, or if you had the right last name, you were accepted by the popular cliques.

Imagine if a new American kid with an ordinary last name, average looks, and a mid-priced wardrobe had a panic attack at the prestigious London school?

There were no viable alternatives here. No options. No escape. *No oxygen.*

Caitlin's thoughts were interrupted by a cry from the window.

"Bird turd!" exclaimed Natalie. Caitlin turned to see her kid sister climbing in through the open window with a camera in her hand.

What the—?

Caitlin pulled the bag from her face and stared wide-eyed at Natalie, who was hopping down from the windowsill. She started wiping globs of green goo from her hair with a damp towel she grabbed from the back of her desk chair.

Natalie's dangerous stunt made Caitlin forget all about her own panic.

"What in the world were you doing out there?" she hollered.

"A pigeon just guanoed on my head."

 Caitlin's forehead crinkled. "Guano?"

"Bird droppings. You know . . . poop!" Natalie stood in front of the window, her mountainous spray of red hair backlit by the spill of daylight.

"Dad would kill me if he knew I'd just let you do that."

Natalie plopped down on the chair and rested her feet on the desk. "Don't be such a wuss. I was taking pictures and investigating. Chill, first-born sister. Where's your sense of adventure?"

Caitlin sniffed. Attending a school dance at a school like Kingshire was, for her, an extreme sport.

"I'm totally adventurous."

"Uh-huh," Natalie muttered, eyeing the paper bag in Caitlin's hand.

Caitlin dropped it and hoofed it under the bed.

"What's up with you?" Natalie asked as she got up to get her backpack from the closet. "You look excessively morbid this morning."

Caitlin exhaled a breath full of despair. "I have some issues."

"I've been telling you that for years!"

Caitlin glowered. She didn't care if the teachers called Natalie "gifted," or if the psychologists declared her a "prodigy" in various academic fields—science among them. To Caitlin, she would always be her overbearing, bigmouthed baby sister.

"That's why I never tell you anything personal," Caitlin said. "You have zero sensitivity."

Natalie slid her camera into her backpack and then hopped onto her bed and began jumping up and down. She moved nimbly, like a gymnast.

"Forgive me, sweetest. I was trying to lighten things up. Go ahead. Vent. I'll be sensitive."

Caitlin was uncomfortable baring her soul, even to Girl Wonder. If Caitlin chose to skip the dance, though, she didn't want Natalie probing for details as to why. She decided to dish out just enough information to throw her off the scent.

"The problem is my social life," Caitlin said.

"You don't have one."

Caitlin shot devil eyes at Natalie, who winced.

"Oops. Severe lapse of sensitivity. My bad. Go on."

Caitlin crossed her arms. "Too late, twerp. For once you tell *me* something."

"Like what?"

"Like that scatterbrained stunt you just pulled—what were you investigating out on the window ledge?"

Natalie's eyes narrowed. "Not sure you'll wanna hear this."

Caitlin rolled her eyes. "Gimme a break."

Natalie stopped jumping. She sat down on the edge of the bed, looking unusually serious. "I woke up in the middle of the night last night. Thought I saw something or someone at the window."

Caitlin blinked and laughed. "On our tenth-story ledge? You were dreaming again."

"That's what I thought. But it's happened before."

Caitlin swallowed. She brushed the hair away from her eyes. "When?"

"Right after we moved here. Night before we started school."

"Why didn't you tell anyone?"

"Like *you* said, I thought I was dreaming or maybe groggy from jet lag. This morning I finally decided to check it out." She slid her hand in her pocket. "I found these." She pulled out her hand and opened her palm.

Caitlin's brow furrowed. "What are they?"

"A peculiar type of domesticated *Cicer arietinum*."

"English, brainiac."

"Chickpeas, aka garbanzo beans."

"Garbanzo beans?" Caitlin laughed. "Who cares? They probably fell off a tree."

Natalie rolled her eyes. "Who cares? *Who cares?* Garbanzo beans grow on bushes in Bombay, not elm trees in central London. Ergo, someone had to have put them there."

"Yeah, the wind. Stop creating drama where it doesn't exist."

"Excuse me? You're the one planning to skip the masquerade ball over some irrepressible drama of your own making."

How did she know that?

"How did you know that?"

Natalie smiled wryly. "I didn't."

Conniving brat!

Caitlin had to think fast. "I can't go. I have an article to write."

She wasn't lying.

"Really? For what?"

"Unexplainablenews.com." Also totally true. And Caitlin was truly looking forward to it. She loved writing. And a popular post could win her some fans online and some fame at Kingshire. Most kids loved that pseudo-news site with all of its arcane articles and bizarre, improbable news stories. Even big-brain Natalie read it.

Natalie took the bait. "What inexplicable story will you be reporting on?"

Caitlin exaggerated a shrug. "That's my problem. Don't have one yet. And I'm supposed to submit the article tomorrow." Partly true. Caitlin was in search of a story, but there was no deadline. She sighed. "Guess I'll have to stay home tonight and write."

Natalie folded her arms. "Bollocks. You're too scared to go."

Caitlin's back went straight. "Such a pie hole you have! Two months in London and you talk like a soccer player."

"You mean *football*. You're in the UK. But smooth misdirect."

"You're a freak of nature."

"And you're demonstrating signs of social anxiety."

Before Caitlin could respond, Natalie continued. "If you're too freaked out to go alone, ask that boy Jack to take you."

That boy Jack. If only.

"That boy Jack" was the ridiculously cute guy in her freshman English Lit class. All the girls shamelessly gawked at him instead of paying attention to Professor Jenkins—not that the professor was some rad, charismatic dude deserving of their attention. But even if, say, Brad Pitt were the substitute teacher for the day, Jack would've given him a run for his money when it came to igniting ogles and giggles from teenage girls.

This was Jack's first year at Kingshire too.

And though Jack was certainly hot, it wasn't the superficial, pop-idol kind of hot. Totally not. Jack had a homespun wholesomeness about him. And a ruggedness. And green eyes and wavy, ash-brown hair. He always looked as if he'd just returned from some uncleared forest after a long day of chopping down pines, shirtless and copper-toned under a mid-August sun. Somehow, inexplicably, Jack maintained that copper tan in overcast London.

Stardom had found "that boy Jack" on his very first day of school. It started when someone screamed, "Fight!" and a swarm of kids congregated in the commons.

Barton Sullivan—a ginormous senior and majorly buff rugby player—started flicking the glasses off poor Erwin Spencer, over and over, just because Erwin was a freshman and a bona fide nerd. Truth be told, most girls thought Barton to be kinda cute and charismatic. But he could also be an ignorant bully on some days. This was one of those days. Derisive comments and cackling from the crowd of onlookers only added to the cruelty.

High school could be so medieval.

Jack happened to enter the yard after Erwin had picked his glasses up off the ground for about the three hundredth time. Amid all the catcalls and laughter, Jack ran over and literally stepped in between Erwin and Sullivan. The hush that fell over Kingshire's schoolyard was deafening.

Big, bad, buff Barton stood there in the silence of the yard and smirked. He towered over Jack.

He cracked his knuckles.

"Lemme see what ya got, ya daft twit," Barton said. He was expecting Jack to cower, like Erwin Spencer had, because Barton Sullivan's family was one of the major benefactors of Kingshire. Because Barton Sullivan had earned his reputation as the toughest senior in *any* London high school—and he was a rugby star to boot.

Not on that day!

Before the brute's next breath, Jack belted Barton on the beak with a clenched fist.

Then Jack handed the brute some tissues to plug the nosebleed.

Then Jack requested an apology.

Barton closed his gaping mouth just long enough to wipe his bloodied nose with one hand and shake Jack's hand with his other. Barton wasn't stupid. Beating up someone that was acknowledged as consummately cool by the entire school wouldn't win him any favor with the kids at Kingshire.

"No hard feelings, mate," responded Barton.

He gave Jack a ticket to a rugby game and almost immediately, they became best buds. They had forged a deep friendship over the past two months. Barton Sullivan totally respected and appreciated Jack, almost like a brother. And he never bullied another nerd again.

Erwin Spencer even began hanging out with them. How

crazy was that? Barton Sullivan consorting with Jack and Erwin Spencer.

And that right there is what made Jack so special. Even though he was considered one of the hipper kids at Kingshire, he wasn't afraid to hang with dorks, mess with misfits, or defend nerds from creeps who bullied nerds. He easily navigated through all the various cliques at Kingshire by bridging opposite worlds. How? Simply by being nice to everyone.

That's probably why he befriended me. It couldn't be because he thinks I'm pretty.

Caitlin didn't want to risk their friendship by making Jack think she might be crushing on him. And she could never dance in front of him anyway. He was a human. Besides . . .

"Girls don't ask boys to masquerade balls," she said to Natalie.

"In this millennium they do," Natalie responded. "Generation Z."

Caitlin crossed her eyes. "Ugh. What planet are you from?"

"See . . . *not* adventurous."

Before Caitlin could stop her, Natalie climbed back out the window into the early-morning light and snapped more photos from the ledge.

"Get back in here, now!" Caitlin screamed.

Natalie smirked while shutting the window from the outside so Caitlin couldn't grab her. Then she snapped a photo of her through the glass.

Caitlin's dad, Harold Fletcher, hollered from downstairs. "Girls, you'll be late for school."

Caitlin darted to the window and shoved it open.

"Get in now or I'm telling."

Natalie was white as a ghost. Spooked.

"What is it?" Caitlin asked.

Natalie didn't answer. She climbed back into the bedroom as if in a daze.

"C'mon," Caitlin snapped, swinging her backpack over one shoulder. "I don't wanna be late."

As she exited her room, Caitlin stole a glance at each of the four corners of her bedroom's ceiling and counted.

One, two, three, four.

She admitted to herself that it was a totally dumb habit. But if she didn't do it, she'd obsess about not having done it all day long.

And today Caitlin couldn't afford that.

She had to resolve her no-win situation by sundown. Otherwise the next twenty-four hours, which included her birthday and Halloween, would wind up being the absolute worst day of her existence on planet Earth.

Caitlin made it down the hallway and stairs before she noticed that Natalie still seemed freaked out. She stopped and tugged her sister's shoulder.

"What *is* it?"

Natalie tilted the back of her camera toward Caitlin. "Look."

Caitlin looked at the small LCD screen. It showed a close-up of her bedroom windowpane.

A helpless, hunted look crossed Caitlin's face.

Thick fingerprints were impressed on the glass. Somehow, someone had placed those strange-looking chickpeas on her tenth-story ledge. Directly outside her bedroom. Only an arm's distance from her.

Inhale.

Exhale.

CHAPTER TWO

CAITLIN AMBLED OUT OF ENGLISH LIT CLASS, HER MIND OCCUPIED with fetching the gluten-free, sugar-free, wheat-free energy bar sitting in her locker.

She pulled out her phone and began typing an e-mail while trying to navigate past the swarm of students milling around and lumbering along the hallways. Caitlin had spoken to her dad prior to English Lit. Told him about the fingerprints. He figured window washers on scaffolding had probably scaled their apartment complex to clean the exterior windows. Perhaps they did a shoddy job on Caitlin's.

Caitlin was composing an email to the property management company. She asked about the last time the windows had been washed. In all likelihood—

Then Caitlin saw them.

Them!

Piper, Paige, and Layla. The worst clique of elitist stuck-ups at her new school.

Layla had an envious mane of thick, black curls, serviced by a jewel-encrusted headband. Stick-thin Paige wore an outfit that looked so expensive it just might as well have been made of euros. And the alpha female, Piper, with her Brazilian blowout blonde hairstyle, looked like she belonged on the *Real Housewives of Rio de Janeiro*. Her laser-whitened teeth were so bright that Caitlin expected moths to appear whenever she smiled. Caitlin was positive Piper had a cauldron somewhere.

These girls were toxic. And they were in Caitlin's direct line of sight.

The energy bar would have to wait.

Caitlin had almost had a socially fatal run-in with them the first week of school. She had been in the third-floor bathroom, in one of the stalls when she overheard Piper and her friends harassing Alicia Saunders. Sweet Alicia Saunders, never did anything mean to anybody. And what had Alicia done wrong? Apparently Alicia Saunders wasn't skinny enough for Piper and her coven. They brought poor Alicia to tears, berating her over her eating habits and severe lack of fashion sense. Piper bluntly told Alicia to stay away from baggy clothes and bold patterns, and to go heavy on black spandex and polyester. She suggested calorie counting and then listed places to shop for plus-size apparel.

Alicia was humiliated.

Some girls just thrive on hating.

Caitlin had planned to exit the stall and confront them, but suddenly she felt a bit light-headed. Perhaps a touch of the flu.

Or maybe it was period cramps. She remained in the stall till Piper, Paige, and Layla left.

Now here they were again. Owning the hallway. Flirting with some boy.

Wait! Some boy?

Some Boy was Jack.

Caitlin's face flushed. She spun and started walking in the other direction.

"Caitlin! Where you going?"

She froze.

The voice belonged to *Some Boy*.

She glanced back as casually as she could manage. Jack was waving her over.

"Caitlin, you need to hear this!" he said.

She swallowed, trying to dissipate her unease. Then she walked toward Jack as confidently as she could while the Kingshire coven perched themselves around him.

"Hey, Jack," Caitlin said. She nodded to the three girls, trying to make eye contact, though she found herself distracted by the light reflecting off their highly glossed lips. "Do you know Piper, Paige, and Layla?" he asked.

The girls nodded at her with cold eyes and pinched lips.

Caitlin offered a friendly smile. "Hi. We haven't met, but I've seen you around."

Girls like these made Caitlin feel like an empty carton of milk, ready to be tossed in the trash.

Piper was gawking at Caitlin's T-shirt with disdain. Without thinking, Caitlin glanced down. It depicted a vintage rendition of Cinderella, flouncing in front of a castle. Her mom had bought it for her when they'd visited the Brothers Grimm Amusement Park in Windsor, Berkshire . . . when Caitlin was seven. The shirt had fit her like a nightgown back then; now she filled it out quite nicely. Or so she thought.

Caitlin often relived that family vacation. It was a welcome reminder of happier times. Times before her mom, Evelyn Fletcher, had gone missing four years ago, on one of their annual visits to London to see her mom's British family.

"Did you hear about these strange sightings at the cemeteries?" Jack asked. "I was just telling the girls about it."

Caitlin nonchalantly wiped away the moisture forming on the rim of her nose. "What sightings?"

"Spirits of some sort. Or ghouls, supposedly roaming about graveyards," Jack replied. "In different countries in Europe, and across the pond as well. At first it sounded a bit dodgy. But then I thought it might make a wickedly cool article for you. For unexplainablenews.com."

Piper snickered. "You write for *that* website?" she asked in a tone peppered with scorn.

Jack's head tilted to one side as he replied. "I fancy that site."

Piper swallowed. Her scheming eyes lit up. "Hey, Jack, why don't we go ghoul hunting tonight at some old graveyard?"

She's bluffing. Just imagine her, in designer duds, traipsing through a cemetery after dark, thought Caitlin.

"What about the masquerade ball?" Jack replied.

Piper faked a clumsy laugh. "Oops. Almost forgot."

This girl is astronomically obnoxious.

Jack smiled. "So, who are you girls going to the ball with?"

"Layla and Paige are going with the Banister twins, Alfie and Piers," Piper answered.

Apparently Piper is their mouthpiece.

Her playful eyes glimmered seductively. "But *I* haven't decided yet," she added. "How about you, J? Who are you taking?"

J?

Is she serious? She's on a first-initial basis with Jack now?

"Actually, no one," Jack replied. "I prefer going solo to these kinds of things. Then I'm free to chat and dance with anyone I'd like."

Piper raised an eyebrow. "I like that. I suppose I'll do the same."

Caitlin wanted to throw up.

"Look forward to chatting and dancing tonight, Jack," Piper said.

She waved her arm forward as if she were Cleopatra and then departed, her lackeys in tow.

Caitlin and Jack stood alone in the hall.

"And what about you?" Jack asked.

Caitlin bit her lip. Then she casually flipped her head, tossing her long, cinnamon-colored hair over her shoulder. "Me? I'm probably not going . . . I might have other plans."

Jack shrugged. "Oh. I was going to suggest that if you *were* going, perhaps we'd go alone together. I should say—each of us could go solo—together. Well, you know what I mean."

Do you mean you're inviting me to the masquerade ball?

Caitlin couldn't contain her glee. She imagined Piper spotting her with Jack. Then without thinking, she blurted out, "I think my plans have been canceled."

Did I just say that? How uncool! How desperate!

"What I mean is, now that you're suggesting we go together, I think I could change my plans. So, sure; I'll go solo with you."

They both laughed.

Jack winked. "Brilliant!"

Caitlin suddenly remembered she didn't have a costume idea yet. "Hey, what are you wearing tonight?"

"Going medieval—an Arthurian knight. Sword. Tunic. Some chain mail. You?"

"I have a few options." She had none. "How about I surprise you?"

"Perfect," Jack said with a smile. "I'll ring you later."

He took off for his next class, and Caitlin walked on air toward her locker. Not only because those pretentious divas would see her with Jack, or because going to the masquerade ball with him would help ease her transition to Kingshire. No. Those were bonuses. What really mattered to her was that Jack was simply a cool and decent guy.

Then it all went flying out the window.

I absolutely, categorically don't dance in front of human beings! Ever!

Caitlin froze.

He'll think I'm lame, a total loser.

Dancing meant not caring one bit what others thought of her.

And that was the crux of Caitlin's problem.

She didn't know how to let go and be happy!

Especially on her birthday.

My birthday!

Emotions stirred inside of her. Caitlin Fletcher's mom had gone missing on her birthday the year she had turned ten years old.

Or perhaps Mom had simply packed up and left?

Caitlin often wondered if her dad was in major denial.

She wasn't sure.

Her dad never talked about it. No one talked about it. And Caitlin couldn't—and didn't really want to—remember the details.

Her pocket vibrated. Caitlin took out her phone. The property manager had replied to her earlier e-mail inquiry.

She chewed her bottom lip as she read.

The exterior windows of their apartment complex were cleaned back in mid-July—weeks before the Fletchers had moved into the building.

Caitlin stared off into space.

Who, then, had climbed the exterior of the building and left those creepy fingerprints on her tenth-story bedroom window?

Along with a batch of strange-looking chickpeas.

Dancing might actually be the lesser of her worries right now.

CHAPTER THREE

CAITLIN WALKED THROUGH HER APARTMENT DOOR AND HEADED upstairs to her bedroom. Natalie was lying on her bed, immersed in her tablet, head propped up by two pillows.

Caitlin pulled off her vintage Cinderella T-shirt. She tossed it over to her kid sister. "This is yours now."

It landed on Natalie's face. Natalie held it up to see what it was, then cast a wary eye at Caitlin but said nothing.

Caitlin took another top from her closet and slipped it on.

Then she froze.

Caitlin visualized it with irrefutable clarity. A totally wicked concept for a costume.

"Nat, hand me the scissors." Natalie opened the desk drawer while Caitlin lifted out the wedding dress. Her mom's wedding dress. It had been in Caitlin's closet ever since she could remember. Even before her mom disappeared.

Or left.

Natalie found the scissors. She held them in her hands and stared at them for a moment. Her brow wrinkled as she glanced up at Caitlin.

"What do you plan on doing with these?" Natalie asked.

"It's for my costume."

"So you *are* going to the masquerade ball?"

"Yeah, totally."

Caitlin's current plan was to "sprain" her ankle when she got there so she wouldn't have to dance.

Natalie shook her head from side to side, jeering at her sister the whole time.

"And you're going to this masquerade ball dressed as your own mom on her wedding day?"

Caitlin rolled her eyes. "Are you psycho?"

Natalie sneered back. "I was afraid *you* were."

Caitlin held the wedding dress against her body. "I'm going as a zombie bride. You can help me do the makeup."

Natalie winced. "Wait, that's even worse." She squinted one eye at Caitlin. "What are the scissors for?"

"To cut the dress. Make it look worn-out and decrepit."

"But your own mom gave you that dress. And also this T-shirt that you just bequeathed to me!"

"First of all, stop saying 'your own mom.' Makes *you* sound like you're unspawned. And Mom's not here. So hand over the scissors."

Natalie tucked them under a pillow. "But then you'll have nothing left of hers."

"I still have all of her old records."

A vague smile played on Caitlin's lips. *The vinyl records.* Caitlin's grandfather, Robert Blackshaw, and her great-uncle Derek were tie-dyed hippie brothers playing in a British rock band back in the olden days. Liverpool. Circa 1968. Like many in their generation, they experimented with——*ahem*——plant-based substances. Unfortunately, groovy Gramps indulged in one too many experiments and never made it to the seventies.

He had left his only daughter, Evelyn, his personal music collection. She had raved about the oldies that had "birthed rock 'n' roll." Caitlin faintly remembered the back-and-forth squabbles her parents had had over which country——England or America——had produced the best rock music during that epic age.

Her dad, born in Brooklyn, naturally argued on behalf of America. Her London-born mom made the case for England, talking about some sort of British Invasion.

When Caitlin packed for the move to London, she had rummaged through the stacks of LPs. She liked all the weird band names: The Doors, The Beach Boys, The Kinks, T. Rex, The Who, and The Zombies.

A soft twinge touched Caitlin's heart. "You can put the scissors away," she said. "I'll just wear some freaky makeup and pin up the dress."

Natalie sighed. "Why'd you really give me your top?"

As usual, Caitlin felt weird telling her baby sister about her personal life. It was times like these when she most missed her mom.

"I've outgrown it."

"Really."

She's not buying it.

"Yeap."

"This morning it was a teen fashion statement. Now it's a junior-apparel hand-me-down?"

Caitlin's nose twitched. "Uh-huh."

Natalie folded her arms. "You got slammed today by some hostile, stuck-up fashionista. And you were too chicken to speak up."

Caitlin looked away. It wasn't that she was afraid of those girls—physically. She wasn't. She would've shoved them aside with a sharp elbow to help Alicia Saunders. Caitlin wasn't afraid to body check older girls at school when playing floor hockey in the gym, either. In fact, she was an exceptional body-checker. One time she flattened Edith Schreckenhauser—who was twice her size and probably triple her weight—with a crushing hip check.

Caitlin Rose Fletcher wasn't afraid of a nosebleed. But she was deathly afraid of blushing from embarrassment. Natalie ambled over to the middle of the rug and smiled at her sister. "You need to let loose, Caity-pie. Shake up your life. Dance deliriously at the ball and stop stressing all the time."

Natalie shook out her arms and legs and swayed her butt, obviously trying to get Caitlin to lighten up.

"I can't," Caitlin said. "I'll look stupid."

"True. But so what? At some point you must overcome the phobias you're trying to hide from the world."

"Leave me alone, mutant brain."

"Have it your way," Natalie said. She closed her tablet and skedaddled out of the room.

Caitlin buried her head in her pillow. A million and one thoughts flooded her mind. Jack. Piper and her coven. Jack. Her favorite top that she'd just given away. Jack. The ball! Her mom . . .

Caitlin clenched her fist in anger. And then she must have fallen asleep, because the next thing she heard in her head and felt on her leg was a buzz and the vibration of a cell phone.

She rolled over on her back and pulled her phone from her front pocket.

A video call. From Jack!

She rubbed the sleep from her eyes and primped her hair. Then she clicked Accept Call.

"What's up, Jack?" she said.

"Hey. I was just texting with Piper."

Caitlin suddenly had an uneasy feeling in the pit of her stomach.

"I need to change our plans."

Her heart skipped a beat.

"Totally understand, Jack." Her voice traitorously cracked, and she cleared her throat. "No worries—I'll make other plans."

"Hold on, lassie," he replied. "Piper texted me about another sighting. Some kid posted it online."

The sun shined inside her again. "Really? Where?"

"Copenhagen. Denmark. The Assistens Cemetery." Jack stroked his chin. "I wonder if anything interesting would turn up on Google?"

The writer inside of Caitlin sprung awake. She grabbed Natalie's tablet from her bed. "How do you spell it?"

"What?"

"The name of the cemetery."

Jack smiled. He spelled it out carefully, and Caitlin promptly Googled it. Then she clicked Wikipedia. Then she scrolled the page, perusing it, and then . . . "You know who's buried there?"

"Who?"

"The Little Mermaid."

"Huh?"

"I mean the author of *The Little Mermaid*, Hans Christian Andersen." She bit her lip gently. "Hmmm. You know what, Jack?"

"I'm way ahead of you," he said with a wily grin. "I'm checking to see if anyone famous is buried in the cemetery in Florence, Italy." Jack's eyes scanned his computer screen. "Bloody hell, Carlo Collodi is buried there, the man who wrote *The Adventures of Pinocchio.*"

Caitlin picked up on the pattern at once. "Check for famous authors buried at the other cemeteries," she instructed Jack.

He was now drumming the keyboard furiously. It only took a moment. "L. Frank Baum. The Wizard of Oz himself! He's in Forest Lawn. Glendale, California."

I knew it!

After one more set of keystrokes, Jack shouted, "Brothers Grimm! They're buried in Berlin."

Caitlin was already writing her article for unexplainable-news.com in her head.

"I have a hunch who might be in Scotland," Jack said. His fingers danced upon the keyboard. "Tickety-boo. J. M. Barrie rests in the Kirriemuir Cemetery."

His face suddenly broadened into a mischievous smile.

"Caitliiinn," he said in a drawn-out, teasing tone.

"Jaaack!" she answered playfully.

"So far, there haven't been any sightings in merrie, olde England."

That comment stopped Caitlin cold. "Oh."

All of a sudden she didn't feel so playful.

Jack kept typing, reading, typing . . .

"Guildford," he said. "Small town just southwest of here."

Thin beads of sweat formed on Caitlin's brow. "What about it?"

"Charles Lutwidge Dodgson is buried there."

"Who's he?"

"He wrote *Alice's Adventures in Wonderland.*"

Caitlin nervously ambled over to the white mahogany bookshelf in her room. She rummaged through the books on the third shelf. *Peter and Wendy. A Wrinkle in Time. The Little Mermaid. Black Beauty.* There it was—*Alice's Adventures in Wonderland.* Her mom used to read it to her all the time. Caitlin missed that. She pulled the book from the shelf.

"Lewis Carroll wrote that."

Jack's adorable dimples deepened as he leaned toward the screen. "Same bloke. Lewis Carroll is the pen name of Charles Dodgson."

But why Guildford of all places!?

Caitlin desperately hoped there was more than one cemetery there.

A thunderclap interrupted her thoughts. Lightning flashes outside her bedroom window followed. A nasty storm was rolling in.

"In which graveyard in Guildford is Dodgson buried?" Caitlin asked.

"Mount Cemetery."

The lump in her throat became more pronounced.

"Um . . . my mom's . . . *dad* is buried there."

"You've been there then? Perfect. You can navigate."

"What do you mean?"

"That's why I called. I thought it might be fun to visit a graveyard after the ball. You know, see if we can spot any ghoulish occurrences. Mount Cemetery is perfect. And it's Halloween. The way these sightings are unfolding, this seems the most logical time and place for the next one to happen. And then you'll have a bloody marvelous story for unexplainable-news.com."

She suddenly realized Jack was staring at her with a concerned look. "Hey, what's wrong?"

She couldn't tell him. She wanted to, but no words could get past her lips.

Caitlin had *never* been to Mount Cemetery. She'd never even been to Guildford.

When Caitlin was thirteen, she had been too panic-stricken to go to the graveyard where her grandfather was buried after the Fletchers had to unexpectedly travel to London. How could she tell Jack she had been afraid because . . . she didn't have her good luck charm with her?

The magic wand.

What a freaking joke. It seemed so ridiculous and juvenile at this moment. The memory alone embarrassed her.

She had bought it from a magic shop to help her wrestle with her fears. The shop owner said that waving the wand would make her fears vanish. Yeah. Sure. Waving a wand. She was nine. *Nine.* A frightened little girl, positively gullible and utterly naive.

It happened to be a charming piece of costume jewelry—a tiny, silver wand with a round, opaque tip. Caitlin had carried it everywhere. When she turned ten, she had suddenly lost it. Her anxiety worsened ever since. Her mom's disappearance, around the same time, certainly didn't help matters. When the Fletchers abruptly flew to London last year, and with the wand long gone, there was no way on earth Caitlin was going to that graveyard!

Another strobe of lightning lit up the white, sheer curtains adorning the window. Another roll of thunder followed. Storm clouds were gathering outside.

"Caitlin, you okay?" Jack asked.

Change the freaking subject, Caitlin.

She blurted out, "It's my birthday today."

Definitely an inappropriate response.

Thankfully, Jack smiled.

"A belated happy birthday wish."

"Thanks."

"Look, if you'd rather not tempt the dead and woo ghouls on your birthday, we can forget about the graveyard. We'll stick to the school dance."

More than anything, Caitlin wanted to be with Jack. And the more time she could hang with him, the better. For some reason, being near him gave her a sense of calm. She dreaded that particular cemetery, but at least she wouldn't have to travel there alone. Also, if she didn't go to the graveyard, Piper, Paige, and Layla surely would try to claw their way into the adventure. Besides, the whole graveyard-sighting phenomenon *would* be a solid story for unexplainablenews.com.

"No, no. The cemetery after the ball is, like, totally cool."

Jack checked his watch.

"Brilliant. Listen, I'm still at school. Maths test. But I'm heading home now. I'll pick you up at seven sharp. We'll arrive fashionably late. Cheers."

Caitlin forced a smile and then tapped the End Call button.

"Cheers," she muttered to herself.

She pocketed her phone and stared at her nails, pondering which one to chew.

Out of the corner of her eye, Caitlin caught sight of something moving. Something was in the bed next to her. Beneath the blanket.

Another crack of thunder shivered through the room.

"I'm abso-blood-lutely coming with you!" a determined voice called out in a thick British accent.

Natalie.

Caitlin threw back the puffy comforter. Her eyebrows narrowed together sharply.

"Don't even think about it, you, you . . . *wiretapper*! And drop the Brit accent and slang."

"But I'll be your photojournalist."

Natalie whipped out her camera and snapped Caitlin's picture.

"Imagine if a ghoul shows up—we'll make Internet history."

"*Not* gonna happen, Natalie," Caitlin said as she blinked away the sting of the camera flash.

Natalie folded her arms and huffed.

Caitlin's phone buzzed. A text from Jack: *Thx 4 sayng yes. Grvyrd 2nite aftr ball will b fun.*

Caitlin smiled inwardly.

"What did he say?" Natalie asked.

Caitlin gave her sister a once-over. She knew the bombastic bundle of brains and cuteness would think of some way to blackmail her.

Caitlin hoisted Natalie up in the air until they were nose to nose.

"None of your business. And if you tell one living soul about any of this, you won't live to see the sun rise."

CHAPTER FOUR

AFTER JACK LEFT KINGSHIRE, HE MADE A SLIGHT DETOUR. HE turned onto Wellington Street and then stopped in at Penhaligon's perfume house—it had been around forever and seemed like the perfect place to buy Caitlin a surprise gift now that he knew it was her birthday. William Penhaligon, an alchemist and the official perfumer to Queen Victoria, had created his first fragrance way back in 1872.

When he had first met Caitlin two months earlier, he ha only wanted to befriend her. But she had turned out to be an and weird and unique in such a cool, sad, and vulnera He couldn't help liking her.

Jack opened the shop door and was met of scents—vanilla, jasmine, sandalwood, aromas.

The hardwood floor of the old Lo

of a rustic walnut. A small fireplace burned brightly, and a large, lit chandelier hung from the ceiling.

The polished, red mahogany cabinets and sparkling glass shelves were stocked with a vast array of perfumes, powders, lotions, candles, and other fancy bottles. Jack had no idea which fragrance to buy for Caitlin, and suddenly felt unsure whether this was a good idea.

Thankfully, a female sales clerk greeted him.

"Welcome to Penhaligon's. Would you care to sample some men's cologne?"

Jack scratched his head. "Actually, I'm looking for a bottle of perfume. For a friend. It's her birthday."

The sales clerk smiled warmly. "How lovely. I have a couple of ideas in mind."

She immediately brought Jack a few testers. There was something intoxicating about the third sample, *Elisabethan Rose*. Jack was no expert on ladies' fragrances, but he knew plants and flowers quite well. He was certain that he detected geranium, musk, chamomile, and, of course, rose petals.

"Could you please gift wrap this one?"

"Of course," the clerk said. Jack took out his mobile, as well as wallet.

rk promptly returned with the wrapped package and Jack to sign. Jack set his mobile and wallet on the handed the clerk his money. Then he wrote a wishing her a truly happy and meaningful

"Cheers," he said as he walked out the door, holding Caitlin's gift in one hand and pocketing his wallet with the other.

Jack made a right turn as he left the shop. About a half block down Wellington, he saw them walking directly toward him.

Piper, Paige, and Layla.

Piper's cagey eyes lit up when she spotted Jack.

"What a surprise! Hello, Jack."

He nodded. "Where you off to?"

"Penhaligon's," Piper said.

"Some last-minute shopping," Paige added. "Buying fancy fragrances for the masquerade ball."

Piper spotted the package in Jack's hand.

"Looks like you've already been there," Piper said. "Is that some new devastating gentleman's cologne?"

Jack chuckled. "No, no. It's a gift for Caitlin. It's her birthday."

Piper's eyes hardened. She seemed to be straining to maintain a smile. She placed a friendly hand on Jack's shoulder. Her fingers straightened his shirt collar.

"Jack, luv, suppose you and I go to the dance together, seeing that we are both dateless at this late hour."

"That's kind of you, Piper. But I made plans with Caitlin."

Piper's arm recoiled. Her eyes narrowed to mere slits.

"I don't wanna sound high-nosed, J, but do you really wanna be seen at the ball with someone like Caitlin?"

Jack smiled. "I'd love to stand here and chat, but I really gotta go P."

And with that, Jack strode off. He felt a bit bad for the pee innuendo. But it was the only way to put Piper in her place. Jack knew, given the chance, Piper would skin alive someone as vulnerable as Caitlin.

"I can't believe he's taking that nerdy Yank to our ball," Piper complained.

Layla nodded. "Agreed."

"Forget about it," Paige said. "One date with her and he'll realize how positively lame she is. Probably tell her to piss off before night's end. Let's go. It's getting late."

The girls arrived at Penhaligon's, where they selected expensive bottles of perfume. Each girl paid with her parents' credit card.

Layla saw it first.

A mobile phone sitting unattended on the counter.

She snatched it. Opened it. Her eyes popped. "It's Jack's!"

Piper swiped it from Layla. She started snooping through Jack's phone—*his e-mails . . . his text messages . . .*

Piper glared at the screen, her lips thinning into blades.

"How romantic. After the ball Jack and Caitlin are going gallivanting about in some graveyard."

Piper suddenly broke out in a crooked smile.

"Why the grin of sin?" Layla asked.

Piper slid the mobile into her purse. "Suppose Caitlin never shows up at the ball? I'll have Jack all to myself." Her smile sharpened. "And Caity will have the fright of her life."

All three girls exchanged conniving looks.

"You're positively evil," Layla said.

Piper admired her manicured nails and smiled.

CHAPTER FIVE

THE CLOCK ON CAITLIN'S NIGHTSTAND SHOWED 4:22 P.M. AS A slanting rain pelted her window and Royal Street below. The Kingshire Masquerade Ball was scheduled to start at 7:00 p.m., and Caitlin still had to dream up some edgy makeup concepts for her zombie bride get-up.

Her thoughts were interrupted by the appearance of a bright red chili pepper.

Caitlin's eyes widened. Natalie was dressed in a life-size chili pepper costume. The bulbous bell of the pepper was a brilliant red, and she wore bright-red tights and a matching long-sleeve, bright-red shirt underneath. It started at the shoulder and fell to a point at the knees. The brown stem of the pepper was provided by a turtleneck.

"I thought you were going to dress up as Alice in Wonderland, with striped stockings?" Caitlin asked.

"I saw this in the costume shop," Natalie said. "It looked more . . . exciting."

"Exciting? You're a freaking vegetable."

"Technically, I'm botanically classified as a fruit. Wanna help me zip?"

Caitlin's cell phone beeped. Another text from Jack.

"Out!" Caitlin shouted at Natalie.

Natalie pouted as she left, and Caitlin sat on the edge of her bed to read the text: *Let's skip dance & go strght to graveyard. Besides, I'm not 2 fond of dancing.*

Caitlin was sort of delighted. No need to fake a sprained ankle, and she'd spend a spooky and kind of freaky fun evening with Jack. However, there was still the issue of the cemetery in Guildford. She didn't have her magic wand to wave. Then again, she'd have Jack by her side and she wouldn't have to go to her grandpa's burial site. Only Charles Dodgson's.

She texted him back: *Awesome. Meet u under clock at Waterloo station?*

Her phone chimed again: *Cant. Need 2 run errand 4 mum. Meet u @ mount cemetery. 7:30. Or should we cancel?*

A terrible dread punched Caitlin in the stomach. It winded her, in fact. Not because she was afraid of gathering up ghouls in a graveyard. Not at all. Caitlin had seen all the *Scream* horror movies. Seen *The Shining* four times. *World War Z* twice. And she devoured vampire books like Skittles.

The solo train ride to Guildford is what caused a wrecking ball to swing in the pit of her stomach. What if she got panicky midtrip, when she was far from home?

Just then, Natalie busted into the room again.

Caitlin had to act fast. She'd be crushed if Jack canceled. So she did the most daring thing she had ever done in her entire life.

She texted him back: *C u 7:30!*

Am I not adventurous?

She stole a peek at the four corners of her ceiling.

One, two, three, four.

Fear was strange. Caitlin was comfortable standing in front of a class or an auditorium and giving a lecture on any given topic. But dancing at parties and worrying what others thought about her always brought forth stifling insecurities.

On a dare, she'd have no problem running through . . . say . . . a pitch-black graveyard in the middle of the night. But the thought of having a panic attack in the school hallway or in the middle of a mall far from the nearest exit, or at a party—well, just the anticipation of potential panic would altogether make her knees go soft, make her beg for relief. Caitlin wouldn't have wished that type of terror even on Piper. No one understood how crippling it could be.

The first time she had an attack, she thought she was dying or losing her grip on reality. The anxiety ran her over like a bus. She had to run to her dad, panicked and wild-eyed, not knowing what was happening to her. Her dad gave her half a Xanax—she only wondered later why *he* had any—and said it was just her nerves.

Just my nerves?

What did that even mean? What nerves was he referring

to? Where were these evil nerves located? Why did they suddenly revolt and shut down her breathing and fill her head with dreadful thoughts and irrational fears and cause her to sweat icicles? How did these nameless, indefinable "nerves" exert that much control over her?

Caitlin couldn't be pissed at her father. Not at all. He was doing his best. He had sent her to bed after she popped half a Xanax. She had hoped she would sleep it off. Yeah. Right.

A fresh roll of thunder stirred Caitlin from her reminiscing. She turned and looked at her window from afar.

The grimy fingerprints were clearly visible, pressed against the pane.

Rain fell softly outside. Raindrops dribbled down the window like tears.

Something gnawed at her. Something drifted at the edge of her mind like a delicate billow of fog as she looked through the window. She couldn't put a finger on it and she knew that if she tried to, the vapor would dissipate.

She let it go.

A heartbeat later, however, the thought sharpened in her mind. The fingerprints!

Why hadn't the rain washed them away?

An icy wave flooded over her, making her skin prickle.

She moved toward the window, warily. She reached her hand out. With her pinky, Caitlin rubbed one of the fingerprints.

Please don't!

It did.

It smudged.

Oh my God!

Whoever left those fingerprints had done so from *inside* her bedroom.

Standing and breathing next to her bed.

While she slept.

CHAPTER SIX

NATALIE SUDDENLY BUSTED INTO THE ROOM AND HER MOUTH FELL open when she saw Caitlin.

"Whoa," Natalie said. "What's with you? You look severely spooked."

Caitlin responded in a grim tone, "Those fingerprints on the window . . . they were made by someone *inside* this bedroom."

Natalie leaned toward the window to inspect. She raised her eyebrows. "Nice work, Sherlock. How'd I miss that?"

"I'm creeped out, Nat. This isn't funny."

Natalie shrugged. "Probably some maintenance worker from the building came while we were at school. In fact, I overheard Dad talking about ordering new window blinds for this room. Yeah, that was it."

Caitlin exhaled. Of course. *That* explanation made perfect sense.

She turned her attention to Natalie's red chili pepper outfit. She snickered. "A bit bright, dontcha think, Lady Gaga?"

Natalie folded her arms. "First you're on the verge of a major freak-out, now suddenly you're cocky and mocking me after I solved your mystery. Could it be you're a bit uptight? A suppressed fear of freaking out in front of Jack? Like you did in front of that skateboard dude last year at the dance?"

Low blow, Natalie Fletcher.

Caitlin's nostrils flared. "I never freaked out, you pretentious, bigmouthed brat!!"

If a tone of voice had teeth, Natalie would've had bite marks on her flesh. Except that Caitlin *had* totally freaked out that night. She really thought she was dying.

Skateboarder Dillon Slater had asked her to dance. Suddenly, as they strode onto the dance floor, the DJ played *that* song. *That song* was "She's Not There" by the British sixties band The Zombies. The same song her mom played all the time while dancing with Caitlin around their house.

When Caitlin heard it at the dance, her body turned ice cold. She ran out of the gym because she felt like she couldn't breathe. Everyone had stared wide-eyed, wondering what was happening to her. But there's always a jerk in every school who degraded others for the sake of preserving his own reputation. That jerk turned out to be Dillon Slater. "Skateboard dude" himself. He hollered a comment that wounded Caitlin deeply as she'd fled.

"Hey look," Dillon Slater had shouted, *"another Fletcher disappears into thin air!"*

The insinuation was cruel. A joke about her mother's disappearance was heartless.

Some other creep then posted Slater's comment on Facebook. Caitlin had been crushed.

Natalie, suddenly contrite, lifted Caitlin's chin with her finger. "I'm not trying to take the piss out of you, sweet sibling. It's just that you were gasping for air when you came home that night."

Caitlin shrugged. "Was not. I just like oxygen."

Natalie rolled her eyes. "It's called hyperventilation."

"Spare me your copious vocabulary. And how about you?" Caitlin countered. "With your intimacy issues? You head-butt instead of kiss good night."

"Not true. I'm tactfully evading infectious germs."

Caitlin heard the sound of their apartment's front door opening.

"Finally," Caitlin said. "I'm ravenous!"

Both girls darted downstairs.

"Guess who's home?" Harold Fletcher called out as he entered the kitchen carrying a large, white plastic bag filled with takeout food.

He plopped the plastic bag onto the counter and then turned to his girls, a warm smile on his face.

"So? How was everyone's day?"

Caitlin leaned across the counter, and her father planted one on her forehead. Natalie made a vinegary face, slid both hands in her pockets and tottered across the kitchen. She offered her dad the very top of her frizzy, red-haired head.

Harold Fletcher surveyed the scalp area in search of a clearing—to no avail. He pecked a shapeless mound of red hair instead.

Caitlin glared at Natalie. "Told you. Head-butt."

Natalie took a seat at the kitchen bar, smiling at Caitlin while throwing a sideways glance at their father.

"I've been trying to help your daughter with her various phobias and anxiety disorders."

"Dad!" Caitlin hollered at the top of her lungs. Their father's smiling face turned solemn.

"Come on now, girls, get along. Natalie, don't blow things out of proportion just so you can start with your sister."

Natalie's eyes popped.

"But the last time she cut her precious hair she was my age. Which explains why it now hangs down to her butt crack. It's called tonsurephobia!"

Caitlin's eyes blazed as Natalie kept up her attack.

"She's had contact lenses sitting in the medicine cabinet for almost as long. Fear of eyes is called ommetaphobia."

Though Caitlin wanted her sister to shut up, she couldn't deny the truth.

She recalled the time she'd had a temper tantrum, which her mom said had hit 7.2 on the Richter scale. It had happened when a salami-breathed eye doctor tried to insert a contact lens in her eye. Caitlin had lost it. She'd flung her arms wildly, knocking over a tray of lenses and freaking him out. Her mom had said her fear was irrational.

Irrational? Mom's disappearance . . . now that was irrational.

And Caitlin had only stopped cutting her hair when her mom was no longer around to take her to the hair salon. How was that her fault? Besides, she adored her long, flowing hair.

Harold Fletcher pressed his lips into a thin line.

"Natalie, another word and you're staying home for Halloween." Natalie zipped it lightning-quick. Her dad then pulled up a tall stool and joined the girls at the counter.

"Who's hungry?" he asked. Her dad opened the takeout container and passed around some paper plates. Natalie and Caitlin stared at the contents of the containers. Puck-shaped slices of black sausage, speckled with blobs of fat, floated on a sea of brown, saucy beans.

"What! Is! That?!" Caitlin asked, wide-eyed.

"Black pudding," her father replied. "With bangers and mash. You had it once a few years ago."

"What's it made of?" asked Natalie.

"Dried, congealed blood."

Caitlin felt her stomach churn. "How wretched." She pushed it away.

"Fascinating," remarked Natalie, leaning in to study it more closely.

"It's a classic dish of English cuisine," her dad said. "People have been eating it for centuries."

Caitlin got up and made herself a nice, familiar tuna salad sandwich.

Natalie stuck her finger into the blood pudding gravy and slurped it up. "Hmm," she chirped, "needs hot sauce."

She reached for the bottle of Upton Cheyney Sweet Chilli

Sauce sitting nearby on the counter. She tipped it over onto her plate . . . and one measly drop fell out. Natalie shook it vigorously up and down. Two drops.

"*Hmmmm.* What's with the child safety cap?"

She turned the bottle upside down and gave the bottom a mighty pound.

GLOOP.

That did it. A spicy wad of hot sauce blurped out of the spout. It covered her entire slice of blood pudding, her plate, the table—and her costume!

"Smooth move, chipotle," gloated Caitlin. "Now you'll stink like a pepper too."

Natalie shrugged, scarfed the black sausage and washed it down with some bubbling spring water. After a few sips, she let out one of her famous hot-dog burps—the family joked that they hung so thick in the air, you could brush a slab of mustard on it.

"Disgusting!" Caitlin lifted the hem of her top over her nose to block out the foul odor. It took a moment for the stench to dissipate, and then the Fletcher family dug into the rest of their dinner.

AFTER SUPPER, CAITLIN SUDDENLY FOUND HER DAD STANDING IN the kitchen with a birthday cake. It was big, it was chocolate, and it was just what Caitlin needed at that moment.

They sang "Happy Birthday," and then Harold Fletcher shared a birthday kiss and hug with Caitlin.

"Congrats on your second year of teenagerdom, Caity-cakes!" Natalie said and gave her a head-butt.

Caitlin's dad handed her a thin box wrapped in silver foil. "I know how much you love writing, honey."

Caitlin apprehensively peeled away the wrapping. Her eyes grew as bright as twin light bulbs.

A mini tablet!

Dad beamed. "Now you can write articles from anywhere. For your blog."

Caitlin was truly grateful. She hugged her father tight.

"Thanks so much, Papa Bear."

"Whattaya say, Caitlin?" her dad said as he cleared away the plates. "Sure you don't want to come trick-or-treating with us tonight?"

"I'm too old for youthful indulgences like knocking on doors in search of sugar."

Caitlin watched as Natalie stretched her bright-yellow rain-coat over the bulbous pod that served as the frame for her ridic-ulously oversize chili pepper outfit. She hooked her pumpkin-shaped candy-collection bucket over her arm and snapped her coat.

"For the record," Natalie said, looking up at her father. "We don't say 'trick-or-treat' in London. Kids here say 'Happy Halloween.'"

Her dad smiled. Then he put on the silliest-looking court jester hat Caitlin had ever seen and left with Natalie.

CAITLIN SPENT THE NEXT HALF AN HOUR DISHING OUT CANDIES TO every superhero, phantom, pirate, princess, and witch who knocked on the door. She also booted up her new tablet to check the London-Guildford train schedules.

When her dad and Natalie returned from their trick-or-treating, Natalie quickly disappeared into the bedroom with her bucketful of treats.

"It's getting late, pumpkin," her father said. He plopped down on the sofa next to Caitlin in the living room. "Shouldn't you be getting ready for the dance?"

Caitlin sighed. "I don't know. I'm feeling a bit tired."

I'm getting cold feet about going alone to Guildford.

Harold Fletcher looked at his daughter with mournful eyes. "Mom would have wanted you to go. She was always so outgoing and spirited."

Caitlin despised hearing about what her mom would have wanted so she shut down the conversation. She knew her father was trying his best—*or denying his best!* She didn't want to say anything that would make him feel worse than he already felt on the anniversary of her disappearance, her birthday aside.

"I'll see how I feel later."

"Whatever makes you happy." He kissed her on the forehead.

Caitlin headed upstairs. When she entered the bedroom, Natalie was passed out, snoring just like her father. Sugar crash, no doubt.

Her bag of superabundant Halloween calories lay at the

foot of her bed with a "don't touch or else" sign on top of it. Sometimes Girl Wonder did act her age.

Caitlin's phone vibrated. A text from Jack popped up on her screen.

C u soon.

Caitlin slumped onto her bed. Her clock read 5:42 p.m. She had to be at Waterloo station by 6:15 if she was going to catch her train to Guildford.

That meant she had to leave right away to make it on time. Caitlin bowed her head and sighed. Who was she kidding? She couldn't pull this off. She'd tried, but there was no way it was going to happen. She picked up her cell to text Jack. She'd say she was feeling fluish. No, she had a migraine. No, it was that time of month.

If he hated her now for bailing on him, so be it.

Caitlin paused. Then she typed on her phone. She exhaled and then she hit Send.

On my way! B there soon.

Without allowing a second for grim thoughts to sabotage her bold decision, she beelined to her closet, looking for a change of clothes. *Am I not adventurous?*

Caitlin preferred genderless fashion so she slid on a pair of her most comfortable jeans, a cozy, oversize, college-boy-style sweater, and lace-up combat boots. As she wrapped a scarf around her neck, she heard a rattling sound. Something had just spilled on the closet floor.

"More garbanzo beans?" Caitlin muttered nervously as she

leaned down to pick up a few. She slipped them into the pocket of her jeans so she could show them to Jack.

"Leaving now!" she called out to her dad as she headed for flat's front door.

Harold Fletcher met her by the door. "Wait, I'll walk you over to the school."

Caitlin rolled her eyes. "Please, Dad. I'll look like a dork arriving with my father. Besides, I'm meeting some friends downstairs."

He chewed his lip. "What time will you be home?"

"Around ten-thirty."

"I'd rather you be home by ten. And what about your costume?"

Think fast.

"It's . . . at school. I'll put it on in the girls' locker room."

He sighed. "Okay. But call me when you get there. And call me before you leave to come home. And please be careful."

"I'm always careful," Caitlin said as she waved goodbye. With a writhing knot in her stomach, she plodded down the hall toward the elevator, turned the corner . . . and came face to face with Natalie.

How did that little faker get past Dad?

"And where do you think you're going?" Natalie demanded. She was still dressed in her chili pepper costume with the yellow raincoat stretched over it. Her camera hung in its case around her neck.

"To the dance—and it's none of your business!"

"Bollocks. You're off to the graveyard. I'm coming."

Caitlin glared. "*Not* gonna happen! Don't even think about it. And if you don't go back into the apartment right now, I'm calling Dad. Then we can both stay at home, and you'll wreck it for both of us."

Natalie clenched her jaw as the elevator door opened. Inside stood a male Queen Elizabeth and a very pretty vampire with fake fangs. Caitlin joined them and pressed L for lobby.

"Fine." Natalie crossed her arms in a huff.

"And next time don't try to freak me out by planting those dumb garbanzo beans in my closet."

Queen Elizabeth's eyebrows arched in surprise.

The elevator door began to close. Natalie looked dumbfounded.

Genuinely dumbfounded.

If it wasn't her . . . ?

CHAPTER SEVEN

ONE, TWO, THREE, FOUR.

Caitlin counted the corners of the elevator's ceiling before exiting it and ambling out the front door of her apartment complex.

A curious feeling overcame her as she stepped out into the night and began the walk to Waterloo station.

She felt as though she was following in her own footsteps, like she was stepping into footprints in the sand. And for the briefest of moments, she didn't feel afraid.

The breath of night was cold and damp against Caitlin's cheeks. She tucked her hands under her armpits and strode briskly along the gleaming, wet streets of Central London.

The atmosphere was charged with Halloween magic. Brooding shadows waited around every corner. Clouds began to shroud a treacherous sky.

On the next block, five drunk and rowdy guys masquerading as bikers and werewolves reveled in the street, brandishing beer bottles and lit cigarettes. They scoped her out as she strode by on the sidewalk, whistling and shouting tasteless remarks.

Trying not to appear bothered, Caitlin casually picked up her pace. Soon she was scampering as fast as she could toward Waterloo station.

Before long she reached a street that was humming with pedestrians and busy shops.

The semicircular Victory Arch entrance to Waterloo station soon came into view.

She darted towards the white-gray stone structure.

When she arrived at the station, Caitlin trotted up the stairs and entered the main concourse. She found Waterloo station's famous four-face clock hanging from the glass atrium roof. It read 6:31 p.m. She scurried to the departures board. Her train was due to leave at 6:40 p.m. She bought a ticket and boarded a half-full train bound for Guildford.

After the train departed the station, Caitlin pulled out her phone and did a Google search for Mount Cemetery. She found a map. Located Dodgson's grave. Marked it. Then she mapped out a route from the Guildford train station to Mount Cemetery. It would be about a fourteen-minute walk. Not too bad.

Caitlin exhaled a big breath, sank into the warm seat and peered out the window. She focused her thoughts on Jack, on the delight she felt when he had asked to her to the masquerade ball. She'd never expected it. And then on Jack asking her—not Piper—to participate in this daring cemetery escapade. She even let herself imagine being more than friends with Jack, imagine it being more than her one-way crush. Suppose if, just maybe, he really did like her?

Charcoal-colored storm clouds sparked with internal flashes of lightning outside her window, interrupting her thoughts.

Caitlin bit her bottom lip.

Her body sensed the vibration of the train riding the rails full tilt. They were long gone from the station. Traveling farther and farther from home. She was alone. Heading to that graveyard in . . . *Guildford.*

Caitlin was suddenly thirteen again. It was one year ago.

Her mouth dried up. Neck muscles tensed drum tight. She picked at a fingernail. Sometimes she would pick a nail till it bled because the shock of seeing her finger bleed took her mind off the breathless panic attack—the lesser of two evils.

There were no paper bags on board this train. There was no getting off this train. And, as utterly foolish as she knew the thought was, she couldn't help thinking that there was no magic wand to wave away the tide of anxiety rising in her chest.

She became light-headed. Her breaths became shorter and faster and more irregular.

She was seized by a sudden urge to flee this wretched train, to get back home at that very instant. To the safety and warmth of her bed.

The train was cruelly indifferent to her horror: it hurtled onward like a bullet.

She sat on her hands.

Caitlin Fletcher was in the middle of a full-on panic attack.

And there was no one to help her and nowhere to go.

CHAPTER EIGHT

Caitlin was certain she was going to pass out any second. Then she remembered a technique she read about in a book on anxiety. *Do the opposite of what your stress-fueled impulses are demanding.*

Caitlin did it. She held her breath. She did it in roaring defiance of a panic-stricken mind that screamed, *Breathe, girl, breathe!*

If she listened to her irrational thoughts, they would control her. If she defied the urge to guzzle air by the gallon, her nervous system would eventually force her to sip oxygen. It would force her respiratory system to function in a calm, regulated manner. At least, that's what was *supposed* to happen.

After about twenty seconds of holding her breath, Caitlin's mouth burst open with a slow, soothing exhalation. As she blew out the deep breath, she immediately felt a sense of calm. She held her breath again. She waited until her body compelled her to exhale. The calmness and depth of her breathing deepened deliciously. She was still shaky, but the insanity was passing. She had survived.

After a few stops in the forty-two-minute ride, the train slowed and braked to a halt at the Guildford station.

Although there were still quite a few passengers on board, only the oddest-looking of the bunch disembarked with Caitlin. One man in particular was rail thin, with an elongated neck, a protruding Adam's apple, and oversize eyes. He reminded Caitlin of an ostrich.

She quickly made her way to a lonely sidewalk. Hulking tree branch shadows, cast by streetlamps, nodded at her as if they knew why she was there. She checked the map on her phone. Mount Cemetery was located atop a hill that overlooked the Guildford town center.

Though it was damp outside, it wasn't very cold. She checked her phone for the time: 7:22. She was late, but at least Jack would be there by now and she wouldn't have to wait alone.

Fallen autumn leaves littered the sidewalk, making it slippery.

After she had gone just a few blocks along Wodeland Avenue, the street began to slope downhill. Thick trees lined both sides of the road. Caitlin then came to a crossroad.

The street crossing Wodeland was called The Mount.

She had forgotten whether she was supposed to make a right or left turn. She lifted up her phone to consult the map. From out of nowhere, a blue British Shorthair cat darted out from the shrubs. The cat shrieked as it ran right in front of her ankles, startling Caitlin and causing her to drop her phone.

At least it wasn't a black cat.

Caitlin retrieved her cell from the sidewalk. Her shoulders slumped. The map was gone. And she no longer had a signal to download another one.

The cat meowed and scurried off to Caitlin's right, disappearing into the dark on The Mount. Caitlin continued on in the same direction.

The Mount was a long and extremely narrow road that ascended to the top of the city of Guildford. Clumps of yellow-and-brown leaves littered the pavement. Caitlin wished there were more streetlamps.

Lining the road to Caitlin's right were detached and semidetached Victorian brick houses clumped together tightly on a rise.

Jack-o'-lanterns lit the sloped landscape.

The pumpkins were perched on garage rooftops, brick gateposts, and on the bottom steps that led up to the houses.

A light drizzle began to fall.

She was anxious to find Jack.

She was soon short of breath—not from anxiety this time, but from the steep trek up The Mount.

The last flickers of candlelight seemed to be dying in the pumpkins as she reached the halfway point up the hill. After a few more minutes of climbing, Caitlin arrived at her destination.

On her left stood its gates. Somehow, she thought, they looked like they were expecting her.

Mount Cemetery.

ONCE UPON A ZOMBIE

The burial place of Charles Dodgson—aka Lewis Carroll.
But there was no Jack waiting for her.

CHAPTER NINE

A BLACK, CURVING, WROUGHT-IRON GATE GUARDED THE COBBLE-stone entryway to Mount Cemetery. Drizzle reflected off its gleaming black bars. The bolted gate was affixed to two red brick posts.

Jack must've arrived early. He must be waiting for me at Dodgson's gravesite.

A sign on the gate read hours of operation: 8:00 a.m.—7:00 p.m. And while the cemetery itself was quite ancient, the lock on the gate was not. After she gave it a few hearty pulls, it was obvious to Caitlin that the gate wasn't going to open until some gravedigger came to unlock it in the morning.

How had Jack gotten in?

Caitlin chewed the ends of her hair as she glanced around. The evening was hushed except for the soft sounds of raindrops spattering pavement and the faint hoot of an owl.

She checked the time on her phone: 7:35 p.m.

Jack might have thought she wasn't going to show up!

A sharp meow interrupted the quiet. The shorthaired blue cat appeared again. The sopping wet feline hopped atop the cobblestone wall and slid between the brick post and hedges, past the gate, and then jumped into the cemetery.

Ever so clever idea, Caity-cat!

Caitlin hoisted herself up the wall and stepped through the same narrow opening.

She sat on her butt, then hopped down.

She was in!

Wide lawns that flanked both sides of a narrow road were dotted with gravestones and a scattering of trees.

Caitlin checked her phone again.

Five bars!

She downloaded another map and searched for the location of Charles Dodgson's burial site.

As she walked the roadway toward Dodgson's grave, she could swear she heard something out of the ordinary. Maybe not.

Wait!

She *did* hear something. Behind her. Footfalls.

Did those sketchy thugs follow me? Was it Jack? It had to be Jack!

Caitlin froze in her tracks. The crisp night air filled her lungs. She called out in a loud whisper, "Jack, is that you?"

The response was a disturbing silence. Something was wrong here.

Caitlin kept moving in the direction of the gravestones. A whining wind brushed the tree branches.

Footsteps were still on her tail.

Rain dripped into her eyes.

Hold your breath, Caitlin. Wait for your body to force the air out of your lungs.

Her sweater stuck to her back, itching her skin.

She heard Natalie's taunting voice in her mind: "Caity-cat, fraidy-cat!"

Indignation gave her the strength to keep stepping forward into the looming darkness.

Caitlin finally located the gravesite up ahead. The plot lay adjacent to a medieval brick chapel and directly beside a thick pine tree.

Still no sign of Jack.

At the foot of the grave was a small plaque identifying the renowned individual resting there: LEWIS CARROLL GRAVE.

Caitlin approached the cross-shaped headstone timidly. She flipped her phone around so that her screen was now aimed away from her. It projected a soft glimmer. She cast the glow onto the base of the headstone. Warily, she kneeled in front of it and read:

REV. CHARLES LUTWIDGE DODGSON,
(LEWIS CARROLL.)
FELL ASLEEP JAN. 14. 1898.
AGED 65 YEARS.

This is so creepy! But it is also sort of cool. I'm standing at the actual burial site of the literary genius who penned Alice's Adventures in Wonderland.

Caitlin's arms shivered.

She checked the time. 7:40 p.m.

Caitlin sent a text to Jack: *I'm at the grave. Where r u?*

No response.

Everything had become eerily silent. No footsteps. No wind. No hissing branches. Not a single sound. Caitlin clenched her fist around her phone.

Better call Jack.

As she lifted her finger to dial, she froze.

A long, irregular shadow began creeping over her … slowly…

She heard breathing. More footsteps. Then they stopped. Someone was now standing directly behind her casting that shadow.

For some reason the garbanzo beans in her pocket came to mind. And the fingerprints on her window.

Her windpipe constricted.

She shot up and turned around, fully prepared to scream like a banshee and run like a deer if it wasn't Jack standing there.

Her eyes widened in total disbelief.

Then her jaw dropped.

She couldn't scream.

And her knees were locked.

It wasn't Jack.

CHAPTER TEN

JACK SPRINTED INTO THE KINGSHIRE ALL HALLOWS EVE Masquerade Ball and began to look around, desperately searching for Caitlin.

He was donning his Arthurian knight attire—fitted gray boots, narrow pants, silver-trimmed tunic, sword, and a chain-mail cowl. And though he looked quite majestic, adventurous, and definitely medieval, his face was a mask of concern.

He had been stunned when he buzzed at Caitlin's apartment and her father said she had already left for the ball.

He wondered if she was bailing on him, or if she mistakenly thought they were supposed to meet at Kingshire?

Jack scanned the crowd. All the faces were covered in masks or heavy makeup; it was nearly impossible to identify who she—or anyone, for that matter—was. And he had no idea what costume Caitlin was supposed to be wearing.

A hand tapped him on the shoulder.

"Greetings, chivalrous knight."

Jack turned. A very sexy female vampire stood there, blood dripping from her fangs. She was holding Jack's mobile in her hand. Piper.

"You left this at Penhaligon's," she said, batting her fake eyelashes. The tone of her voice radiated heat. "Now I'd like to collect my reward."

Jack took the phone, nodding his thanks. "Have you seen Caitlin?"

Piper's eyes widened innocently. "I thought she was coming with you?"

Jack didn't have time for Piper's BS. He left her standing there as he waded into the sea of masked partygoers. He checked his mobile to see if Caitlin had called.

Nothing.

Then a new text message arrived.

From Caitlin: *I'm here at grave. Where r u?*

Jack's heart skipped a beat.

He glanced back at Piper. Her pale vampire face went a shade whiter as their eyes met. She promptly turned away and melted into the mob of masqueraders.

Jack tore out of Kingshire, hell-bent and determined. He dashed toward Waterloo Station.

He couldn't believe what a cruel prank that was to play on Caitlin.

When Caitlin gets to that tombstone . . . all by herself . . . Bloody hell, she'll positively freak out.

His legs pumped harder. He called Caitlin on his mobile as he raced through Central London. Voice mail.

Jack quickened his pace.

He was utterly grateful when he reached Waterloo station and saw that he was just in time to board a train bound for Guildford.

He only hoped it wasn't too late.

CHAPTER ELEVEN

THE LONG, DARK SHADOW THAT HAD CREPT OVER CAITLIN WAS A whole lot larger than the small, bright, yellow-and-red figure who had cast it.

"Perhaps there's some adventure in you after all," giggled the shadow.

Natalie!

She was still in her red chili pepper costume and yellow raincoat. Her wet red hair flowed like a frizzy lion's mane.

"What are you doing here?" Caitlin screamed. "Dad would freak if he knew you came all this way by yourself."

"You forgot to bring your birthday present," she said.

Her tablet!

"Don't worry; I have it," Natalie said as she yanked it out from inside her coat. It was wrapped in pale-blue, plastic take-out bags. Caitlin was glad to have it, but she was upset that

Natalie had tagged along and traveled to Guildford all alone at night. Nonetheless . . .

"I owe you," Caitlin said.

"Don't we know it." Natalie held up her camera. "Here's your first photo op. Standing at the grave of Lewis Carroll."

Caitlin shook her head and scowled.

Click.

"Isn't Jack supposed to be here?" Natalie asked.

He certainly was. Caitlin checked the time again on her phone, and as if on cue, it rang. Slick from the rain, it slipped out of her hand. It dropped right in front of the headstone! Right on top of Dodgson's grave.

"Whoops. Sorry, Charles," Caitlin said as she kneeled to pick it up.

As her hand reached for the phone, the grass shifted.

That's weird.

Then it rolled like a wave. Instinct always seeks the logical, and Caitlin's first thought was that a sinkhole must be forming from the pounding rain.

A second wave rumbled the ground. Caitlin willed herself to believe it would be the last one, the same way she always willed herself to wake up from the throes of a nightmare when it was about to overwhelm her.

Not this time.

A small mound of grass thumped, as if being punched up from beneath the surface.

An earthquake then? Unlikely.

The rest of the cemetery grounds had remained motionless.

Natalie took cover behind the wide trunk of the pine tree next to the grave. She crouched down, out of sight, camera poised. She was ready to photograph whatever happened next.

Caitlin's mind floundered for a rational explanation.

Rain must've flooded the grave.

Mud beneath the ground is being pushed to the surface.

How absurd to even think for a moment that a body might be clamoring to get out.

Caitlin again reached for her phone.

A pile of soil suddenly spit up like a geyser.

A shimmer of ice-blue light spiked through Charles Dodgson's grave.

Then a white, bony hand broke through.

Caitlin's terrified scream rang out into the night.

The pale, cold hand seized her wrist.

Caitlin's body iced over with spindly needles. Her eyes grew wider than two full moons. She jerked her hand wildly and screamed again. "Let go of me!"

Powered by adrenaline, Caitlin yanked herself free. In the moment that followed, there was an uncanny quiet.

A voice broke the silence.

"Caitlin, are you there?"

Jack!

His voice was coming from her phone. Hearing it stopped Caitlin from losing it, momentarily.

A second pale, dead hand rose from the dirt. Two arms groped upward toward the sky, emerging from beneath the glowing muck and soil. Long, slender limbs, with scars and stitches cut into the forearms, began pulling at the ground—clawing, raking away globs of mud. Both palms then pressed against the soil for leverage.

Caitlin went numb. Charles Lutwidge Dodgson was climbing out of his grave. *This might actually be more terrifying than dancing in front of people!*

Natalie stood behind the tree trunk, her camera flashing away.

A jagged arc of lightning cut through black clouds. The corpse's spindly fingers dug deep into the dirt, working to extract their body from the bowels of the earth. Natalie's camera flashed bright. Through the sharp camera light and cold, blue glow seeping from the grave, Caitlin observed something that struck her as even more bizarre.

The fingernails on those rotting hands were elegant and manicured and actually quite pretty.

Huh?

These were not the hands of a dead man who'd been buried for nearly two hundred years.

They were the attractive hands of a girl!

And she was now climbing out of the grave!

CHAPTER TWELVE

In the charming and historic town of Guildford, on the night of October 31st, the evening of Halloween, a dead *girl* was apparently climbing out of a *man's* grave in the old Mount Cemetery. She finally uprooted herself completely from the dirt, leaving a large gaping hole in the ground.

From behind the pine tree, Natalie snapped away.

"Caitlin! Are you there?" Jack was still on the phone, calling to her from a mound of mud. Unfortunately, a certain obstacle separated Caitlin from her phone.

A beautiful dead girl who now seemed very much alive.

Caitlin let go of the breath she didn't realize she'd been holding. Blood found its way back into her knuckles. Her tensed shoulders slackened.

It finally dawned on her, though she had already intuited what was going on in the back of her mind the whole time.

Caitlin was the victim of a Halloween prank brilliantly

orchestrated by Jack. He probably had majorly buff rugby leg-end Barton Sullivan dig that massively deep hole.

Ha, ha, ha.

The dead girl pulled her long, slender legs up from the ground and dusted off the dirt. Caitlin noticed that her blonde hair, though, stretched back into the grave. As the girl pulled it up, it kept on coming. And coming. And coming. Caitlin stared at the full length of her exquisite, long, braided locks. They seemed to flow on forever into the depth of the grave. Her hair wasn't decayed like the rest of her body. It was silky and golden. Shimmering. A tumble of hair that Caitlin would die for—no pun intended.

"Excellent zombie makeup and costume," said Caitlin with a hint of nervousness in her voice. "So, where's Jack?"

The long-legged, long-haired zombie girl turned slowly. She made eye contact with Caitlin.

"Kudos," Caitlin continued. "A brilliantly executed prank. Scared me half to death."

The girl didn't respond. She simply stared back with cold eyes.

What's her problem?

Then the girl reached out her right hand. Caitlin flinched. The zombie gripped the collar of Caitlin's raincoat with her bony fingers.

"Hey!"

She effortlessly lifted Caitlin straight into the air. A good four feet off the earth.

Oh my God!

Faster than lightning, she yanked Caitlin toward her so they stood face to face. Except, of course, Caitlin was hanging by her collar.

Her veins pulsed with blood.

The dead girl's strength was inhuman!

The more Caitlin struggled, the harder it became to breathe. Finally, Caitlin let her body go limp. She dangled there by the scruff, her collar gripped tightly in the strong grip of the female ghoul.

The dead girl then uttered four words. Four words that Caitlin never expected to come out of a zombie's mouth.

"I need your help."

CHAPTER THIRTEEN

CAITLIN SWAYED IN THE NIGHT AIR AS THE DEAD GIRL'S COLD, DAMP breath hit her in the face like a winter wind. Unlike warm human breath, which produced a white cloud when exhaled into cold air, no steam rose from this girl's mouth.

And her breath . . . there was no odor to it. It was cold and scentless like ice. That fact unnerved Caitlin to the bone—as if she wasn't already scared to death.

Natalie, unfazed, stayed hidden behind the tree, clicking her camera. The dead girl did not seem to notice the flashes. Caitlin tried to signal her sister to stop before this creature caught sight of her.

The dead girl's gaze was unwavering.

The corners of Caitlin's mouth began to tremble. "What do you want?"

"I'm hungry," she said.

Caitlin struggled frantically.

"But I'm not here to eat," the dead one said. "Not if you can help me."

Caitlin calmed down slightly. The dead girl was forthright and spoke with a British accent.

"I could help you a lot better if you'd kindly put me down," Caitlin said.

The ghoul lowered Caitlin gently to the ground. Caitlin lunged for her cell.

She pressed the phone to her ear. "Jack?"

Silence.

Caitlin hit the Call Back button, but before it could connect, and before Caitlin could even see it coming, the dead girl's lightning-quick finger tapped the End Call button.

"No calls," said the zombie. "I came here to find someone."

"Who?"

"Someone named Caitlin Rose Fletcher."

Caitlin's heart stopped cold.

"Hey, that's you!" Natalie shouted from behind the tree trunk.

Way to go, Natalie.

Caitlin's mouth fell open, partly because a real-live dead person was looking for *her* and partly because her kid sister had just thrown her under the bus!

Natalie snapped pic after pic as the dead girl's eyes scanned Caitlin from head to toe.

Caitlin dried off her phone and stuck it in her jacket.

She turned to the ghoul. "How do you know my name? And why are you looking for me?"

"I need you to slide down into that hole." The zombie pointed to her own long rope of hair, which still stretched down into the depths of the gleaming grave.

Natalie broke out in laughter. "Hey, zombie chick, my sister would rather face an *army* of walking dead than plunge herself into that glowing pit!"

"Zombie Chick's" head swiveled, zeroing in on Natalie. Anger flared from her pretty, dead eyes. Natalie cowered behind the pine.

"Back off," Caitlin said. "That's my kid sister."

The zombie girl's expression softened.

Natalie fearlessly emerged from behind the safety of the tree.

"That grave doesn't even belong to you!" she shouted.

In her stylish yellow boots, Natalie stomped over the muddy mound and right up to the zombie. "You're not Charles . . . Lewis . . . Carroll . . . Dodgson . . . or whatever his name is. So what are you doing messing with his grave?"

Caitlin's kid sister was half the size of the zombie, but that didn't stop her from getting up in her face.

"Where I come from," Natalie continued, "we call that invasion of privacy. And trespassing."

Natalie had finally moved close enough for Caitlin to yank her out of reach of the zombie.

"Charles has been resting in peace for more than a century," the dead girl said. "I'm borrowing his grave as a sort of off-ramp."

"Off-ramp?" Caitlin exclaimed. "Off-ramp from what?"

"The wormholes."

Caitlin's brow scrunched. "Excuse me?"

Natalie's eyes flickered like fireflies in the dark. *"Wormholes* are shortcuts," she said to her sister. "They bridge distant regions of the universe by traversing the space-time continuum."

Sometimes Girl Wonder does come in handy.

The long-haired dead girl smiled and explained, "Certain graves in your world are the gateways into the wormholes. They connect distant dimensions and faraway worlds."

"Which graves are you talking about? Caitlin asked.

Long-haired dead girl smiled. "The ones belonging to the storytellers."

Caitlin glanced over at the plaque posted at the foot of the grave. A gleam lit her eye.

"You mean like Lewis Carroll?"

"I do. And JM Barrie. And Hans Christian Andersen. And the Brothers Grimm. Do you understand?"

She did. Caitlin saw it clear in her mind's eye. And it made her skin tingle from awe. The graves of all the great story-tellers were not just ordinary graves. They were portals into the mythic kingdoms and wondrous worlds found in the beloved fairy tales of childhood.

Natalie obviously got it as well. Her eyes had opened like a book. "We're totally going, sibling."

"There's no freaking wa—"

Caitlin's phone buzzed.

Jack!

Caitlin desperately wanted to tell him that the sightings were positively real.

She lifted her finger to accept the call when a movement she saw out the corner of her eye made her pause. She pivoted. Her heart stopped.

Natalie was sliding down the zombie's luminous locks. She was headed straight into the wet, muddy pit of the grave.

"Natalie! Don't!"

Caitlin dove across the mud-drenched ground to grab her sister's hand. But she only managed to break Natalie's grip on the zombie's hair. Caitlin watched, horrified, as Natalie fell into the glowing tomb. She vanished quickly, leaving only a fading scream behind her.

"Yippeeeeee!"

CHAPTER FOURTEEN

THE ZOMBIE FIXED HER DEAD, ENCHANTING PUPILS ON CAITLIN AND sighed.

"You have a choice: slide down my hair or fall into the hole like the little one just did. Which will it be?"

Another crack of lightning split the sky. Caitlin felt her chest vibrate as thunder shook the humid air. A split second of silence, then—*pow!* Bucketfuls of rain poured from the dark sky.

"Hurry," warned the zombie, "before the rain pushes the dirt back into the passage and the poor kid is stuck there for good!"

Caitlin bit off a sliver of thumbnail.

"What's actually down there?" she asked.

Long-haired registered a coy smile, which only amplified Caitlin's anguish.

There's no choice here. None. My sister is somewhere down that hole. That's all that mattered at that moment.

Caitlin set her tablet against the tree trunk next to the grave. She slid her mobile into her front right pocket.

Then she scrunched up her face and climbed onto the zombie's shimmering strands of hair. She slowly lowered herself into the grave, fully expecting to wake up from the bizarre dream at any moment.

The passageway smelled like a wet dog. She clung to that rope of hair for dear life, her fingers gripping it till her knuckles gleamed white.

Am I really sliding into a grave on a cable of golden, braided hair?

Her mobile rang.

Jack!

But she didn't dare let go of that rope to retrieve her phone.

"You have to keep moving!" said long-haired dead girl. "You can't just hang there."

Inch by inch, Caitlin submerged herself into the hole, holding her breath for as long as she could, then sucking in what she believed every time might be her last gulp of oxygen. Mud pressed against her sopping wet body, and pasty, cold lumps of it clung to her arms.

"Slide!" the zombie shouted from above. "We don't want the walls to close around us!"

No, we don't!

Caitlin inhaled. She closed her eyes. She unclenched her grip ever so slightly.

She began her descent.

The lower she dropped, the faster she fell. She was sinking

and sliding along the twisting braids The silken tresses massaged her palms as braided folds slipped through her stiff-but-slightly-open fists.

As she continued down the hair, the muscles in her body relaxed.

She opened her eyes.

The mud on the tunnel walls was now dry and hardened. And bathed in pale blue. Bright orange-and-pink streaks of light leaked through narrow cracks, and the faster Caitlin slid through the extraordinary passageway, the faster the streaks of light shimmered by, until she was sliding so fast they ran together into glowing, wide ribbons of color. Downward she whooshed, past lambent waves of light.

She heard a distinct, though distant, *meow* echoing from high above her.

That cat!

The cry amplified, and a second later the blue British Shorthair whizzed by, heading downward.

The tunnel, now awash in bright color, took a gentle curve, and Caitlin turned with it. The light shifted into swirling greens and twisting pinks.

She finally landed with a *thud*.

There was an uncanny silence.

Caitlin took a couple of big breaths. She looked around. She was in an old barn. It appeared to be empty except for the cat, which had landed cleanly on all four paws.

Before she could move, the cat bolted from the barn, leaving behind only the echo of a fading *meow*.

Caitlin glanced around again. Then she surveyed the hole she had fallen through.

Her hands turned clammy. She breathed in extra air to compensate for the lack of oxygen in her lungs. There was no escape, nowhere to run, nowhere to hide. No way to get back up that portal. No Natalie.

Caitlin forced herself to take stock of her surroundings. To settle down. The slatted, chipped walls showed more bare boards than paint, and the wood appeared to be rotting. Bales of hay were stacked to the ceiling, and piles of straw filled the corners. A pitchfork lay on the ground next to an overturned, rusty metal bucket. A faintly cheesy smell tickled her nose.

There was something extra peculiar about this barn. Then Caitlin realized what it was: it was uncommonly small, as if it had been built for a child. Caitlin's head almost bumped into the ceiling as she stood up.

Where the heck was she? Where on earth was Natalie?

Caitlin opened the barn door.

Daylight!

But it was a hazy, gray daylight.

She checked her phone for the time: 1:37 p.m.

Wow, well past noon! Definitely not my time zone.

Before leaving the barn, Caitlin snuck a quick look at the four corners of the ceiling.

One, two, three, four.

Then Caitlin stooped and maneuvered through the pint-size doorway. She stepped outside—into extreme heat, and into what appeared to be a miniature, abandoned village. Most of the buildings were shorter than she was. A row of cozy, thatched-roofed cottages circled a child-size, covered well. Caitlin could tell there had once been bright colors here. But now the colors were muted.

The windows on all the houses were broken. The walls seemed to sag against each other. Brown, patchy grass covered cracked, dry dirt, and the only green things she saw were weeds. Despite the intense heat, a murky sheet of fog hung between the sun and the clouds.

Caitlin took a few tentative steps. Tall weeds tickled her knees. She glanced back a few times at the barn door. A tiny grasshopper hopped across her path. She let out a shriek.

"What took you so long?" came a familiar voice.

Caitlin glanced up fast.

Her fists opened.

Her jaw unclenched.

For the first time in a long while, she was overjoyed to see her sister. The little twerp looked just fine. She was perched on top of a miniature brick schoolhouse, her camera swaying around her neck.

"I say we slide down that hole again!"

Caitlin shook her head. "Get down from there right now."

Natalie out stretched her arms, reaching for a flagpole on the front of the building and she slid to the ground. A frog abruptly hopped right over Natalie's feet while letting out a large *croak!* Then, with a few bounding leaps, the frog vanished into a mass of tall weeds.

"Cute!" Natalie exclaimed.

Caitlin checked her phone again. No bars, no signal, no way to reach Jack or emergency rescue.

Suddenly, a loud clunk. The barn shook. A moment later, long-haired dead girl emerged through the barn's crumbling double doors, her silky locks trailing behind.

Now, in daylight, Caitlin was able to get a good look at her. Though her attire was tattered and decayed, you could tell it had once been a stunning, purple-blue royal gown, embellished with a gleaming, gold V-shape belt. Her complexion was white as chalk, and the rims of her eyes dark as ink.

That hair!

It still had a fabulous glistening sheen. As if it contained magic.

"You still trying to call Jack?" the zombie asked.

How does she know about Jack?

"Actually, yes. But I lost my signal," Caitlin said.

"I'm not surprised."

Caitlin checked her voice mail.

Yes! A message from Jack.

"Caitlin, where are you? There's something I gotta tell you. Please listen. My ph—"

The message died. Her phone must've cut out as she'd slid down that grave hole.

"You'll get no signal in this place," the blonde ghoul said.

No signal? No phone? No texting? No communication with the outside world?

A frantic Caitlin suddenly felt like a castaway.

Abandoned. Stranded. Shipwrecked on some god-forsaken island far out in the ocean, cut off from . . . well, everything!

Her panicked eyes welled up with tears. She turned to the long-haired one. "Please. We have to go back up there. Now."

"But we need your help, Caitlin."

Caitlin shook her head. She wanted to get out of there—fast. The strange world felt like it was closing in on her. But she knew she shouldn't show that she was panicky.

"My dad will have the whole city searching for me if we're not home by ten. He's probably already got Scotland Yard out looking for Natalie."

Natalie elbowed Caitlin. "Technically speaking, Dad doesn't even know I'm gone."

Good one, Natalie.

Caitlin's breathing grew erratic. She started seeing spots. She crouched on the ground and put her head between her knees. The feeling eating her up inside was profoundly awful.

"Ugh. I'm trapped in the middle of nowhere. And I'm the worst sister on earth. I need to get out of here!"

Natalie crouched beside her. "Relax, Caity-pie. I'm guessing this is some kind of alternate reality or parallel universe that's congruent with the known laws of physics. However . . . "

"Will you shut up!" Caitlin yelled as she tried to stay focused on her own misery.

Natalie shrugged. She rose up and marched over to the zombie. "I'm thirsty. And zonked. It's way past my bedtime."

The zombie girl unhooked a leather bota bag that hung from her belt and handed it to Natalie.

"Thanks," said Natalie. "What is it?"

"Drinking pouch. With water. Until we find something more substantial."

Natalie tipped the spout of the kidney-shape pouch into her mouth and chugged.

"Drink up, little one," the zombie said. "Then we'd better get a move on. I'll explain everything when we find the others."

Natalie stopped drinking. "Others?"

CHAPTER FIFTEEN

CAITLIN AND NATALIE FOLLOWED THE ZOMBIE GIRL TO THE OUT-skirts of the village. They stepped over the crumbled remains of a thick stone perimeter wall and other ruins that still surrounded the town. Outside the village, drooping plants leaned into each other for support. An orange, parasitic-looking fungus covered crooked trees, climbing up their trunks and smothering their already-petrified leaves. Giant flowers that had clearly been enchantingly colorful and beautiful once had lost their luster and bloom. Jumbo dried mushrooms of faded purple, lime, and blue littered the landscape. Thick rotting tree stumps sat, lonesome, on abandoned grasslands.

As they crept onward, Caitlin glanced up at the sky and . . . and . . . and . . . she freaked!

"What is *that*?"

"The sun. Why?"

Caitlin couldn't believe it. It shone like the sun back home.

Even had the same color. What it didn't seem to have was the same shape.

Caitlin squinted through the veil of fog at the bright, odd thingamabob-shape solar orb in the sky. Though it was oddly shaped, it still somehow seemed familiar to her.

A walnut? No. *A closed fist?* Not really.

Then it hit her.

That had to be it!

The sun's glimmering form sort of resembled a translucent brain!

Is my mind playing tricks? Is it a mirage? An optical illusion?

Caitlin was reminded of an amusing game she'd played as a child. She'd stare at puffy clouds in the sky. Soon familiar shapes would appear in them, as if by magic.

Likewise, this sun seemed to project a shimmer in the shape of a brain.

How imaginatively weird!

Suddenly, two dainty, cold, dead hands latched onto her shoulders.

Caitlin was yanked backward.

She felt a frosty nose sniffing the back of her neck.

"Don't you dare, Cindy!" the long-haired girl called out.

"One taste?" came the voice attached to those dainty hands.

"One taste is never enough," the long-haired said. "It only makes us want a bigger second bite. I mean it, Cinderella! Let her go!"

Wha—?

Cinderella?

The dainty, dead hands spun Caitlin around. She was now staring directly into the face of the real, live . . . Cinderella? Only Cinderella wasn't really *alive*. She had the silvery-white complexion of death and the slightly sunken cheeks and dark-rimmed eyes of a ghoul risen from the grave. And yet she was elusively beautiful. And even though she was decomposing, her blonde hair and polished nails seemed well-groomed. Caitlin had always adored the tale of Cinderella. She gazed at her with awe.

Natalie's eyebrows practically popped off her forehead.

"This gets more surreal by the moment," Girl Wonder said.

Cinderella released Caitlin with a huff. Caitlin stood there, mouth agape, certain now that she was in the middle of some epic lucid dream. Perhaps, when she had fallen asleep in her room after school, she had gotten a high fever that was fueling these curiously symbolic imaginary events.

Long-haired dead girl flashed an apologetic smile.

"Please, forgive me. Where are my manners? I never did introduce myself. My name's Rapunzel."

The little girl in Caitlin was now doubly star struck—and surprised.

How could I not have recognized Rapunzel after seeing those exquisite, long, golden locks?

"Where am I?" Caitlin asked.

Rapunzel smiled. "A universe of extraordinary kingdoms and spellbinding worlds . . . at least they were before this degenerative affliction broke out."

Natalie elbowed Caitlin. "Aka zombification."

Cinderella sauntered over to chili-pepper Natalie. She circled her as if perusing a buffet. Then she turned to Rapunzel. "Perhaps a nibble on the hot and spicy one?"

Natalie swung her arms in the air. "Stay back, royal zombie chowhound!"

Rapunzel shot a disapproving look at Cinderella. Just then, another zombie appeared as if out of nowhere. This one was gracefully slender, with midnight-black hair, cherry lips, and a pale, metallic-white complexion.

Like . . . like . . . snow? It couldn't be! Could it?

"I'm Snow White," she said as she curtsied. "Pleased to make your acquaintance."

Caitlin blinked.

Natalie just sighed. "The hypnagogic hallucinations keep on coming."

Caitlin's vacant stare faded as the corners of her mouth curled into a wide smile. She forgot about being frightened or angry as a warm and pleasant feeling arose inside of her.

"I feel like I've known you all my life."

Rapunzel smiled broadly. "You must meet our other friend; look behind you." Caitlin whirled around. A captivating, ash-blonde zombie stood a few feet away.

Caitlin's eyes sparked with wonder. "Sleeping Beauty?"

Beauty held out her pale hand. "An honor to meet you, Caitlin."

Something must've clicked for Natalie, because her eyes grew big as billiard balls. "Are you guys, like, authentic flesh-eating zombies?"

"Indeed we are," Snow White said, her voice warm and gentle.

Natalie spun around to Rapunzel.

"You mean you're not wearing special-effects makeup and costumes? For Halloween?"

"Nope," said Rapunzel. She pinched a stitched scar seared into the pale flesh of her arm. "It's real."

"How radically intriguing," Natalie said.

Cinderella folded her arms across her chest. "Being dead is hardly intriguing." She eyed Natalie hungrily. "Especially when you're always famished!"

Sleeping Beauty pulled out a compact mirror and began patting her nose with a small powder puff. "Our complexions are always under the threat of mold. *You* try living up to the name 'Beauty' when your face is susceptible to mildew."

Natalie smiled at the zombie princesses. "I think you're hauntingly beautiful."

Caitlin also found it strange that these dead princesses had managed to remain attractive and regal. She always thought of zombies as slow-moving, drooling corpses—a walking gorefest of blood, decayed flesh, and rotted, spotty teeth.

Cinderella's face had the delicate features of a hand-painted porcelain doll. Her shimmering, pale-gray complexion was accentuated by a splashy pink-and-baby-blue dress—the kind that would turn heads in a royal ballroom. She also moved about gracefully on slender, bare feet.

Snow White's tousled coal-black hair and wide, deep-set, chocolate-brown eyes were absolutely gorgeous. Her skin was pale as fallen snow—and just as cold. The compassion in her eyes, however, would put anyone at ease. Her tattered top was golden yellow, her shredded skirt cobalt blue, and she, too, pranced about barefoot.

Sleeping Beauty was indeed worthy of her name. She was also shoeless, though breathtaking in an elegant pink-and-blue gown, which somehow managed to look stylishly tattered. A frayed sash hung smartly around her waist. Her hypnotic baby-blue gaze penetrated deeply; Caitlin thought she might be able to peer right into her dreams.

And Rapunzel? Rapunzel was clearly the leader of the group. The stunning zombie girl with the flowing, blonde locks was like a walking sunset. Endless ribbons of golden hair shimmered behind her like the sun setting over the horizon.

A look of shock overcame Caitlin's features as she caught Cinderella once again sniffing the neck of the red-hot chili pepper.

"Back away, Cindy," said Rapunzel, who shook her head, obviously frustrated by her friend's insatiable appetite.

Cinderella stepped back sulking.

"You know I crave spicy food."

Rapunzel turned to Caitlin. "It's not easy controlling these impulses. They never stop. And we're slowly losing control. Which is why we need your help."

"But why me?" Caitlin asked.

Snow White chimed in. "It's not about just helping *us*. This concerns all the subjects of this kingdom, including all the living things of the forest."

Snow bent down. She caressed the drooping stem of a fern with the back of her hand. The plant slowly opened its leaves and wrapped them around her arm, like it was giving her a hug.

"What happened to all of you?" asked Caitlin. "And what happened to this place?"

Rapunzel sighed and slowly shook her head. "That's what you're going to help us find out."

CHAPTER SIXTEEN

"ONCE UPON A TIME, OUR WORLDS EMBODIED PERFECTION," Rapunzel said. "Everyone lived happily in Wonderland. Life was genuinely joyful in the Emerald City, truly delightful in the Enchanted Forest, serene and content in Camelot, Neverland, Oz, Munchkin Country, Lilliput, and all the fairy-tale kingdoms. Then it happened."

"What?" Natalie asked.

Rapunzel's eyes darted around suspiciously. She placed her hands on Caitlin and Natalie's backs and nudged them forward.

"We need to keep moving."

Rapunzel led the way. "Staying in one place too long allows them to pick up our scent."

Caitlin lengthened her stride. "Who?"

"The Blood-Eyed."

Blood-Eyed? Blood-Eyed what?

Caitlin didn't want to know the answer. She tapped the back of Rapunzel's shoulder.

"So what happened after all the contentment everywhere?"

"Sleeping Beauty fell asleep."

Natalie and Caitlin exchanged puzzled looks as they scurried along.

Snow interjected while nodding toward Beauty. "She foresees things in her dreams."

"As I was saying," Rapunzel went on, "Beauty fell asleep. Upon waking, she told us of a strange dream she had—about the colors of the sun."

Caitlin's forehead scrunched. "What colors? Sunlight is white."

Natalie shook her head. "No. Sunlight includes *all* the colors of the rainbow. Each color is a different wavelength of light. Red is the longest wavelength. Blue is the shortest. The smaller rays scatter when the sun is low, which is why it sometimes looks only yellow, red, or orange, and violet—"

"Enough. Showoff!" Caitlin said with a scowl. She turned to Rapunzel. "So what happened to your sunlight?"

Rapunzel nodded at Beauty who immediately stopped in her tracks. She reached into the ruffles of her skirt and pulled out a sparkling, triangular-shaped crystal. She handed the crystal to Rapunzel.

Natalie's eyebrows arched. Rapunzel held the glittering gemstone up just above eye level. Then she delicately angled it toward the sun.

"See for yourself," Rapunzel said. A shaft of sunlight struck the crystal.

Now it was Caitlin's eyebrows' turn to bend up like bows.

From the bottom of the crystal, a rainbow of seven colors fanned out onto the ground: red, orange, yellow, green, blue, indigo, and violet.

A prism!

"Only six colors are shining in full splendor," Rapunzel noted, pointing at the top and bottom of the rainbow with her long, slender fingers. "One color is dimming."

She ran a finger through the green light, and Caitlin could see that its radiance was far weaker than the rest.

Natalie appeared fascinated by the phenomenon. Caitlin stared intently at the fading green shimmer.

"What does it mean?" Caitlin asked.

Snow White frowned. "We don't know yet. But Beauty foresaw it all in a dream, including the arrival of the Blood-Eyed. Isn't that right, Beauty?"

Silence.

Snow looked around. They all looked around.

"Beauty?"

A soft snoring was coming from the tall weeds to their left.

"She might have more to tell us when she wakes," Rapunzel said.

"What was that about us standing in one place for too long?" Caitlin asked.

Rapunzel sighed. "Occupational hazard; it's impossible to

rouse her. Be on alert until she wakes. And, actually, it was through one of Beauty's inconvenient, prescient dreams that we were instructed to come find you."

Caitlin forced herself to ask two dreadful questions. "But *why me?* And what are the Blood-Eyed?"

"And where is everybody?" Natalie added. "This place, and that undersized village for people of slight stature are deserted."

The zombie girls fidgeted nervously. Caitlin looked over at Snow, who avoided eye contact and rubbed her neck. Rapunzel pretended to fuss with her hair.

"And why are you all so jumpy?" Natalie asked.

Rapunzel swallowed. "The Queen of Hearts."

"From Wonderland? You mean she's real?" Caitlin asked in a jittery tone.

Cinderella laughed. "As real as the beings inhabiting *your* world. Probably *more* real."

Snow White cringed. She covered Cinderella's mouth with her hand. "Don't go there, Cindy. Not now. You're liable to frighten her."

Caitlin glanced back and seriously contemplated grabbing Natalie and making a run for it. Except Natalie was grinning like a Cheshire Cat. Nothing would delight that red-haired dork more than a discussion on the nature of reality.

Rapunzel raised her hand to silence Snow and Cindy. She then turned to Caitlin.

"Listen close. One morning, the queen's herald banged a gong from atop the castle keep, then the queen raised her royal

scepter to the sky. She waved it east, west, north, and south."
Rapunzel swallowed. A tinge of sorrow glinted in her eyes.
"From that moment on, everything changed. Beauty had seen it
happen in her dream."

"What changed?" Caitlin asked.

Snow's face became solemn. "It started with the vegetable
kingdom. Plants. Trees. Flowers. They started decaying."

"A few days later," Cinderella added, "the queen slammed us
with a second wave of her scepter."

"That's when the decay spread to the animal kingdom,"
Snow said.

Cinderella nodded. "Yeah. The three Billy Goats Gruff
turned into billy goat ghouls, and the three little pigs grew
scars like Franken-ham."

"It was horrible," Snow said. "The food supply almost completely dried up."

Cindy looked back at Rapunzel.

"It was the third wave that affected the highest thinkers.
The Munchkins. Dwarfs. Pirates. Fairies. Elves. All forms of
people—even Pinocchio, and he's made of wood."

Rapunzel exhaled. "After that third wave, the affliction
sparked a relentless urge."

"For what?"

Rapunzel's commanding eyes hardened. "Anything. At first,
people started taking things." She shook her head. "Thieving.
Stealing. Then the bodies soon began decaying. At first, it only
affected people's outward appearance—their clothes and flesh.
But then it started to creep inward. Empathy and decency were

drained from the heart. The urge to survive grew stronger. Strange, dark cravings arose. *Savage* cravings. Bright twinkling eyes turned dark, like hot coals."

Even Natalie gulped. "The Blood-Eyed?"

The zombie girls nodded in unison.

"And with those burning crimson eyes," Cinderella said in a tone that grew grimmer with each spoken word, "there came unspeakable yearnings to consume anything . . . especially flesh and blood."

Caitlin shuddered.

Cinderella looked her in the eye. "The populace became like mindless automatons, operating under the complete control of their depraved impulses. Enslaved by their diabolic desires. They had become remorseless, bloodthirsty ghouls."

Caitlin squeezed Natalie's hand tightly.

Snow waved a finger. "With positively no manners and not a trace of dignity."

Cindy's eyes narrowed like a fox's. "They're dangerously agile. And deceptively quick. They're also clever as weasels when it comes to hunting down food."

"B-b-ut, what about you girls?" Caitlin said with a quiver in her voice as Cinderella eyeballed Natalie again. "Your eyes are still . . . *so beautiful.*"

"Royal blood. It gives us more resilience to resist the urges."

"I'm only royal by marriage," Cinderella noted. "Thinner blood . . . " She leaned in toward Natalie. "Which explains why your scent remains succulent to my senses."

Natalie shrugged her off and muttered, "Pays to be a princess."

Snow said, "Our eyes won't be clear for long, though." The zombie girls exchanged worried glances as she continued. "If Beauty's dream is accurate, the queen's herald will sound the gong again on Halloween Night. Tonight. At midnight. And then she'll wave her scepter for the fourth and final time." Her eyes welled up. "We'll never survive it."

Beauty stretched and yawned, as she awoke from her catnap.

"Right now," Rapunzel said, "we can control our cannibalistic urges by satisfying our appetites with spicy food."

Cinderella whipped out a long, red sausage. "Pepperoni, anyone?" She bit off the tip and chewed heartily—while leering at Natalie. "And little you," Cindy continued, caressing the edges of her chili pepper costume, "stuffed inside that pungent pepper outfit. What a delectable snack for *moi*!-"

Natalie glared. "You're excreting saliva on my shoulder."

"Shut it down, Cindy," Rapunzel ordered.

Caitlin was now convinced she needed to do whatever it took to get out of here before Natalie wound up in some ghoul's digestive tract. And if that meant helping these zombie princesses, so be it.

"I had another dream," Beauty said.

Ears perked up and the group gave Sleeping Beauty their full attention.

"He's ready to help us," she said. "He knows how to end this malignant affliction!"

"Who?" Caitlin asked.

"A wise, old sage," Beauty replied. "A master of metamorphosis. The one who appeared in my dream. The one who instructed us to fetch you. He's demanding that we bring you to him in person."

Caitlin gulped.

"At once."

CHAPTER SEVENTEEN

NATALIE FLETCHER NODDED PENSIVELY AS SHE MASSAGED HER CHIN.

"Hmmm. A master of *metamorphosis*," she said. Her face brightened. "I'm betting he has twelve eyes. Am I right, ladies?"

Beauty nodded with a smile and said, "He's a wise caterpillar. And he can transform chaos into order."

Natalie pumped her fist in the air. "I knew it. The hookah-smoking caterpillar! From Wonderland. How cool."

"Okay," Caitlin said, "So where and why does this caterpillar need *me*."

"He usually hangs out at the Ali Baba Ganoush Hookah Lounge," Cindy said.

Snow frowned. "Oh, no! That place is most unsavory. We cannot bring children in there."

Natalie crossed her arms in a huff, obviously offended.

"Don't worry," Beauty responded. "The caterpillar gave up the hookah. He's an organic tea drinker now. In my dream, I saw him hiding in a cave near his mushroom. He's trying to steer clear of the Blood-Eyed."

"There's proof of his wisdom," Natalie whispered to Caitlin.

"I saw a boulder," Beauty said. "Covered in moss. It sits by the hidden entrance to his cave. We'll recognize it by large clusters of four-leaf clovers surrounding it."

"Is he a caterpillar or a leprechaun?" Natalie muttered.

"How do we find it?" Rapunzel asked.

"I can get us there," Snow interjected in a solemn tone. She closed her eyes and raised a hand to catch the soft warm wind. She caressed it with her fingers.

An exasperated Caitlin stamped her foot. "Will someone please tell me *why* you need *me*?"

Beauty gently put an arm around Caitlin's shoulders. "Only he knows that. That's why you must go to him."

"Can this caterpillar help me get back home?"

Natalie smirked. "Sounds like there's a yellow-brick road in our future."

Beauty gave Natalie a blank look. "No. That belongs to another kingdom, rather far from here."

"I was being irreverent."

"Oh." Beauty yawned.

Snow White opened her eyes as she turned to survey the vast landscape. She pointed southward. "Zeno's Forest lies that way."

Zeno's Forest?

When the zombie girls saw the direction Snow was pointing, their faces became a collective mask of concern.

"You sure you wanna go that way?" Cindy asked.

Snow shrugged nervously. "No choice."

AFTER A GOOD HALF AN HOUR OF HIKING UNDER A BLISTERING SUN, the girls came upon an expansive meadow overrun with bamboo plants; large, green flowers; and rows of odd-shaped plants that were mostly the same size as Natalie—though some were three times her size.

The blooms of the green flowers were oval-shaped and their petals were mainly all closed. They were attached to thick, succulent stems. When the large, elongated pods did open, they did so unexpectedly and on their own, like magic books.

Crimson glistened on the insides of the pod petals. The leaves were lined with long, graceful wisps. From a distance, they looked like fluttering eyelashes, delicately opening and closing.

Caitlin wondered why these flowers had remained green— they were not decaying.

"Better get ready to dance and dash," Cinderella said as they drew close.

Dance and dash?

Snow explained. "The flora here rely on something besides water and sun for nourishment."

"Yeah, like rodents," Cindy said. "Those plus-size pods could easily hold a few rats."

"*Hehhhhhhhh.*"

A weird hiss was audible as they drew closer to the flower field.

Caitlin jumped. "Snakes!"

Her bulging eyeballs scoured the withered grass beneath her feet.

"*Hehhhhhhhh.*" A louder hiss.

The bulbous head of a green flower suddenly unhinged like a jaw. Saw-blade sharp, polished fangs glistened in the sunlight. They dripped thick mucus.

"*Hehhhhhhhh!*" The flower hissed like a python, pivoting its eyeless face toward the girls. Caitlin shuddered. Those graceful wisps they'd seen from afar were in fact spindly, pronged teeth. They studded the inner edge of each pod half. The flower opened its jaw. A hot-pink tongue lashed out at Caitlin.

"*Sssssssss!*"

Natalie took out her camera and snapped a couple pictures of the monstrous plants. She seemed thoroughly intrigued.

"What are these ghastly creatures?" Caitlin asked.

Natalie lowered her camera. "They appear to be some exotic form of *Dionaea muscipula.*"

"English, please."

"Venus flytraps."

Cindy elbowed Caitlin. "*Ravenous* and *carnivorous* Venus flytraps."

Caitlin rocked back and forth on her heels. "You mean, like, flesh-eating plants?"

"I do," Cindy replied. "And those razor-sharp teeth also secrete venom."

Caitlin swallowed.

Deeper in the meadow, Caitlin could see more unfamiliar

and fierce-looking plant life. All species were supersized and scattered thickly across the dry grassland.

Natalie snapped another photo and said, "It's the meadow from hell."

"Got that right," Cindy said.

"What's that disgusting, foul odor?" Caitlin asked as she suppressed a gag reflex.

"Corpse flowers," Natalie said, aiming her camera at the flower patch. She snapped two more pictures and said, "They stink like rotting corpses. The stench attracts blowflies and beetles, which feast on decomposing flesh. Don't get too close. If that putrid smell invades your nostrils, you'll be projectile vomiting lickety-split."

Cindy lifted her chin. Her nose twitched. She was sniffing the air. "But I sense something sweet too," she said.

Natalie pointed. "Over there. The carnivorous pitcher plants." The meat-eating plants had huge pitcher-shaped digestive tracts easily big enough to hold a frog or two.

"Their leaves are moistened with sweet nectar," Natalie said, "But it's a deathtrap. When a bug comes to taste, it lands on the slippery rim of the pitcher. The insect slips into the pitcher and drowns in a pool of digestive enzymes."

Ugh!

Natalie suddenly squinted and knitted her brows together in bewilderment.

"What is it?" Caitlin asked.

"Cannibal tree."

Caitlin followed Natalie's line of sight. There it was: a

twenty-foot-high tree with a thick, pineapple-shape trunk stood tall in a grove. Long, slithering tendrils moved around like octopus arms.

Natalie slowly shook her head in amazement. "It's called the Madagascar Tree. Some call it the Devil Tree. Except this particular species is not supposed to exist. At least not where we come from."

"What are you talking about?" Caitlin asked.

Natalie was clearly in her element.

"Karle Liche."

"Who's he?"

"A German explorer. He visited Madagascar back in the late 1800s. He came upon a cannibal tree. Said it possessed some kind of demonic intelligence. With his own eyes he watched the tree snatch a primitive tribeswoman. Wrapped her up in its tendrils. Kept her wrapped up like that for a week. When the tree finally let her go, all that was left of her was her smiling skull. Except someone claimed that Karl Liche never existed. And that the whole story had been made up. A fabricated myth."

Caitlin relaxed her shoulders. But Natalie remained spellbound as she pointed vigorously at the Devil Tree.

"Except *that's* the tree from the story." She poked her finger in its direction. "It fits the description to a *T*."

Cindy smiled guilefully. "Welcome to our world."

Caitlin felt the blood rush from her face.

Natalie shrugged. "Stop worrying. Just steer clear of the tree. It's the garden of Venus flytraps on that winding path in front of us that you need to worry about."

Natalie suddenly handed her camera to Cindy and slid out of her yellow boots. She plunged barefoot into the deadly flower patch, dodging and dancing between the snakelike stems of the stabbing flowers. Caitlin could only watch, slack-jawed.

"Natalie!" shouted Caitlin in panic.

Thankfully, her kid sister made it safely to the other side of the patch. But instead of appearing pleased with herself or cocky about her deft maneuvering, Caitlin could see that Natalie had turned white as a ghost—a rarity for Girl Wonder.

"Natalie, what is it?" Caitlin shouted. Natalie didn't answer. She only pointed toward a particular flytrap in the middle of the patch.

Caitlin clutched her chest.

A furry blue cat's tail dangled from the plant's throat. Then a sickly, morbid meow seeped out of its jaw.

My God! The blue British Shorthair cat!

Natalie whimpered. Caitlin stared helplessly.

"That poor kitten," Snow White said. "We have to help her."

"Poor *us!*" Cindy replied. "We might be next."

Before Snow could run to assist, the cat's tail disappeared down the plant's throat leaving only a deathly silence behind.

Rapunzel shook back her hair and raised her chin. "Don't worry. I'm armed."

Snow White's brow furrowed. "Rapunzel . . . you promised."

"Stop whining, Snow. Did you see what that . . . that *thing* did to little blue kitty cat over there?"

Cindy nodded decisively and muttered, "Fanged that unfortunate feline to kingdom come."

Rapunzel turned to Snow. "I'll only use it as a last resort. Now let's get going."

To everyone's shock, Cindy suddenly began to hike up her skirt. She exposed long, bare, sexy legs.

"Cindy, really!" Snow scolded. "That's not very dignified or courtly."

Cindy paid her no attention. She hiked her skirt a bit higher. Then she knotted the hems above the knee. Snow's look of disfavor suddenly gave way to a knowing smile.

Snow now gathered the edges of her own skirt. She unashamedly slid it up to her thigh, and tied it firm and tight. Rapunzel and Beauty exchanged wary looks, then followed suit. Rapunzel then reeled in her long flow of locks and bundled her hair up in a bun. She tucked it under her arm like an oversized football.

Caitlin sighed gratefully as she patted her skin-tight denim. With so many needle-like fangs nipping at them wildly, the flytraps would surely snatch up loose garments.

The girls approached the carnivorous flower patch. One at a time, with meticulous and precise footing choices, they darted and hopped through the flesh-eating obstacle course. Snarling jaws snapped mere centimeters from their legs.

One beefy flower suddenly arched its stem, cobra-style. It pounced on Snow White.

Whhhiiippp!

Its vicious mandible clamped down on her foot.

It tightened. Twisted.

Snow dropped to the ground. She landed in a patch of moss. The flytrap's fangs sunk deep into her ankle. Snow wailed in pain.

Horrified and dumbstruck, Caitlin stumbled. She teetered over a patch of hissing flytraps. She regained her balance and froze, contorting her body to barely avoid snapping fangs.

Rapunzel reached behind her and into a narrow bag strapped across her back. She extracted a long, metal baton. It had a shiny, golden tip.

"No!" Snow screamed.

Cindy winked at Caitlin. "The zapper."

"That hideous flower has you in its jaws," Rapunzel said. "How can you have compassion for these . . . *things?*"

"They feel pain. And you promised."

"I promised I would only use it as a last resort."

Snow cried out again as the flytrap tightened its bite.

Rapunzel's frown sharpened. "And this is a last resort."

"Help Caitlin first!" Snow screamed as beads of sweat trickled down her face. "We need her."

Rapunzel brandished her baton and tipped her head toward Caitlin. "Don't move. Not an eyelash. When I give you the word, run. *Fast!*"

Caitlin stood perfectly still, struggling to maintain her impossible pose.

A flytrap opened its head. Its set of needle-sharp fangs prepared to strike. Caitlin's flesh tingled. Rapunzel thrust her prod into the flytrap's head just before it bit. The flower stiffened from electroshock! It convulsed, sizzled, smoked, and then fell limply to the ground in a crumpled heap.

"Now!" Rapunzel shouted. "RUN! NOW!"

Caitlin dashed for her life between beds of biting flower heads.

"You can do it!" Natalie shouted.

Caitlin felt Rapunzel close at her heels. Crackling sounds sizzled behind her. She stole a backward glance. Hordes of vicious flytraps were flinging themselves at them, trying to plant their razor-sharp teeth into her legs. Rapunzel fried them one by one. Short puffs of smoke ignited with each zap as plants drooped over, one after another. The acrid smell of roasted petals burned in Caitlin's nostrils.

She picked up her pace. Her calf muscles burned as she weaved and bobbed her way to the other side, finally reaching Natalie and safety.

Rapunzel turned back. She raised her weapon. Like a Roman gladiator, she fenced her way back across the flower patch, leaving behind a scorched trail of wilted, wounded flytraps. The seared plants lay limp; their toasted heads flopped in all directions, wet, pink tongues hanging out in defeat.

Cinderella scrambled back through the patch of broiled plants, heading for Rapunzel. Caitlin and Natalie followed.

SLEEPING BEAUTY, IN THE MEANTIME, WANDERED OVER TO A SMALL clearing of grass as a heavy sleepiness descended upon her. She made a pillow out of some fallen leaves. No sooner had she laid her head upon on the withered leaves, though, than two snakelike tendrils slithered under her arms and coiled around her shoulders. Simultaneously, a third tendril wormed around her head, roping her mouth shut before she could react. Beauty screamed, but only muffled squeaks slipped out.

The tendrils belonged to the Devil Tree. And they began dragging a bug-eyed Beauty back toward its trunk.

CAITLIN, NATALIE, AND RAPUNZEL RUSHED OVER TO SNOW, NOW facedown in the moss. The flytrap's fangs were still lodged in her flesh. Rapunzel poked the plant with the cattle prod.

Zzzzzzzt!

The fangs recoiled from Snow's leg. Rapunzel closed her eyes in relief.

Caitlin glanced about. "Hey, where's Beauty?"

"Sleeping, no doubt," Rapunzel replied.

Caitlin turned back to Snow White. Snow still wasn't moving. Alarmed, Caitlin nudged Rapunzel, who then shook Snow by the shoulders. No response. No movement.

Caitlin grimaced. "Is she dead?"

Cindy rolled her eyes. "We're all dead. Not the problem here."

"She's comatose," Rapunzel said. "She'll sleep for eternity if we don't extract the venom from her bloodstream."

Caitlin and Natalie exchanged nervous glances.

"Step back," Cindy said. "I'll suck the poison out of her."

"No!" Rapunzel shouted. "With your uncontrollable appetite, you're liable to eat it. Then *you'll* slip into a coma."

"Such a pessimistic princess. How about little certitude in *moi?*"

Cindy elbowed the girls back. She then leaned over the deep gash on Snow's ankle. Just as she was about to lower her lips onto the open wound, Natalie shouted, "Wait!"

Cindy glanced up. "What?"

"Germs."

Cindy rolled her eyes. "I don't care about a few germs."

Natalie stood firm. "There are hundreds of different species of bacteria in *your* mouth. And about twenty billion microbes. *You* could infect *her.*"

Rapunzel threw her hands up. "Now what? We're running out of time."

Suddenly Natalie's brow brightened. "Wait a sec!" She ran over to one of the bamboo plants and carefully broke off a shoot. She dashed back to Cindy, who took it from her with a grin.

"Bamboo shoot straw—good thinking, chili pepper."

Cindy carefully inserted the bottom end of the shoot into the wound on Snow's leg. Caitlin winced as blood-tinged mucus bubbled around its edges.

Cindy flung her hair back and hunched over the ankle. She wrapped her lips around the tip of the shoot and drew a deep breath to create suction flow. She opened her mouth, exhaled, then drew a second bountiful breath.

This time her face crinkled like a dried prune as liquid poison poured into her mouth. She leaped to her feet and stood on her tippy toes, arms jettisoned behind her. She then spit out a wad of neon-green, venomous blood. It sailed a good five feet through the air.

"Girl's got lungs," Natalie quipped.

Caitlin suppressed a gag as Cindy went back for a second sip of poison. After filling her mouth, she jumped up and spurted another mouthful of venom into the air before it splattered on the ground. She went two more rounds before Rapunzel put a stop to it.

"That'll do it. It's pure blood you're spitting now."

Rapunzel rolled Snow White onto her back. She put her hands on her cheeks and patted. "Wake up, girl."

"C'mon, Snow," Cindy said as she leaned close and gave her a hearty jostle by the shoulders.

Snow White opened her long-lashed eyelids. She was groggy. She sat up slowly. Then she gave Rapunzel a steely glare.

"I told you not to electrify those flowers!"

Rapunzel smiled and kissed Snow on the forehead. "You are truly unconditional. Now let's get Beauty and get out of here."

Caitlin quickly realized that she hadn't seen Beauty anywhere. No one had.

"Wake up, Beauty!" Rapunzel screamed as her eyes swiftly scanned the meadow. There was no response.

"The Devil's Tree . . . " Natalie muttered under breath. She screamed: "Hurry, over to the cannibal tree!"

Rapunzel's face went a shade paler. The girls dashed toward the grotesque, wooden carnivore. Rapunzel spread her arms to stop them about twenty feet in front of the tree. Their collective mouths fell open.

Beauty was pinned to the tree trunk, roped and gagged with oily, green tendrils. She was unconscious.

When they tried to approach, the tendril that was laced around her neck tightened viciously, as if in warning. Beauty was suffocating.

Caitlin *also* couldn't breathe. She began to step backward ever so slowly . . . she turned discreetly . . . and then she cut loose.

Caitlin raced back to the flower patch. She fetched the bamboo shoot from the ground, the one Cinderella had used to suck venom out of Snow. Caitlin dipped the shoot into the toxic blood still pooled on the ground. She sucked. When the venomous liquid filled the shoot, Caitlin plugged both ends using her forefinger and thumb. Then she gave a hearty spit.

Caitlin ran back to the tree, but this time she cut a wide arc, sidestepping pitcher plants and accidentally running through a patch of stinking corpse flowers. The stench of death was profoundly awful. Nausea rose in her throat. She plugged her nose as she sprinted. It didn't help. Caitlin turned her head left and projectile vomited.

Splat!

She weaved out of that wretched flower patch and breathed in fresh air to clear out the stench from her nostrils.

Natalie saw her coming from a distance.

Caitlin swung far around the cannibal tree and then slowly snuck up behind it. One of its many tendrils swayed lazily in the air—slowly enough for Caitlin to be able to grab hold of it.

She exhaled.

Fears are crazily irrational.

Nameless monsters in the night never caused Caitlin Fletcher much anxiety. Dancing in front of others, the fear and feeling of not being able to breathe, or worrying about a possible panic attack at school—all these scared the devil out of her. The grim fact that the Devil Tree was now suffocating Sleeping Beauty dared Caitlin to come to her aid.

She closed in on the swaying tendril, moving as quietly as a drifting feather.

She snatched at the tendril with both hands. It went rigid. Then it slithered violently like a serpent wriggling to break free. Caitlin stabbed the bamboo shoot into its slimy flesh. She blew on the shoot. Then she let it go, turned and ran.

Caitlin tripped. She hit the ground hard. Another tendril had snagged her by the ankle, coiling around her shin and pulling her foot out from under her.

With her other heel, she frantically tried to scrape it off her leg. It squeezed tighter, cutting off her circulation. Another tendril crept toward Caitlin. It slid up her torso and twisted around her neck. It tightened. Again. And again.

Just as it began to cut off Caitlin's air supply, the tendril loosened its grip. And then, just like that, it went limp as a wet glove. All the tendrils on the Devil Tree, in fact, suddenly drooped into slumber. The poison had taken effect.

The girls were clamoring with relief on the other side of the tree. Caitlin uncoiled the tendrils from her neck and ankle. She scurried around the thick trunk to where Rapunzel and

Cindy were now holding Beauty by her underarms and trying to wake her.

"Nice work, fearless sibling," Natalie said proudly. "You just saved the life of the authentic Sleeping Beauty." Caitlin was delighted for the simple reason that Beauty was finally breathing normally again.

Beauty opened her eyes. She stared blankly at her friends. A vacant look remained in her eyes.

"I had another dream."

CHAPTER EIGHTEEN

SLEEPING BEAUTY, HER EYES HAZY, STARED STRAIGHT AHEAD AS IF in a trance.

Rapunzel took her hand and patted it. "What did you dream?"

Beauty raised her glassy eyes to the sun. "I saw what has already happened. The Queen of Hearts. How the affliction began. The death and decay." Then she raised her hand, her palm pressed to her mouth as her face registered a profound horror.

"It was *him*." Her voice barely registered a whisper. Beauty rocked gently as she began to reveal the queen's tale.

THE QUEEN OF HEARTS HAD SUMMONED *HIM* TO HER CASTLE. THE kingdoms had still been a place of goodness and honor and benevolence, and the Queen had still been lovely and gentle-hearted.

The man—if she dare call him a man—dressed and moved

like a shadow. Attired in a sinuous ebony robe, he swayed like windblown curtains in the night as he walked.

He was known as the Enchanter. The Queen of Hearts feared him, but the Enchanter possessed hidden knowledge of their universe, so she had no choice but to summon him. She believed that surely such an enigmatic being could halt her degenerative blindness and failing memory. She became frightened when she realized she was confused and alone.

A lone crow cawed, announcing *his* arrival. The queen met him in the throne room.

His eyes held her like quicksand, and the more she tried to turn away from him, the deeper she sank under the influence of his commanding gaze. The Enchanter held up his gnarled hands so that his bone-white palms faced the queen. He moved his fingers in a circular motion, as if strumming an ancient, dark space.

"Your blind fury brings on your physical blindness and inner distraction," the Enchanter said.

His woeful prognosis kindled desperation in the queen. She had never experienced blind fury before; what was he talking about? Nonetheless, she humbly beseeched him to devise a cure and promised him a great reward if he could deliver one.

He did.

The Enchanter presented her with a peculiar pair of eyeglasses. She was awed by their opulence. The lenses were oversized and as darkly shaded as the Enchanter himself. They were cut in the shape of two hearts—a perfect match for the queen's heart-shaped bouffant hairdo.

After a moment, her head began to spin. The glasses brought on a dizziness that made her queasy and faint. It took a few moments for her to adjust to it and for her strength and balance to return.

When they did, the blurriness vanished.

But her world went black.

She was now blind as a spotted bat.

For the first time in her life, the Queen of Hearts felt a raging fury. She flung the glasses from her face, and threw them across the throne room.

"What have you done?" she shrieked. She frantically waved her arms about, trying to find his scrawny neck so she could wring it. "You diabolically deceitful cretin!"

The Enchanter seized her by the wrists. He hung on tight as her arms flailed. "Your Royal Majesty, you are fine. Calm down. I have given you something far more powerful than physical sight."

"What have you given me, Enchanter?"

She flapped her arms wildly, trying to break free of his grip. "Tell me before I send you to the gallows, and off with your head!"

"I have given you what you asked for."

She jerked her arms in zigzags, but the Enchanter kept his firm grip on them.

"Blindness?" she yelped.

"Vision," he replied in a seductive tone.

She flicked her wrists, frustrated at remaining caught in his clutches. "I'm blind, you fool."

"I speak not of ordinary sight but of something far greater."
She swung her arms up and down. "And what is that?"

The Enchanter paused. Then he said, "Clairvoyance."

The queen stopped flailing. The Enchanter released her wrists. She exhaled a long breath.

"Go on," she said.

"You will learn to see through the mind's eye," the Enchanter said. "Your vision will reach across the kindgoms and into the minds of every one of its creatures. You will know their innermost thoughts and the deepest secrets of their hearts."

The queen settled down. Her breathing slowed.

"Fetch me the glasses again," she said.

The throne room floor creaked as footsteps crossed it. A moment later, frigid fingers turned her hand upright. The glasses were set in her open palm.

She slowly raised the spectacles to her face. But before she could set them on her head, the cold, spindly fingers stopped her.

"Before you proceed," the Enchanter said, "know that once Your Royal Highness masters the use of these glasses, they must never leave your face. If they do, your clairvoyance will be lost forever."

The queen nodded. Gently and methodically, she slid the arms of the glasses over her ears and set the frame down on the bridge of her nose.

She glanced around the room. She saw only a long expanse of nothingness.

"Do not *look*, Your Highness. *Feel*."

She closed her eyes. The explosion of colors was

immediate—a celestial fountain of incandescent light. Amid the blaze of fireworks, a whirlpool emerged. The colors twisted and swirled into a vortex, leaving in its wake an eerie darkness, a horrid gloom blacker than death.

"Now I see *you*, Enchanter," the queen said.

His chuckle was grim. "It's not me you sense, Your Royal Highness."

"What, then, is this wretched blackness?"

"An impending rebellion against the throne. You sense the individual who will lead it. A young girl. And the others, of royal blood, will aid her. Together they will plot to turn the collective kingdoms against you."

She dug her fingernails into her palms, seething. "Off with their heads," the queen declared.

That icy hand seized her wrist again. This brazen sorcerer desperately needed warm blood, she thought.

"Open," said the Enchanter.

She unclenched her fingers. He pressed a cold, metallic staff into her palm. She wrapped her fingers around it.

"What is this?" she asked.

"A scepter."

"What's it for?"

"Behead everyone in the kingdom, and there'll be no subjects to rule, no kingdom to rule over. Instead, use the scepter to *control* their minds and, in turn, the world."

This Enchanter was dangerous and too clever. The queen couldn't wait to be rid of his foul presence.

"I'm listening," she said.

"There is a realm *beyond* this realm. A mysterious and primordial place known as *the Red Spectrum.*"

"Sounds forbidding—why tell me of it?"

"It is the source and font of all fear."

"Where is this ghastly place?"

"That knowledge was revealed to me on the promise that I take it to the grave, Your Royal Highness."

"Then I shall impale your head on a spike, and you may keep your promise."

The Enchanter grabbed hold of her hand. He pressed it against his jugular vein. "If it be your wish."

She hissed. Then she snapped her hand away from his scrawny throat. "I admire your conviction."

I'll take his head some other time, she told herself.

The queen took her seat on the throne. "Kneel."

The Enchanter knelt.

"Tell me," she said, "why should I concern myself with fear?"

"Fear is a potent weapon with which to rule."

Her pinky finger tinkered with her earring as she swallowed his words. "Tell me more."

"We do not choose fear. It comes to us freely."

The queen grinned. "Like hunger?"

The Enchanter smiled, revealing crooked and rotting teeth. "Magnify fear and your rebellious subjects will fight to survive! They'll turn on one another instead of turning on the throne."

A glint appeared in the queen's eye.

"You're devilishly shrewd, Enchanter," she said.

"Only in service to the throne, Your Grace."

She wagged her finger in front of her shaded eyes. "As I said . . . shrewd. Now tell me how to accomplish this."

"You control the multitude by manipulating the Red Spectrum and afflicting the kingdoms with unrelenting fear."

"But how?"

He laid his cold, gaunt hand atop hers again suddenly.

He squeezed.

In turn, her hand squeezed.

Cold, hard electrum alloy pressed against her palm.

A buzzing tickled her fingers.

The scepter!

CHAPTER NINETEEN

BACK IN THE TOYLIKE MINIATURE VILLAGE, THE WALLS OF THE TINY barn shook with the thud of another tremendous impact inside. The doors swung open. Out stepped a dusty and very flushed Jack, wide-eyed and cautious—and still clad in his Arthurian Knight armor.

He was covered in mud and hay.

He stepped into the sunny town square and glanced around at the squalid village, grimacing at its dilapidated condition.

"Caitlin! Hello? Caitlin? Anybody?"

"I'd certainly call myself more than 'anybody,'" came a man's deep voice from below. "And by not being anybody, I'd say I was most certainly 'somebody.'"

"Who said that?" asked Jack, looking around warily.

"It is I, Alfonzo Thadius Bertram the Second. Prince of Farmlandia, at your service."

Jack looked down. In the tall weeds at his feet was a frog. He had a feathered cap in his hand and was bowing with a flourish. On his arm, he wore a fabric band embellished with a family crest. His skin was pale and his eyes darkly shaded.

Jack rubbed his eyes and looked again. "You're a damn toad? How weird is this?"

"I've been called many things, amigo, but *toad* is not one of them. I am a frog. And if you do not wish for my help, so be it."

Alfonzo began to hop away.

"No, please, Your Highness. I didn't mean to be rude; I was just surprised, and I—"

Alfonzo hopped onto Jack's shoulder with one mighty leap. "It would be an honor to be of assistance, as I am starved for noble action."

"I need help rescuing a damsel."

Alfonzo eyed Jack's knightly attire. "You're certainty dressed for that mission."

"Can you assist?"

"Absolutely, amigo. My specialties lie in the art of love."

"No love arts for now. I just need to find my friend. Any chance you've seen a girl named Caitlin around here, with a little sister tagging along?"

"Indeed I have, amigo. She left a while ago with some others. A curious bunch. I will tell you all about it on the way. It should be very easy for me to follow their tracks." Alfonzo gestured in one direction with his arm. "Let the quest commence." And with that, he hopped out of sight.

"Wait!" called Jack.

Alfonzo was back in a flash.

"I'll never be able to keep up with you. You're too fast."

The frog sat for a moment, as if in thought. Then its amphibian eye winked. "Come," the frog instructed as he skittered off.

Jack followed him past a run-down miniature schoolhouse and up some broken boards that served as steps into the town sheriff's office. Floorboards creaked under his feet.

"Now, where is it?" said Alfonzo, hopping around.

A huge spider descended from the ceiling on a long, silky thread. It settled on a drawer handle on the sheriff's desk. Alfonzo zapped the spider with his tongue. As he retracted it, the drawer also stuck to it and slid open. Inside sat a small blue bottle labeled "drink me."

"Mmm, that's it," said Alfonzo, munching down the spider. "Have a sip."

Jack took off his chain-mail cowl. He held the bottle up to a beam of light that was streaming through the cracks in the boarded-up window. He grinned from ear to ear, like a Cheshire Cat.

"Sweet! I know what this is."

CHAPTER TWENTY

SLEEPING BEAUTY'S ENIGMATIC DREAM HAD LEFT EVERYONE WORD-less. They felt even more pressure to find the caterpillar—fast.

Caitlin surveyed the northwestern horizon as the group marched onward. A flat expanse of brown, parched grass stretched for miles under the blisteringly hot and hazy sky.

The flavorful hot-sauce aroma from the spill on Natalie's costume had intensified with the warming sun. Licking her lips and twitching her nose, Cinderella sidled up to her.

"You're smelling sweet and delectable, young chili pepper. We'd better find something to dine on quick. Not sure I can control myself much longer." Cindy poked her nose close to Natalie's neck.

Natalie lifted her hand. "Keep your distance, glutton."

Sleeping Beauty shook her head and sighed. "I'm sorry to say that I'm starting to feel the same way." She smiled awkwardly at Caitlin. "And I'm a vegetarian."

Rapunzel and Snow White exchanged troubled looks, as if to say they all were experiencing an increasing hunger.

"We should hurry it along, dontcha think?" Caitlin said.

Snow knelt on the ground, closed her eyes, and scooped up a handful of earth. She allowed a few grains of sand to spill out between her delicate fingers. Her brow furrowed in concentration.

"The entrance to Zeno's Forest is about two hundred paces that way." She pointed east. "Just past that bridge."

Caitlin and Natalie squinted and turned their gazes eastward too. A small footbridge about as long as a school bus arched over a rushing stream. Wooden slats that formed its deck curved up and over the babbling water, and its railings were intricately constructed from woven vines and branches.

When they approached, they could see that the slats were thickly coated in a splatter of bird droppings.

"Please don't tell me we have to cross doody bridge," Natalie lamented.

"*Doody* isn't the only reason we should avoid that bridge," Cinderella noted.

As she spoke, ten meaty, black crows landed on the bridge railings. Their beady eyes burned like red embers as they perched on the vines and glared at the group.

Caitlin gasped. "Why don't they attack us?"

"You sound disappointed," Cindy said.

Rapunzel took hold of Caitlin's hand. "Black crows are the queen's eyes. A pack of living-dead wolves are her teeth. The crows signal the location of her prey, and the wolves hunt them down and retrieve them for the queen."

Zombie wolves?

"We need to cross by fording the stream," Rapunzel suggested. "Better hurry. We're now on their radar."

Snow pointed across the stream. "I can see the entrance to Zeno's Forest over there."

The girls quickly made their way to the bank of the stream.

"Hold hands," Rapunzel said. "The water is only knee-high, but the current will knock you flat unless our fingers are locked tight."

Slowly and steadily, the girls eased themselves into the rushing stream. Natalie's eyes bulged as she immersed herself waist-deep into the frigid waters. "I-I c-c-can't b-b-brea—"

"Can't breathe?" Caitlin said, finishing her sister's sentence.

Natalie nodded briskly while flapping her hands.

"M-m-my sympathy f-for your anxiety h-h-has g-grown i-immensely."

Hand in hand, the girls waded across the cold river.

When they were safely on the opposite bank, Snow White unhooked her canteen. "How delightful. Fresh water. We should fill up our water pouches." The princess ghouls opened their bota bags and immersed them under the water until they were bulging.

Suddenly a sharp, clamping sound followed by a crackling noise ending in a thud rang out from over by the tree line. Snow's head whipped left to right, scanning the area.

"Did you hear that?" she whispered.

"Loud and clear," Cindy said.

"What was it?"

"It sure wasn't the drip of the water from my skirt landing on my feet."

Snow tilted her head. "Sounded like the rustling of leaves."

"Or maybe the bloody babbling stream of death," Cinderella said with a smirk.

"No, shhh. I'm not kidding," Snow said. "Stop for a second. Listen."

Snow cupped her hand to her ear. "It's more than just wind and twigs. Can't you hear it?"

Caitlin and Natalie looked at each other in bewilderment.

"Sounds like moaning," Snow said. "Like someone's in pain. This way."

Snow tore off toward a cluster of decrepit white oaks on the edge of the forbidding forest.

"Wait!" Rapunzel called after her. "You can't just detour from the mission!"

Too late. Snow had already scurried down to the edge of the woods.

"Well," said Rapunzel, putting her hands on her hips and spreading out her wet skirt to let it dry, "we can't just leave her here alone in the big, bad woods."

The girls detoured to follow the direction Snow had run. They came to a tangle of trees on the edge of the forest whose trunks were contorted in ways that made them look nearly human. Their lower branches resembled old limbs, and their topmost branches fanned out like sprouts of three-foot-long hair. Fallen leaves, seedpods, and broken branches shrouded the ground. The place had a vinegary, woodsy scent.

Clearly, the trees were barely alive. Sap oozed from upper branches as if the trees were crying.

"What is this place?" asked Caitlin.

"More like what *was* this place," Cindy said. "Whatever it *is*, it appears to be enchanted."

"Snow, where are you?" Beauty called.

The girls looked behind trunks and under branches.

"Not the time for games, girl," Rapunzel said. "What could possibly be so important as to—"

She froze in her tracks. There, on the ground, panting and wheezing among crushed leaves and busted twigs, lay a Blood-Eyed zombie wolf powdered in dirt!

Caitlin's mouth fell ajar.

One of the wolf's hind legs had been caught in a rusted iron bear trap.

Metal jaws were clamped tight around its ankle, piercing its flesh. The wolf had obviously struggled to flee, making the wound worse.

Snow stood a few feet back, just out of reach of its front paws. She stared at him concerned. "If we don't help him, he'll bleed to death."

"That's the idea," Cindy remarked.

Snow glowered. The wolf whimpered and tears clouded its

ruby eyes. Its head flopped down on the dirt so that its snout lay sideways on the ground. It was hard to make out the wolf's features as the dirt dusted and covered its face and torso.

But then it opened its mouth. Two rows of polished fangs glistened clearly. A frothy glob of saliva dribbled from its mouth, pooling on top of the dirt.

"Snow, have you gone mad?" Rapunzel was livid. "This Blood-Eyed would like nothing more than to tear you up, limb from limb. I cannot allow you to do this. I forbid it."

Snow White's chest heaved. "This creature is in pain!"

Beauty pointed her finger. "Snow, if you open that trap, he'll kill us all!"

Natalie shot a wide-eyed, meaningful glance at Caitlin. Caitlin shrugged nervously. She wanted to get out of there, fast. Except there was *another* part of her . . .

The wolf writhed as the metal clamps dug into its bone with a crunch.

"We can't just leave him here to suffer," Caitlin said, regretting the words as they left her mouth.

Cinderella clucked her tongue. "If we don't kill it, it will kill us. At best, he'll take a chunk out of one of our legs. One of us will wind up a Blood-Eyed, just like the rest of them."

Snow looked up at Rapunzel. "I'm not leaving until you help me open this trap."

A small pack of vultures appeared in the sky above the forest canopy.

Rapunzel squinted at the sky. "They smell blood."

"Don't vultures eat *dead* things?" Caitlin wondered aloud.

Natalie nodded. "Gyps bengalensis. White-rumped vultures. They eat carcasses."

"And aren't you all *technically* dead . . . ?" Caitlin said.

"We must leave. Now," Rapunzel ordered. "Snow, pronto."

Snow huffed stubbornly. "Not until you help me free this wolf."

"Tenacious as a Taurus," Cindy said, shaking her head.

"I'm afraid I'm on Snow's side," Caitlin said.

Cindy popped a squat next to the trap. "Okay, I'm in." She eyed the group. "But as soon as we open the trap, this canine ghoul will be on us like ivy on oak. Bread on butter. Flame on a wick. Fleas on a—"

"Okay, we get it," Rapunzel said.

Cindy pointed to Rapunzel's head.

"I'll need one of your luxurious long locks, pretty princess."

Rapunzel loosened a braid and handed it to her.

Cindy tied it around the top jaw of the clamp.

"We'll pull it open from a distance. That way, we'll have a solid head start when we run for our ever-lovin' lives."

Rapunzel pointed to a tree at the edge of the woods.

"Caitlin, Natalie, I need you two over there, please. Now. These wolves run fast. That leg wound might not be enough to slow him down."

After tying a final knot, Cindy let out the line of braid and trotted with the girls to the edge of the woods. She handed the tail end of the rope to Snow. "You do the honors."

Snow wound it twice around her hand. She tightened her grip.

"Get ready to run," Cindy said.

Caitlin knelt, racing-block style. Natalie too. Rapunzel, Cindy and Beauty crouched forward, one leg in front, arms swung back like jet wings.

Snow pulled the rope of hair. Though her face reddened with the effort, the clamp only opened a quarter of the way. "Someone help."

Cindy scooted over, taking hold of Snow's hands. Caitlin felt adrenalin rushing through her veins. She twiddled her fingers. Tilted her head right, left. She was itching to run.

Together, Cindy and Snow pulled . . . and pulled . . . and pulled . . .

The clamp snapped open.

The wolf let out a hair-raising yowl!

It slowly stood on its hind legs. Like a human! Then it shook off all the dirt.

"It's him!" Cindy screamed. "The Big Bad Wolf."

He leered at them with narrowed red eyes.

Caitlin had never seen such a horrific-looking werewolf in all her life!

They took off, running for their lives, and leaving behind a whirlwind of leaves and a billowy cloud of dirt.

CHAPTER TWENTY-ONE

IN THE UNDERSIZE DILAPIDATED VILLAGE, JACK HELD THE SMALL, blue bottle in his hand. Alfonzo the Frog Prince watched impatiently.

"Save the toast for the wedding, amigo. We must hurry if we are to catch up with your friends."

Jack took a big swig. His face contorted as the liquid struck his taste buds. Bile was less bitter. He swigged again. And again. Then he chugged the whole wretched bottle dry.

"That should do it," he said. "Hmmm. I'm not thirsty any-more either."

Jack's left hand suddenly cramped in morbid pain.

"Whoa—that was fast."

A moment later his arm began contracting into his shoul-der. It shrank perversely quickly. It felt to him as though the limb was being crushed in a vise.

"Bloody painful!"

His other arm cramped in racking pain, and he almost wailed like a babe as it shrunk before his eyes. Next went his right leg. The stabbing pain robbed him of breath. This was followed by the contraction of his left leg; it felt like his thighbone was being sawed off.

He tipped over onto his side from the weight of his suddenly oversize torso, feeling like a mutant. Finally, the muscles in his stomach twisted into a knot so tight he almost heaved up the previous night's dinner. Then his torso popped into proportion, causing him to break out in convulsions and a cold sweat. A moment later the convulsions seized. His body temperature warmed.

"I was worried there for a second." He stood up slowly and examined his new, ten-inch-high form, still feeling a bit wobbly. "Think I might've swallowed too much."

"Not at all, amigo," Alfonzo replied.

The small frog now appeared like quite a large one to Jack, since they were almost the same size. Alfonzo's eyes were as big as Jack's fists; they bulged from his head and their glazed surface reminded him of the eyes of some exotic, reptilian alien.

Alfonzo smiled. "If you were any smaller, perhaps you'd be tempting to eat." He waggled his long tongue at Jack. "Ha, ha, ha. But I'd never do such a thing. For I am a frog of honor."

"Now what, mate?" Jack asked.

Alfonzo crouched. "On my back. And please make sure that sword of yours doesn't puncture my hind legs."

Jack climbed up onto Alfonzo's slimy back and held tightly

to a meaty fold of neck flesh. The Frog Prince's skin was secreting mucus, so Jack tried to dry it up with his sleeve.

"Stop, amigo! You'll suffocate me. Frogs breathe through the moisture on their skin."

Jack winced. "My apologies." He spit into his palms, rubbed them together, and smeared the lube over Alfonzo's neck and back.

"Ahh, much better," the frog announced as he inhaled fresh air.

Together, the two of them hurdled over the crumbling wall and bounded out of town at breakneck speed.

"Good news, amigo," the Frog Prince announced. "I smell sweet sap in the air. Delectable plants and flowers await us just up ahead!"

CHAPTER TWENTY-TWO

CAITLIN, NATALIE, AND THE ZOMBIE PRINCESSES STOOD AT A NARROW entrance to what seemed to be an endless forest. Streaks of white sunlight penetrated its tall canopy of tangled branches, which filtered falling sunlight and turned it blue as it spilled into the forest.

The expanse of trees stretched far and wide in both directions—there was no apparent way to skirt the woods. The woodlands were so thick, in fact, that when Caitlin tried to look between the tree trunks, all she saw was a mass of bark bathed in blue.

Some trees had retained a bit of their green, though most were pale and covered in decrepit, bone-dry leaves.

A couple of hand-painted signs hung from a wooden post right where the path they had followed from the "doody" footbridge stopped at the tree line. The sign on top of the wooden post read "Zeno's Forest." Below that were smaller signs shaped like arrows. Each arrow pointed to a different destination:

The Enchanted Forest
The Emerald City
Camelot
Neverland
Wonderland

Practically every kingdom from every fairy tale ever told was represented by its own arrow.

But there were no paths leading *through* the forest.

No paths? Huh?

"How are we supposed to know how to get to where we want to go if there's no path to lead us there?" asked Caitlin as her palms moistened and her chest tightened. Just the thought of getting lost in some unknown, isolated forest was enough to arouse overwhelming dread.

Rapunzel pointed to the arrows. "All these kingdoms are interconnected by this forest. We can journey through it to any place quickly, no matter how far away it is."

Caitlin held the air in her lungs for a prolonged moment. Then she breathed out slowly. She was glad the journey would be quick, but she scratched her head. "How's that possible?"

Snow cracked a smile. "In Zeno's Forest, the farther away your destination, the quicker you arrive."

How odd is that!

Natalie perked up visibly. "Zeno, huh? Is this forest related to Zeno's paradox? And the tale of the tortoise and the hare?"

Showoff.

"Who—or what—is a Zeno?" Caitlin asked in a tart tone.

"Greek philosopher," Girl Wonder responded. "He tried to demonstrate that all motion is an illusion."

Whatever!

Cinderella cast a hard glance at Rapunzel and motioned with her head toward Caitlin. "Better warn her," she said.

Caitlin stiffened. "Warn me about what?"

An uneasy look passed between the four princesses.

Snow put her arm around Caitlin's shoulder.

"There's something you need to know before you step foot inside this forest."

Caitlin blinked rapidly and nodded.

"You must have your destination firmly planted in your mind—*before* you enter."

"Why?"

"Because if you don't, you run the risk of not being able to move once you're among the trees."

Rapunzel leaned in between Snow and Caitlin, her eyes expressing caution. "You could get stuck in Zeno's Forest. For hundreds of years!"

Caitlin's heart fluttered in her chest. She recalled the time she had gotten trapped in a crowded walkway when exiting a baseball stadium. She was eight, so she couldn't see over the heads of the adults towering over her. The ramp out of the stadium had become congested, people jamming up at the exit. The crowd literally stopped moving. Caitlin was trapped. Stuck. It lasted a good ten minutes, but felt like eternity. That was one of the first times she felt claustrophobic and panicky.

Rapunzel signaled to Snow White, who strolled over to the signpost. Beneath it was a plaque with writing carved into the wood: HOW TO NAVIGATE ZENO'S FOREST!

Caitlin leaned in close to read it.

> THE FARTHER YOUR DESTINATION, THE FASTER YOU ARRIVE. WHICH MEANS THE CLOSER YOUR DESTINATION, THE LONGER IT TAKES TO REACH. WHICH MEANS IF YOU DON'T KNOW WHERE YOU'RE GOING, YOU'LL NEVER ARRIVE AT YOUR NEXT STOP.

Caitlin grasped the gist of it. Her next step would be so close it might take eons to get there, based on the laws of logic that governed Zeno's Forest. But one question kept nagging at the back of her mind, so she decided to ask.

"How does the forest know where I'm going?"

Rapunzel winked sweetly at her girlfriends, then turned to Caitlin. "What's your world made of?"

"Ooh, I know!" said Natalie, jerking her arm in the air as if she was raising her hand in the back row of a crowded class-room. "Particles called *atoms*."

Rapunzel's eyebrow curved up sharply. "Now, what do you suppose this universe is made of?"

Girl Wonder suddenly seemed confounded by the question. *A rare occurrence, indeed.*

Caitlin thought about it for a moment. The book *Alice's Adventures in Wonderland* came from the mind of Charles Dodgson, aka Lewis Carroll.

Cindy then discreetly pointed to the odd, brain-shaped sun.

"Particles of imagination?" Caitlin answered, positively unsure of herself.

Rapunzel smiled generously. "Excellent, Caitlin."

Even Natalie seemed impressed.

Rapunzel placed her hand on Caitlin's shoulder. "So your imagination and Zeno's Forest are made of the same stuff. The forest always knows where you are and where you want to go."

"How awesome is that?" Caitlin said. "A mind-reading forest."

"Can it pick winning lottery numbers?" Natalie chirped.

Caitlin's head abruptly tilted to one side. "Hey, I have a question."

Rapunzel nodded, encouraging her to ask.

"The atoms in our world," Caitlin said, "They're made up of protons, electrons, and neutrons. So what are the particles of imagination made of?"

Natalie eyes lit up. "Yeah—excellent question."

Rapunzel and her friends shared a troubled look. Rapunzel then turned back to Caitlin. "That's one of the reasons why you need to see the caterpillar. He'll have the answer to such a question."

Sleeping Beauty tugged at Rapunzel's shoulder. "We're losing time."

Rapunzel nodded and looked Caitlin straight in the face.

"Now concentrate hard, Caitlin. Think about where you want to go."

Caitlin responded with an expectant look. "To the hideout of the caterpillar, correct?"

Rapunzel's face soured. "Sounds more like a question than an answer. That's just the kind of doubt that will leave you stuck in the woods for a couple of centuries. You have to be certain about where you're going!"

Caitlin's eyes darted around, restlessly surveying the expanse of forest. She had to get this right.

"I'm going to see the caterpillar. Pronto!"

Rapunzel grinned. "Better." She turned to the group. "Everyone ready?"

Caitlin wasn't sure if she'd ever really be ready for this. She had no idea where the caterpillar's hideout was or why they were going there. The only thing she knew about the caterpillar was that he appeared in *Alice's Adventures in Wonderland*, which her mom had read to her almost every night when she was younger. Caitlin remembered that the caterpillar smoked a hookah. And now, apparently, she learned he had given that up in favor of drinking organic tea. But to her, the idea of getting stuck in a forest for centuries was unsettling to say the least— and total claustrophobic hell at the very worst!

Inhale.

Exhale.

Caitlin rotated her head around and around, relaxing her neck muscles. "Yeah, okay," she said. "I'm ready."

She took a hesitant step toward the edge of the tree line. Zeno's Forest loomed large before her.

The six girls simultaneously stepped into the ominous blue forest, first with one foot, then the other.

Before Caitlin could blink, Rapunzel, Cindy, Beauty, Snow, and Natalie blurred into twisting, liquid forms, and then at hyper-speed—

SWOOOOOSH!

They were gone!

The memory of Rapunzel's voice hovered like particles in the air around Caitlin, a dreamy tone with a hollow echo.

Caitlin kept walking, but she didn't generate any motion, like in a nightmare. The dread of paralysis toyed with her mind, pushing her toward total panic. She tried running, but no scenery passed her by. She remained imprisoned in the same spot. Her muscles stiffened like cement. She opened her mouth to holler for help.

Before she could, another twisting, blurry form streaked toward her at lightning speed.

SWOOOOSH!

The blur thickened until it looked like pudding. Standing there before her were Natalie and the zombie girls. They stared at Caitlin in bewilderment.

Profoundly relieved, Caitlin threw her arms up into the air. "What happened?"

Rapunzel shook her head. Cinderella put her hands on her waist and exhaled. Snow stared at Caitlin with sympathetic eyes. Beauty was admiring a few green pines still left in the forest.

Rapunzel extended her arm. "Still too much skepticism. Push your thoughts aside and take my hand. I'll help you through the forest. Until you get the hang of it."

And with that, *SWOOOOOSH!*, off they rocketed at unfathomable speed, deep into Zeno's Forest on their way to the secret hideout of the wise caterpillar.

The one who traded his hookah for a teacup.

CHAPTER TWENTY-THREE

JACK RODE FAST AND HARD ON THE BACK OF HIS NEW FRIEND ALFONZO the Frog Prince. His vaulted, jarring strides made Jack feel as though he were riding a riotous bucking bull.

"How long 'til we get there?"

"Worry not, amigo, we will find this Caitlin of yours."

Together they leaped and bounded through a tall jungle of brown-bladed grass. The air was humid and thick. Sweet nectar—one of the last few nutrients still to be found in this decaying universe—scented the wind.

Alfonzo wove in and out of blades, some wide and withered, some gaunt and narrow. Tall, sapling-like stems suddenly appeared. The stems were a pale shade of green, thicker than the dead trunks of grass. The whole area was somewhat shaded.

Weird. Is this place alive? Jack wondered.

"I am famished from overexertion," Alfonzo said. "The

honeyed nectar is coming from a plant a short hop away. I shall refuel before we continue our quest."

Jack slid off Alfonzo's back. The frog then hurdled his way toward a sweet-smelling pitcher plant.

Jack heard an ominous hiss rustle through the stalks.

"Hehhh . . . Hehhh . . . "

He quickly realized the hissing was coming *from* the stalks.

He cast his glance farther up the meadow. He watched as Alfonzo leaped on top of a large pitcher-shaped plant. When he landed atop the rim, he began licking up puddles of nectar. A split-second later, the Frog Prince's legs were scurrying in place, as if he was running on a treadmill at breakneck speed.

Alfonzo began sliding down the inside wall of the pitcher. Despite frantic attempts, his feet could not gain traction to push himself back out. Suddenly the Frog Prince slipped and vanished from sight, leaving behind only a fading croak.

Jack's eyes bulged.

And then, without warning, Jack was swallowed up in one rapacious gulp by a snarling Venus flytrap! Ensnared in its cruel mouth, he felt the oxygen draining out of his lungs fast. Jack jammed his arm between the fangs of the flytrap. He pulled as hard as he could, trying to separate the jaws. He wrenched harder. The jaws widened, and fresh air brushed Jack's face.

Mucus dripped from the fangs and seeped under his palms. Jack's hands went slick, and he lost the grip. The jaws snapped shut.

The walls of the plant suddenly began secreting what Jack knew must be digestive juices. The level of liquid on the inside began to rise. Within seconds, Jack was ankle-deep in fluid. He pounded on the plant.

No way I'm dying in the mouth of some flower!

The liquid rose to his knees.

Jack drew his sword. He locked both hands on the hilt. He raised his weapon like a skilled and stalwart knight. He swung that sword with a mighty blow hard against the fangs.

It shattered into a thousand slivered pieces.

Jack had forgotten his sword was a harmless novelty Halloween prop, not a lethal, unsheathed weapon of steel.

No wonder it was pulverized.

The digestive fluids now reached his waist.

Jack reached up and took hold of a narrow slice of plant tissue jutting out from the roof of the plant's mouth. He hoisted himself up in the air and began to swing, back and forth. When he gained enough momentum, he swung himself full force into the fangs, feet first, kicking as hard as he could. This time he shattered the flytrap's teeth, crashed through, and leaped out of its mouth. He fell to the ground. His knight outfit was smoking slightly. He rolled in the dirt to wipe off the digestive juices.

Jack stood, grabbed a nearby vine, rolled it tight, and raced over to the pitcher plant. He tied one end of the vine to the base of a plant stalk. Then he tied the other end to his wrist.

Jack heard something. A faint, muffled cry. Coming from inside the plant.

"Help!"

Alfonzo!

"Save me! Amigooo . . . !"

Jack started climbing the carnivorous plant. When he reached the slippery rim on top, the honeyed scent of nectar kissed his nostrils. It was so sweet it was almost intoxicating.

What a deadly trap this is!

Jack hung onto the rim for dear life, trying not to slide inside. He glanced up. On the other side of the rim was a large centipede, almost the size of Jack. It began crawling along the rim—angling straight for him! Suddenly, the centipede's fleet of legs started skating on the slick surface. Jack shook the rim. The insect lost all of its footings and plunged down into the pool of digestive enzymes.

"That multilegged arthropod nearly landed on my head!" shouted the Frog Prince from down below. "But I am grateful nonetheless, amigo, for you have kindly come to my aid. Now please get me out of here."

Balancing as best as he could on the perilous rim of the plant, Jack lowered his upper torso deep into the pitcher cup.

This better be worth it.

He kneeled down so he could reach even deeper. He extended his arms as far as he could.

Alfonzo grabbed hold of Jack's hand—and that was all it took.

Jack lost his balance and slid down the greasy, leafy wall. He splashed into the pool of acid.

The centipede was next to Jack, struggling to stay afloat, and quickly losing the battle.

Alfonzo treaded gracefully in front of him. He dripped with gastric juices, though, and a thin drift of smoke rose from his flesh. "I have about a minute—and you amigo, have perhaps two minutes—before we disintegrate to the bone and become lunch for this most unpleasant plant."

The vine was still tied to Jack's wrist. He pulled it taut and began climbing back up the wall. "Grab onto my leg, and I'll pull you out."

Snap!

The vine split, and Jack fell back into the pool.

Now he was *really* getting angry.

"Bloody hell, frog, how about *you* try getting us out of here? My skin's starting to burn."

"Well," Alfonzo said with a sudden gleam in his eye, "wade around to my backside." Jack swished his way through the thick liquid and stood behind the frog prince. "I usually like to save this move for the ladies," Alfonzo pointed out, "but here goes."

Prince Alfonzo began to puff out his vocal sac into the bulging shape of a ball. He puffed some more, inflating his throat until it expanded like a giant hot-air balloon. As the membrane swelled, it pushed back the liquid enzymes in waves. Alfonzo kept puffing until the swollen sac pressed against the inside wall of the plant.

The plant began to inflate. It doubled in size, then tripled.

It swelled and expanded outward until the pitcher cup finally exploded.

Jack and Alfonzo rode a gushing shock wave of digestive fluids out, soared momentarily in the air, and crashed to the earth in a tumbling roll.

Jack leaped up and stripped down to his skivvies, wringing out his smoking tunic and pants.

"I smell fresh water, amigo," Alfonzo said. "Climb aboard, quick."

Jack quickly bundled his knight garb under his arm and slid onto the frog prince's back.

Alfonzo made a beeline to a soft-flowing river coursing through a low-lying section of the meadow. Without stopping at the edge of the riverbank, the frog prince plunged straight into the water with Jack still riding on his back. They dunked under the cold water and splashed around, washing the acidic juices from their bodies and garments.

When they finally emerged from the river, they stretched under the sun-swept sky.

"In no time the sun and wind will dry us like a desert sand dune, amigo."

A puzzled look then crept over the frog's face.

"But I am sorry to say that I think I have lost the trail."

Jack dressed back up in his knight costume, all the while shaking his head as he wondered how he was going to find Caitlin.

A pleasurable "Ooh" emerged from Alfonzo's mouth as a big blowfly bumbled by. The tip of Alfonzo's sticky red tongue snatched the bug midair, then quickly rolled back into his mouth. Alfonzo gulped it down.

"*Eating* lunch is far better than *being* lunch."

Jack winked. "Wouldn't mind a snack myself."

Alfonzo nabbed another fly. He held it out to Jack, presenting it ceremoniously on the tip of his tongue. The fly was still alive; it wriggled back and forth, trying to unstick its wings from Alfonzo's tongue.

Jack gave a dismissive wave of the hand. "Thanks anyway."

Alfonzo picked the fly off his tongue with two digits on one of his front legs. He held the bug up in front of his eyes, admiring the winged delicacy. "Well in that case, I'm ready for my dessert."

"Stop!" the fly shouted. "I beg you not to eat me."

"Flies are a nuisance," Alfonzo replied to the insect. "You serve no purpose beyond pestering people."

"I can help you," the fly pleaded.

Alfonzo laughed. "How could *you* possibly assist *me*?"

"Not you," the fly replied. "*Him*."

Jack's eyebrows rose. "Me?"

The fly nodded. "Let me live, and I'll reveal vital information. The whereabouts of two humans and a royal foursome."

Jack fist-pumped the air.

Alfonzo let the fly go. The insect flew over to Jack and landed on his right shoulder.

"They spoke of visiting the great caterpillar, Lord Amethyst Bartholomew."

Jack turned excitedly to Alfonzo. "Do you know how to find him?"

"I most definitely do."

CHAPTER TWENTY-FOUR

THE CATERPILLAR'S HIDEOUT MUST HAVE BEEN DREADFULLY FAR away, because the girls traversed Zeno's Forest in a matter of moments. In less than a minute, it seemed to Caitlin. She had taken about three actual steps; her feet had barely touched dirt. The scenery had zoomed by her eyes like a wet landscape painting smeared on the walls of a narrow tunnel. And Caitlin had been like a bullet hurtling through that tunnel.

They were stopped now, standing in the magical, timeless, spaceless heart of Zeno's Forest, somewhere just north of Wonderland and south, east, and west of . . . every place, everywhere.

Caitlin's eyes swept over her new environment. Thick woods of wide ponderosa created a brown wall of timber that encircled them. The branches above filtered the sunlight bathing the woodlands in emerald green. Trunks as wide as Caitlin's bedroom at home and covered in knotty bark rose majestically through a ground cover of thorny brambles that covered a snarling landscape of tree roots and sharp-edged rocks.

"Not exactly smooth terrain," Caitlin said. "Thanks for the ride."

"Yeah, really," said Natalie. "Imagine if we had to cab it?"

"So," Rapunzel said to Snow White, "where's this hidden entrance to the caterpillar's safe house?"

Snow scoped out the area for a moment, then broke out in a smile and pointed. "Over there."

A fair-sized sandstone boulder sat in a grassy tract of woods by a dead pine only a short distance away.

"The tunnel to his cave is underneath the rock," Beauty said.

Tunnel?

Caitlin picked nervously at a fingernail as they tramped toward the boulder.

"Hey," she blurted out, "maybe we can communicate with the caterpillar without paying a personal visit? Like, maybe we call first . . . or something."

The girls paid her no attention.

They reached the boulder and, sure enough, the huge, oval rock rested in a prolific patch of shamrock-green four-leaf clovers.

Caitlin had never seen so many lucky four-leaf clovers in all her life. Natalie seemed mesmerized too. Though the leaves were withering, all four leaves seemed to be intact on every clover.

Natalie bent down and picked one for good luck. "You

sure that insect is sipping organic tea down there and not Irish whiskey?"

Rapunzel rolled the boulder away from the base of the dead pine. A pitch-black, narrow tunnel entrance loomed before them.

Are they kidding?

"Hey . . . " Caitlin said, still fidgeting with her nails. "Let's send just one person down there. Like on a reconnaissance mission. She'll locate the caterpillar and bring him back here."

Beauty, ignoring Caitlin's plea, peered down the entry shaft. "I'll go down first. Someone else follow me."

She got down on her hands and knees—beautiful tattered dress and all—and crawled into the muddy hole. Next went Cinderella, then Natalie.

"You'd better go now, my dear," Snow said to Caitlin.

She had started rocking back and forth on her heels and chewing the split ends of her beloved cinnamon-colored hair.

"Hey, I have another idea," Caitlin said. "Suppose we—"

"Hush up, girl," Rapunzel said sternly. "You're next."

Caitlin approached the entrance timidly, leaned slightly forward, and peered down the shaft. "It's, like, totally dark down there. How will we see in the tunnel?"

Snow smiled. "Glowworms."

Her smile seemed sincere, but Caitlin had no clue how slimy worms could help ease her dread of the dark. Natalie had already disappeared down the hole, though, and Caitlin couldn't leave her unattended. So despite her considerable trepidation, she crawled into the shaft and got swallowed up by the blackness.

When her feet touched bottom, Caitlin crouched on her hands and knees in the pitch dark. She peered down the length of the tunnel, expecting to see another stretch of blackness.

A galaxy of green, twinkling lights reflected in her eyeglasses. They glittered in front of her down the full length of the seemingly unending passage.

This isn't scary. This is extraordinary!

Snow was absolutely right.

Caitlin stared in awe at the countless speckles of emerald light shining as far as her eyes could see; they were like a glittering ocean of stars from a distant spiral galaxy.

These green, glowing insects are beautiful and sort of disgusting at the same time.

Caitlin began to crawl on all fours, following her sister. Lime-colored jewels of light cast irregular shadows onto the dirt beneath her. As she maneuvered deeper into the tunnel, Caitlin's heartbeat sped up. Her breath grew shallow—though not for lack of oxygen. She simply realized there was no turning back. She was too far into the tunnel.

"Pick up the pace!" Rapunzel shouted from behind. "We need to get there today."

A glowworm suddenly poked through the surface of the tunnel ceiling, startling Caitlin. It squirmed mere inches above her head.

"I despise worms!"

"Technically," Natalie said, "The glowworm is classified as an insect. They're a species of beetle."

The bright-green, segmented body curved and wiggled side to side within its armored exoskeleton.

Caitlin cringed. "Oh God, please don't notice me. Pleeease!"

The slimy beetle must have sensed Caitlin's approach because, at that very moment, it turned to face her directly. It poked the air with its pointed front tip, searching for a surface to crawl on.

"Oh God, please don't crawl on my face," Caitlin begged.

The glowworm dropped onto her head.

She shrieked.

It scuttled down her forehead and onto her cheek . . . then onto her neck . . .

"Get it off me!"

Natalie craned her head backward. "Just pick up that freaking incandescent insect and place it back onto the dirt."

"You do it!"

"Just to shut you up, I would, but this tunnel's too tight to turn my butt around."

Caitlin was paralyzed.

The glowworm crawled in circles on the front of Caitlin's neck.

"Agh! Get it off me! Use the friggin zapper or something!"

The beetle suddenly scurried down her top.

Don't you dare!

It wiggled across her chest and then downward, crawling along the rim of her bra!

"Aaaahhhh!" Caitlin's ear-splitting shriek shook the whole tunnel.

"We have no time for your neurosis!" Rapunzel shouted from behind. "We've been spotted by the crows, and the clock is ticking. Now pick up the bloody beetle and move it before I zap *you*."

Caitlin had forgotten how forceful the long-haired dead girl from the cemetery could be. And, somehow, being ordered to move the vile and slimy glowworm made it easier for her to do it. She tugged the neckline of her sweater and stretched it outward. She slid her other hand down her top, fingers probing for the bug. By now it had passed over her belly button and was heading toward her pant waist. The dogged beetle then began nudging its way down her pants.

She snatched the slippery beetle up by its abdomen, then pulled it out of her sweater and plunked it back on the tunnel wall. The glowworm slithered along the soil, heading happily off into the tunnel.

Caitlin sighed in relief.

With that nasty catastrophe resolved, the group continued to shimmy their way through the narrow crawlspace.

They tunneled on their hands and knees through tangled tree roots and around a banked curve. The crawlspace began to get even narrower.

A thin wisp of smoke suddenly wafted through the tunnel. Caitlin smelled something peculiar. She coughed.

"Head toward the smoke," Rapunzel said.

Caitlin recalled the old adage: Where there's smoke . . .

CHAPTER TWENTY-FIVE

THE CRAMPED TUNNEL SOON OPENED OUT INTO A WIDE, CAVERNOUS pit. A large entryway with a narrow stained-glass skylight above allowed rays of sunlight into the cave, enlivening the space with blues, violets, and reds. More glowworms lined the walls, providing ample hues of greens. Candles mounted in bronze sconces on the cave wall shone yellow candlelight. All these colors together gave unexpected life to the cave.

The second surprise was that the cave itself was a luscious underground garden. Unlike the zombified plant life above-ground, the flora here was far from struggling. Vines full with tomatoes and cucumbers climbed the walls. Bean plants with stems chock-full of beans grew in abundance out of the ground. Clusters of grapes in purple, green, and red hung from the ceiling. Passion fruit vines clung to shoots of corn and artichokes and tall sunflowers. Pumpkins and carrot greens carpeted the floor. There were cloves of garlic, wasabi plants, and thick horseradish roots. Lettuces and kale and purple-and-yellow chard sprung from pockets of soil between other plants. Even a lemon tree grew here.

Caitlin didn't know much about plants, but she was pretty sure peppermint was growing somewhere too—minty fumes scented the cavern.

"Wow, this place is like a garden of earthly delights," Natalie said. She ran her finger along a vine. "So where's the caterpillar? Looks like the only things here are plants and glowworms."

At the far end of the cave, they noticed a long sofa with purple pillows and a large decorative mohair blanket spread out cozily.

Wisps of the minty smoke wafted from a stick of incense perched on a mushroom near the sofa. The mushroom, Caitlin noticed, was as tall as the bookshelf in her bedroom, and even wider.

"Ahem," came a small voice.

The girls approached the mushroom. Seated on top of its cap, sipping tea from the smallest porcelain teacup Caitlin had ever seen, was a three-inch-long, royal-blue caterpillar.

"You must excuse me," the caterpillar said. "I was not expecting you for another minute and thirty-seven seconds."

He dug one of his pin-size hands into the mushroom cap and pulled up a chunk of mushroom. He took a bite, chewed, and . . . began to inflate! He steadily increased in size like a carnival balloon, inflating and growing and expanding.

"Ah, three feet precisely," the caterpillar said. "Or 91.44 centimeters. A very good height indeed."

He reached under his mushroom and pulled out a new, more appropriately sized teacup and chair. Using one of his spare lower hands, he poured himself a fresh cup of tea. Minty steam rose from the cup and filled Caitlin's nostrils.

Yup. Teacup. Definitely not a hookah.

The caterpillar's face identified him as old, solemn, and wise, though ashen from the zombie affliction. Tiny spectacles were fixed firmly on the far tip of his nose, making him look like a distinguished scholar, and he wore a thick tweed vest and bow tie.

"Allow me to introduce myself. I am Lord Amethyst Bartholomew, but do please call me Amethyst. No need for formal titles, considering our current state of affairs."

His voice was midtone and hoarse, as if he had sand in his throat. He had a wispy beard made of fine threads like spun silk the color of ivory. Age lines graced his forehead and temples, and crow's feet around his eyes became pronounced when he smiled or spoke, drawing attention to them—they were darkly shadowed around the rims.

The grand old caterpillar ignored Caitlin and spoke directly to Rapunzel. "I see you've brought the girl," he said.

She nodded. "Yes. And we're running out of time."

The caterpillar raised his hand pensively. "Ah, look at how we mindlessly react to Father Time, Your Highness, without ever asking, *what is the meaning of time?*"

Natalie butted in. "Though time and space are unified as per Einstein's space-time continuum, time itself might best be defined as the distance—"

"Silence, child!" he scolded in his raspy voice. "It was an allegorical, metaphorical, rhetorical question."

Amethyst turned slowly and peered deeply into Caitlin's eyes. "Who . . . Are . . . You?"

Caitlin remembered this question from her *Wonderland* book. She knew the caterpillar would try to engage her in all kinds of nonsensical wordplay.

Not gonna happen!

"My name is Caitlin—not Alice—and you know exactly who I am. I suppose you're now going to show me how to grow and shrink?"

Natalie raised an eyebrow in response to Caitlin's unexpected assertiveness.

Amethyst ran a finger through his silken beard. "So you choose to accept the literal meaning of *grow*, as opposed to the deeper meaning."

"The deeper meaning?"

"It suggests growing on the inside, not the outside. As for 'shrinking,' I suppose you thoroughly understand that word, speaking internally, of course."

Did he just insult me?

Lord Amethyst nodded sublimely toward Rapunzel and the princesses.

"I suppose you have questions pertaining to the dire state of the kingdoms?" he asked.

"Ya think?" Cindy quipped.

Amethyst raised a finger. "First, you must eat. We must fuel the body to fuel the mind."

Cinderella's stomach rumbled. So did Natalie's.

Amethyst beckoned with his hand. "By all means, eat until you are satiated. And be sure to take some for the road."

Like a band of ravenous soldiers, Natalie and the royals dove into the food supply. They stuffed their cheeks and their pockets with carrots, potatoes, lemons, and as many leaves as could fit. Cinderella smiled at Natalie as she picked a handful of jalapeño peppers from a vine.

"Pay dirt." She popped a whole pepper into her mouth and chewed. "Whoo! Spicy!"

Rapunzel came up behind Caitlin and nudged her in the direction of the caterpillar. "Talk to him."

Caitlin plucked an asparagus growing horizontally out of the wall. She was famished. She needed strength. She crunched a bite and then tentatively approached Lord Amethyst. He smelled like a mixture of fresh-cut grass and peppermint tea.

"Sleeping Beauty had a dream that told her you can help us?" Her tone was timid.

"Perhaps." With one finger, the caterpillar slid his spectacles higher on the bridge of his nose until they were parallel with his eyes. He gazed at Caitlin as if peering into the depth of her being.

"You had some difficulty gaining traction in Zeno's Forest?"

Caitlin blinked twice, then she cleared her throat.

"Well, sort of. Ya."

"Why do you suppose that is?"

Caitlin's back straightened. "Now you're going to tell me that I lacked certainty. Conviction."

"On the contrary," Amethyst said softly stroking his beard. "You *already* have perfect certainty and total conviction."

Caitlin's brow crinkled.

Amethyst pointed a finger. "Your problem is that you have perfect certainty in your doubt. You possess total conviction in your disbelief. So when you choose to not believe, then *nothing* is what you achieve."

He smiled.

"But let's save that conversation for another time."

Caitlin furrowed her brow.

Snow White approached and posed a question.

"My good Lord Amethyst, what about the su—"

The caterpillar raised his hand.

"No need to say it, Your Grace. You wish to know the secrets of our sun and the mystery of the affliction that affects our world."

Natalie elbowed Caitlin in the ribs. "A psychic caterpillar. Think he can bend spoons?"

Amethyst then pointed one of his many fingers at Caitlin. "And *you* wish to know what particles of imagination are made of?"

Caitlin's eyebrows popped up, as did Natalie's. How could he have known what they'd discussed before they entered Zeno's Forest?

"Imagination is the building block of our universe," Amethyst said. "Everything you see, both material and immaterial, is made up of particles of imagination. Except, my child, they are not really particles, but rather *waves*. Particles are found in your world. Not ours."

Natalie's mouth opened in awe. "That's one highly intelligent caterpillar, sis. He's referring to the wave-particle duality."

Caitlin wasn't sure what Natalie and the clever caterpillar were talking about. She shushed her sister because she wanted to hear more.

Amethyst winked at Natalie, then refocused his attention on Caitlin.

"In your world, when you probe into the atom you find electrons, protons, and neutrons. Your question is about what happens when we probe into the waves of imagination that erect all the kingdoms of our world, and give form to all of us?"

Lord Amethyst pointed upward toward the skylight, where rays of sunlight shone through.

He turned to Sleeping Beauty. "The crystal. The one in your pocket."

Beauty slid her fingers into the ruffles of her skirt and pulled it out.

Amethyst gestured upward again. Beauty angled the crystal toward the skylight so it would catch a ray of sun. The crystal prism split the sunbeams into a bright rainbow.

All eyes fell back on Lord Amethyst, who studiously removed his reading spectacles with one of his left hands. He gestured with his glasses as he spoke.

"These are the seven sacred wavelengths that bring forth existence," Amethyst said. "This light is made from waves of imagination that shine forth from the human kingdom."

A twinkle gleamed in Caitlin's eye. All the dots were starting to connect. Their curious brain-shaped sun. The minds of

Lewis Carroll, J.M. Barrie, and all the other writers, who wrote the stories that produced these imaginative worlds.

Amethyst pointed to the glimmering reds and oranges of the rainbow. "Now pay attention. From the Red Spectrum comes fear, lingering doubt, worry, and intolerable woe."

As if on cue, the forbidding caw of a crow echoed through the cavern, raising the hairs on Caitlin's arm. It came from outside.

A Blood-Eyed crow?

Amethyst ignored the caw and dipped his spectacles in the shimmer of blues, indigos, and violets.

"From the opposite, violet, end of the Spectrum there comes sublime courage, contentment, sheer joy, and splendid calm."

Next Amethyst waved his glasses through the middle of the rainbow, in the green and yellow color spectrums.

"Here lies the great power of the will. Our will decides which fears will be allowed to compel us into action and which will be repelled and banished from our being. But as you can see, the green is fading and losing strength."

He placed his spectacles back on the tip of his nose.

"Why not banish the entire Red Spectrum?" Caitlin asked.

"You mean all the fears, my child?"

She shrugged sheepishly.

"Fear of fire is a healthy fear; would you agree?"

She nodded.

"But a fear of a fire-breathing dragon living under your bed is a needless one. Therefore, the will repels the dragon fear. But it allows the fear of a burning house to endure, which serves to remind us to blow out the candles before retiring to bed."

Natalie had been listening with rapt attention. "He's deep," she whispered.

The caterpillar stroked his silky beard.

"Do you understand, my child?"

"I think so."

For some reason, what came to Caitlin's mind just then was a girl from her old school. Penny Robbins. She was a sweet kid who desperately wanted to be popular. At one point in the school year, she got really, really thin. Anorexic thin. She wound up in a hospital and missed a ton of school before she was well enough to return. Then, another situation popped into Caitlin's mind: a nasty stomach flu that had been going around back in September. Natalie had been very afraid of catching it. She had even cut out eating sugars and junk food and started eating a ton of vegetables and other "healthy" stuff that made Caitlin wanna gag. So, she reasoned, maybe Penny Robbins's fear of being unpopular had messed up her eating habits so much that she made herself sick. While Natalie's fear of getting sick had changed her eating habits in a way that kept her from needing a barf bowl at her bedside for a week.

Crazy. One fear had an awful outcome. The other prevented a puke-fest and a case of the runs.

That caterpillar is pretty freaking smart.

Caitlin was intrigued.

Sleeping Beauty's beautiful, pale face looked strained. "May I put my arm down now?"

Amethyst nodded apologetically. Beauty pocketed the crystal prism, and the rainbow of colors vanished.

Caitlin twisted a few of her long, cinnamon strands of hair around her finger.

"How do you light up the Violet Spectrum?"

Amethyst's demeanor took on a decidedly gladdened turn. Then the antennae on his head stiffened. And as he opened his mouth to answer, a bloodcurdling cawing sound echoed fiendishly into the cavern—this one louder than the previous.

Rapunzel winced.

Amethyst's mood turned on a dime. He nervously turned in circles on his mushroom.

"The black crows!" Amethyst said with a grim tone. "Blood-Eyed ghouls of prey." He set his cup down on its saucer with trembling hands. "Where there are crows, the demonic howls of the wolves follow. We must hurry. You need to know what happened here before it's too late to save the kingdoms."

What about saving us?

Even brave, nothing-fazed-her Natalie began to rock nervously on her feet. "My guess is that a fear of zombie wolves falls under the category of healthy fears," she whispered to Caitlin.

CHAPTER TWENTY-SIX

JACK—STILL THE SIZE OF AN INCHWORM—BREEZED ABOVE A STRETCH of decaying brown fields, balanced like a surfer on the face of a dry, brown maple leaf that was sailing through the air on a warm wind. Two dabs of sap kept his feet firmly secured to the leaf's surface.

Jack cupped his hands around his mouth and called down to Alfonzo, who hopped below him on the ground, keeping pace. "You were right!"

Alfonzo looked up at him.

"I can spot the forest from here," Jack said.

Jack dipped down on his leaf-board, skimming the tops of blades of withered grass next to Alfonzo.

"If anything happens to Caitlin, I swear I'll die. It's my fault she's here without me. If only I hadn't forgotten my blasted phone."

"We have not the time for regrets, amigo. Just lead the way to the forest. I can't see a thing through this tall grass."

The wind blew hard at Jack's back. He pulled the tunic from his knight costume off over his head and stretched it between his arms to create a sail. A gust of wind caught the sail and increased his speed. His arm and chest muscles strained as he held the sail firm against the wind and tried to steer. His golden-brown hair whipped around his head as currents of air carried him along.

He and Prince Alfonzo sailed and hopped toward the forest's edge until a babbling stream came into view.

The wind abruptly changed direction. Jack wobbled as his leaf-board began to whirl out of control. He crouched, trying to balance, but the wave of air was too strong. Wipeout! Jack spiraled out of control and landed hard on a burger-size rock, which compared to him, was like a small mountain.

Jack was pulling his tunic down over his chest again when Alfonzo hopped up to him.

"Amigo," Alfonzo whispered, "I would advise a slight detour by way of the stream."

Jack raised his eyebrows and pointed straight ahead. "But the forest is right there!"

Sure enough, only one thing separated Jack and Alfonzo from Zeno's Forest: a wooden bridge laden with crows.

"I'm too small to swim in that current," Jack said. "I'd get swept away. Or eaten by a trout."

"Shh . . ." whispered Alfonzo. "You need to be careful not to wake the troll."

"Troll?"

The idea of meeting an authentic troll did not delight Jack. Nevertheless, with no other option, he decided to forge ahead on land.

"You take the stream," Jack said. "I'll risk the bridge. We'll meet on the other side."

Alfonzo bowed with a flourish. "You are braver than I, amigo. Till we meet again on the other side . . . I hope."

And with that Alfonzo hopped toward a section of the stream that flowed far from the crows.

Jack proceeded on foot to the narrow bridge leading to Zeno's Forest.

How scary could this troll be, anyway? The black crows napping on the bridge rails don't seem the least bit afraid of him.

Jack held his breath. He took a cautious first step onto the edge of the bridge. The crows erupted with caws. Wings flapped. Feathers flew. The blood-eyed birds scattered. They swarmed together under slowly darkening clouds and flapped off in an arrow formation over the tree line of Zeno's Forest.

A guttural growl suddenly rose up from beneath the bridge's deck.

"Who woke the birds?" a belligerent voice bellowed.

A giant foot swung out from beneath the bridge. Then another. A colossal, scaly, and callused body followed. Jack hid behind a handrail. He crouched. Then he peered out to see what kind of monumental force he was up against.

The stink of troll body odor blasted his nostrils.

The troll in all his horribleness loomed over him. A hulking wad of muscle and muck and machismo. His gray skin had a reptilian, bumpy texture that reminded Jack of a lizard. It appeared to be covered by a crusty layer of green-and-white bird droppings. Daggerlike tusks protruded from his face. Pointy goat horns grew from the top of his head above his ears. Thorny spikes accented his brow.

And if that wasn't enough, drool bubbled out from between his swollen lips as he chanted: "Fe, fi, foe, fum. I smell the blood of an Englishman."

Jack flinched. "Cheeky fellow."

The troll's giant big toe landed on the edge of the bridge with the impact of a falling tree. He began walking across it. The rotting, wooden slats jumped with each thunderous stomp.

Wiry hair grew out of his nostrils in an upward curl.

This bloke's a minger.

Strands of nose hair were so long that, if one got close enough, Jack suspected they could be twisted into a fine braid. The curved-up nose hair appeared to be the only thing about this dodgy character that resembled a smile.

Jack crouched, perfectly still. He needed to get across, but he also needed to not die. His mother had once told him that the best place to hide was in plain sight.

Jack clambered up the side of the bridge. He took a running start, then jumped right onto the giant's mountainous snout.

The hideous troll was stunned. And in that moment, one that seemed to pause and last a lifetime, Jack caught sight of his reflection in a giant, glowing eye. The troll tried to squash Jack like a zit. But Jack was nimble. And he was surely quick.

He jumped over the troll's nostril and dashed across his rugged cheek. The troll, in reflex, walloped himself on the nose, which made his eyes water.

The troll stumbled and grunted loudly. He swatted at his nose again.

"I'll nab you, yet!"

He stomped his humongous foot.

"Come out, come out. Come out of my snout."

But Jack, of course, was not in his nose.

He took cover in the troll's ear, pressing his body flat against the waxy canal. A bitter, dung-like smell assaulted Jack. Hairs brushed against his back and coated his shirt in oily wax. Jack tried to pluck out one of the hairs, but he only came away holding a glob of wax—altogether nauseating.

The troll tried to jam his stubby fingers in his ear. Too thick.

Jack wiped his waxen hands on his jeans. He yanked the hair again. He plucked it out! Jack almost hurled.

"Agh!" screamed the mighty troll.

The troll tipped his head to the side and boxed himself in the other ear, trying to knock Jack out.

Jack seized the moment.

He slid down the giant's earlobe and, grasping on tightly, kicked the troll's earring out of its hole.

"My earring!"

The troll bent down. He searched for the earring atop the knotty boards of the bridge.

"Time to bugger off," Jack muttered. He jammed his arm through the piercing hole and clamped on tightly. He rocked back and forth on the loop of flesh. After three pumps to gain momentum, he let go.

Jack flew through the air.

He tumbled hard to the ground. Then he leaped up and ran as fast as he could across the swaying bridge.

A razor-sharp pain stabbed his leg like a knife. He began to limp severely. A warm, syrupy substance oozed atop his skin.

He looked down.

His own fractured bone had sliced through his flesh. The creamy-white tibia protruded between his knee and shin.

Jack realized he would no longer be running to Zeno's Forest.

He would have to hobble his way there.

CHAPTER TWENTY-SEVEN

THE EMINENT CATERPILLAR, LORD AMETHYST BARTHOLOMEW, took a hurried sip of tea. Then he set his porcelain cup on top of the faded orange mushroom that served as an end table. A fresh peppermint aroma wafted through the cavern as mint fumes spiraled up from another stick of incense.

"The Blood-Eyed are closing in," Amethyst said. "Come closer and sit." He clasped his hands while Caitlin and the girls hastily found spots to settle near him.

He whispered in a scratchy voice, "It's time to reveal the secret of the queen's power and to learn why Caitlin has been summoned here."

At last!

Everyone leaned in, intrigued.

"The queen had called upon a devious man of the occult. He knew well the colors of the sun, from which thoughts are born. But as darkness detests light, the Enchanter loathes the sun."

Caitlin rubbed the dryness from her eyes. She hadn't blinked since Amethyst began talking.

"He gave the queen the dreadful royal scepter and the cursed glasses she wears. The lenses of those glasses are not of this world. They were fashioned out of the Red Spectrum. Without any other color included. Now pay attention: Red is at the opposite end of the color spectrum from violet, and thus the Queen sees everything good as its opposite. She perceives the reverse of reality, the opposite of actuality. Especially when she peers into one's imagination and heart."

Caitlin felt a tingle on her forehead.

"These tools of darkness," Amethyst continued, "caused this once lovely and honorable lady to become the grim Seeress who now wreaks havoc upon our world. Because of those Red Spectrum lenses, where there was sweetness, the queen perceives bitterness. Where affection bloomed, she senses ill will. Where loyalty remains steadfast, she sees the seeds of rebellion."

Natalie nodded to Caitlin. "Sounds like Mr. Gandelmeyer, my old social studies teacher."

Caitlin nudged her sister with an elbow.

"The queen's vision swept across the kingdoms," the grand insect said. "She saw people scheming and plotting to overthrow the monarchy while, in fact, they were praying for her well-being and hoping she would regain her true self and identity."

Caitlin swallowed, feeling a slight twinge in her heart.

Natalie tapped her shoulder. "I'm craving buttered popcorn. You?"

"Shh!" Caitlin whispered.

"And so it happened," Amethyst went on, "to weaken and control the masses, the queen waved her scepter skyward. And that's when something changed in the hues of the burning sun."

Lord Amethyst turned to Sleeping Beauty. On his cue, she again took out the crystal prism and held it under the skylight to catch another sunray. A rainbow lit up the cavern.

"The green wavelengths weakened. This, in turn, brought the weakening of our will."

He pointed out the red in the rainbow.

"The red wavelength magnified. Fear intensified. For there was no will to restrain it."

The red color flared just then, as if responding to Amethyst's words.

"Unbridled fear has a raging appetite. As it grew, hunger grew . . . until its appetite included flesh and blood."

The hideous cawing of many crows pierced the cavern, sending a cold shiver down Caitlin's spine.

Amethyst waved his hand, signaling Sleeping Beauty to lower the prism. He rubbed his chin.

"The truth is, fear is free and abundant. The Red Spectrum shines all by itself. It comes to us easily. But courage comes hard. The Violet Spectrum must be kindled to shine. It takes effort. That's the secret of the spectrum."

A lump swelled in Caitlin's throat.

She avoided nearly everything that frightened her.

I never stood up for Alicia Saunders!

She had hid from Piper and her coven in her bathroom stall. She had wimped out. Because it was so easy to. She was mindless, like a zombie. Enslaved to her fear. At least, according to a zombified insect, who was less a zombie than she but far more compassionate to boot. How humiliating.

"How do you ignite the Violet Spectrum?" Caitlin asked again with wishful eyes.

Amethyst raised a finger. "That, my child, is for you to discover."

"But I need to know *now*," Caitlin pleaded.

Amethyst cocked his head and gave her a withering look.

"Impatience also comes free and easy," he said. Caitlin slunk down.

Amethyst's tentacles stiffened in alert, as if he sensed something awful about to happen. A split second later a ghastly Blood-Eyed crow swooped out from the tunnel and into the cavern! It squawked like a demon.

Everyone ducked.

Caitlin screamed.

Natalie gasped.

Cindy leaped up and grabbed a thick throw blanket from the sofa. She flung it over the winged creature. The weight of the blanket sent the crow crumpling to the ground. Cindy jumped on top of it.

"Be careful you don't get bitten," Rapunzel screamed.

"I'll bite this Blood-Eyed bird myself," Cindy replied in outrage. She bundled the blanket up and tied the four corners into a knot. The crow poked and prodded frantically inside.

Amethyst gestured with his chin toward the chest of drawers. Cindy held the blanket with her arm extended far from her body as she walked to the wood-and-brass cabinet, opened a drawer, and stuffed the blanket inside. She slammed it shut.

"Check for scratches," Rapunzel said.

Cinderella examined the fronts and backs of her forearms and hands. "I'm good."

Everyone stood back up—except for Beauty, who was catching another forty winks.

Amethyst exhaled. He stroked his beard. His soulful eyes fell on Caitlin.

"All I can tell you, child, is that the secret for kindling the Violet Spectrum is found in the will."

"Which we're desperately short of," Rapunzel noted.

Amethyst nodded. "And so the scepter continues to breed fear and stoke this horrid degenerative affliction."

Caitlin chewed on the ends of her hair.

Cindy cocked her head. "Is the queen's scepter more powerful than the force that brought our worlds into existence?"

Natalie seemed impressed. "A deep and fundamental question," she muttered to Caitlin.

Amethyst cracked a sly smile. Apparently he concurred with Natalie.

"A most compelling inquiry, Your Grace. The answer—"

Sleeping Beauty interrupted him. "The Blood-Eyed wolves are on the way," she said in an ominous tone. There was cold fear in her beautiful, dead eyes. She spoke as if in a trance. Wait—she *was* in a trance. Beauty was *still asleep* as the words poured out. "They've been called by the crow that detected our royal blood. It was not our fear that gave us away, but our noble courage."

Amethyst nodded somberly with each word she spoke. He raised a pointed finger.

"She speaks truth. The queen is bent on ravaging this world by draining it of every last modicum of courage. Her crows can detect courage and royalty anywhere." He pointed to the chest of drawers. "That's exactly how this last ghastly bird found us."

The zombie girls exchanged nervous glances. Beauty lay back down for a nap.

"To return to your question, Your Grace," Amethyst continued, "the truth is, the scepter has no power over the sun. Darkness is powerless in the presence of light. The Enchanter applied a cunning deception to deceive the queen."

Natalie gave an elbow shot to Caitlin. "This insect has an answer for everything. Let's take him home with us."

"Shh!" Caitlin said, elbowing her in the ribs.

"Like a trick?" Cindy asked.

Amethyst nodded. "Indeed. The scepter is not some magical instrument or supernatural weapon. And certainly no enchanter is more powerful than the transcendent waves of imagination that are the very fabric of our reality. The Enchanter simply blocked out a portion of the light."

"Like a large cumulonimbus," Natalie stated as she chewed her cucumber.

"Excuse me?" Cindy intervened.

Amethyst smiled. "She means to say, like a scattering of dense cloud cover. The scepter created an interference wave that blanketed the atmosphere. And at this moment, it is filtering out the green wavelength of our sun."

"Diabolically simple," Cindy said, shaking her head.

"To be sure." Lord Amethyst pointed up.

"Each new wave of the scepter released another layer of cloud cover, so to speak, in the sky. It continued to thicken until it became so dense it operated just like a blackout curtain. And just like that, our will was vanquished. So, my friends, there is no unearthly curse. No zombie contagion. The sun is still there in its full supernal splendor. There is only an interference pattern. A thick curtain. We just happen to be on the wrong side of it. The red side. However, the royal-blooded among us, though dead, live to fight on. A small remnant of compassion in our hearts strengthens our will." Lord Amethyst bowed his head graciously to the zombie princesses.

Then his gaze made a full sweep of the group seated before him.

"Only the bite of a Blood-Eyed ghoul will turn a human or a royal into a Blood-Eyed—which is how we lost so many of our brave. All the knights. Princes. Kings. Most were bitten during that first battle of the Zombie Wars."

Caitlin's hands went clammy.

"However, even you royals will not survive another wave of the scepter. The queen has that planned for tonight. Should it happen, we'll lose our remaining power to resist the Red Spectrum."

Cindy flexed her fingers, then cracked her knuckles. "We'll snatch the scepter from her."

Amethyst shook his head dejectedly. "You'll never get near it—not even within a few meters."

"Why not?" Rapunzel asked.

"Crows. They can smell the scent of courage and royal blood from vast distances."

"Who cares," Cinderella replied. "We'll storm that wicked wench and overpower her. I'll wrestle the scepter from her myself."

Rapunzel nodded in agreement as she rolled up her sleeves. "Yeah. Six of us, one of her. I'll take those odds."

Caitlin bit a nail.

Amethyst waved a dismissive finger.

Natalie was looking for something else to munch.

"You're forgetting about the wolves," Amethyst said. "They guard her and protect the scepter. As do all the other Blood-Eyed. To get to the queen, you need to be able to get past a kingdom of ghouls without getting bitten."

Rapunzel slumped down on a boulder. "Which is impossible."

Natalie found a carrot and took a nibble. "Now tell us the bad news."

"If that scepter is raised at midnight," Amethyst replied, "Our eyes will turn as red as the blood we'll crave."

Natalie tossed the carrot aside. "And we'll all be living the zombie life."

The chilling caws of a close murder of crows reverberated into the cavern.

Caitlin shoved her hands in her pockets to warm them. She heard another grim wail. Or she thought she did. It sounded like the baying of wolves—faint howls that seemed to ring right through the rock of the cavern.

What had the smart caterpillar said before? Where there were crows, the demonic howls of the wolves followed.

Her eyes darted around the cave. Had the others heard it too? Or was she imagining it?

She felt like she was sitting on a butcher block.

Like a fresh piece of meat about to be eaten.

CHAPTER TWENTY-EIGHT

THERE SEEMED TO BE NO FEASIBLE WAY TO GET CLOSE TO THE QUEEN so they could snatch the scepter.

Resolve glinted in Rapunzel's eyes. "I don't care about wolves and crows—or my own life. I'm going after the scepter."

"Me too!" Cindy cried out.

Amethyst wagged a finger. "Your self-sacrifice, noble as it may be, won't work. No hand born of our world can remove the scepter from the queen's grasp. Only the human hand has the power to take hold of it."

A pregnant pause quieted the cave. All eyes fell on Caitlin Rose Fletcher as Caitlin Rose Fletcher almost fell over on the dirt floor.

That's why I'm here?

"But you just said the crows guard the queen," Caitlin responded in a nervous tone. "Even from humans!"

Amethyst cracked a discerning smile, his eyes betraying his crafty intelligence.

He crawled on his many legs over to the large chest of drawers. He opened the bottom drawer, reached inside, and took out an object. A translucent pyramid about the size of a walnut was fixed between two of his fingers. "*This* prism," Amethyst said, holding it up for all to see, "is made of fused quartz."

Cindy eyed it hungrily. "What's so special about fused quartz? Is it edible?"

Amethyst tilted it to and fro. "A quartz prism disperses invisible wavelengths of light."

He snapped the quartz prism into a clamp located at the top of a tall, thin candelabrum beside his mushroom. He turned his attention to Caitlin.

"Come, child."

Her eyes sprung open. She swung her head to look behind her, hoping he was talking to another child—perhaps Natalie? She turned back and met his gaze.

Uh-oh.

Caitlin tried to speak, but no words came forth. She mouthed soundlessly: "*Who, me?*"

Amethyst nodded. It figured. Caitlin's walk was hesitant as she moved in the direction of the caterpillar She stopped short of the candelabrum. She felt that was close enough.

"Closer, child."

Caitlin glanced back at Natalie. Her sister nudged her chin up, encouraging her onward.

Caitlin crept a little closer.

"A bit more," Amethyst instructed.

When Caitlin was close enough for his liking, he raised his hand. "Stop there, child."

Rapunzel nodded as a canny smile broke at the corners of her mouth. She said to the girls, "This must be why he sent us to find Caitlin."

Amethyst adjusted the angle of the quartz prism, slanting it toward Caitlin's forehead.

"I shall refract your aura."

My aura?

With one of his many hands, he turned a knob. Blackout blinds obediently rolled down to cover the skylight. "Works better in the dark." He turned to Rapunzel. "Please blow out the candles." She blew out the flames flickering in the sconces on the cavern walls.

The cave went dark.

Except for a single phosphorescent maroon glow.

Natalie's mouth fell open. She stared bug-eyed at Caitlin.

"Natalie, what is it?"

Her response remained her open mouth.

Caitlin glanced upward. With her peripheral vision, she could see a faint, radiant field glimmering around her head. It was tinged in shades of red.

"Oh my God! Is that my aura?" she exclaimed. "For real?"

"It is," Amethyst said. "As I hoped. No green. Barely any yellow. This girl is all fear. She's awash in worry. Perfectly petrified of . . . well, practically everything."

Caitlin felt like crying.

How freaking depressing!

"How wonderful!" Amethyst said hopefully.

Caitlin gasped. "I don't understand!"

And I'm not sure I want to . . .

"Your fear will cloak you in a shield of invisibility," Amethyst said.

"Huh?!"

"The crows can only sense courage and royal blood."

"Huh?!"

"The crows will never sense you coming. You'll be like a ghost. You'll be invisible. Even when you're close enough to smell the queen's breath."

Caitlin snapped out of her shock. "But how about all the Blood-Eyed wolves and zombies who surround her?"

Amethyst scratched his head with one of his left hands. "Haven't figured that one out yet."

That comment drained the blood from Caitlin's face.

"I cannot do this!" Caitlin whined.

Amethyst fixed his narrowed eyes on her as his manner turned gravely serious.

"Be careful of the thoughts you express. Our entire realm is one endless wave of imagination, my child. When you complain and worry, our world will bring you more to complain and worry about. When you appreciate, the world brings you more to appreciate. It's in our own hands. It's in *your* hands, my child."

A hair-raising wolf howl roared into the cavern, frightening Caitlin so much she completely emptied the air out of her lungs.

The awful wolf's call was no longer echoing from some faraway ridge outside the cave. It was coming from *inside* the tunnel!

"Oh my!" Lord Amethyst announced, hands on his cheeks. "They've found the entrance!"

The cavern went silent. No one moved.

Wind whistled through the tunnel.

Then a whining gust of foul air whirled into the cavern, scattering papers, stirring up dust, and rattling vines.

"Nature has not produced this wind," Amethyst whispered. "It gestates evil and possesses depraved intelligence."

Caitlin blew hot breath on her fingers. Then she rubbed her hands together.

The snarling of the wolf drew closer.

Amethyst massaged his chin with one hand after another. Caitlin hoped those eyebrows of his would arch in a sudden flash of inspiration, because their group needed an exit strategy, fast.

The clawing noise of paws tracking along the dirt grew louder. Closer.

Natalie was running a finger through her hair, twisting loose strands around and around and around. It was a nervous habit of Caitlin's, but she'd never seen Natalie do it even once— before now.

Another draft of wind brought the rancid odor of wolf breath into the cavern. It smelled like one of those stinking corpse flowers mixed with blood.

Caitlin's mouth ran dry.

No spit. Zero saliva.

The hellhound was nearly at the door.

Amethyst became still. His antennae sprung to alert. The ghoulish, guttural growl was about to enter his cavern.

Caitlin flattened both palms against her ears, hard. She couldn't bear to hear that bone-chilling snarl again. She kept her eyes glued on the caterpillar, waiting for him to proclaim a miraculous solution.

Amethyst looked peaceful. He seemed to be accepting his fate.

What?

The grand old insect turned to his frightened guests.

"Evil has arrived."

CHAPTER TWENTY-NINE

CAITLIN DISLIKED DARKNESS—IN FACT, SHE WAS SCARED STIFF OF it—so closing her eyes to avoid seeing what was about to come into that cave was not an option. Instead she sat down on the small boulder. She lifted her gaze, fixing it determinedly on the ceiling.

Please, please don't let me see it! Don't let me see it!

As if not seeing *it* would somehow prevent *it* from seeing her.

Her nails clawed the sides of the boulder as she sat, muscles tensed. She clenched her fingers into fists till her knuckles went white. Her eyes remained locked on that single spot on the ceiling.

Cold wind drifted around her ankles and snaked up her back. The wind was vile and alive, just as Amethyst had said.

No one in that room dared to move a finger, steal a breath, or even blink an eye.

The stench of wolf breath was thick in the air.

It was moving.

Caitlin felt the urge to look. The not knowing gnawed at her. *Not* looking would torment her. But looking, she knew, would also freak her out.

Caitlin lowered her eyes.

The wolf roamed right past her, making the hair on the back of her neck stand on end.

Its eyes glowed a deep red as it lurked about the dim cavern, fangs bared.

Its black fur was thick in some spots, but elsewhere the skin had rotted right through, exposing its innards.

A tract of rib cage.

A strip of leg bone.

A patch of newly decayed flesh.

When it prowled past the quartz prism clamped atop the candelabrum, the creature's aura dispersed into a rainbow that quickly became no rainbow at all! It shimmered only black—all the colors were *gone*!

Caitlin's skin crawled.

She thought she had known fear before this moment. But never before had she been able to taste it on her tongue, like now. Her other phobias paled in comparison to what she was feeling now—a cold fright biting her to the bone.

Saliva speckled with blood, possibly from a fresh kill, dripped from the wolf's mouth as he leered at the bountiful meal before him. He seemed to relish deciding which one of them he was going to devour first.

Her head still as a statue, Caitlin shifted her eyes to her left.

Rapunzel was quietly reeling in her long, golden rope of hair. Caitlin thought it looked like she was preparing to twist it into a lasso.

No, that'll never hold him!

A sharp sniff issued from the snout of the creature as it sized up Sleeping Beauty.

She is asleep?!

Caitlin stiffened as a medley of howls rang out from afar.

Others were coming!

Horror rose like bile in Caitlin's throat as the wolf reared, preparing to lunge at Beauty. The carnivore reared up impossibly high, then did something utterly chilling . . . the creature stood upright!

On its hind legs!

Like a man-turned-werewolf . . . like the hideous Big Bad Wolf that they had freed from the trap!

Her eyes went all flashbulb.

She called to Snow, "It's him!"

Beauty suddenly opened her eyes in silent terror.

Snow White leaped to her feet before the wolf could leap on Sleeping Beauty.

"Wait! Stop!" she cried as she waved her hands.

The wolf whipped its head around to face her. Its soulless eyes were like stone-cold rubies.

"We helped you! Don't you remember us?"

The wolf tilted its head to one side.

"Snow! Are you crazy?" Rapunzel screamed. "You can't reason with it! It's an eating machine!"

"She's right!" Cindy added. "Stay back!"

Snow continued, undeterred. "Those vultures would have eaten you alive if it weren't for us," she said to Mr. Big Bad.

It glared at her, sniffing, snarling, saliva dripping from its jaw. A low, vicious growl rumbled through its fangs. It seemed to know the scent of royal blood.

The wolf arched its back. Its leg muscles contracted like a spring. It was preparing to pounce.

Snow White's brow furrowed. "And you never even said thank you!" Her words were laced with a tough-love tone. "You think you're so big and bad? Well, it's easy being a big, bad, *ungrateful* wolf. It's much tougher to be an appreciative one— especially when it's your life that was saved!"

Out of the corner of her eye, Caitlin saw Rapunzel preparing to toss the lasso. She gave Rapunzel a swift shake of her head, worrying that being snared might make the wolf really lose it.

Rapunzel lowered her arm.

Thank goodness!

The yelping of the coming wolf pack grew louder.

It was almost here.

The Big Bad Wolf howled in response. He turned his crimson eyes on Natalie. He glared at her. Inhaled her smell. She stood helpless in her little red chili pepper outfit.

Little? Red? Uh-oh!

Cinderella jumped in front of Natalie, arms spread wide in a protective stance, her eyes lit with anger. She grabbed the candelabrum and wielded it menacingly. "Back up, werewolf," Cindy warned, "or you'll be wearing this around your neck!"

The wolf snarled like a demon. The fur on its back spiked upward.

"Don't antagonize him," Snow said. She then smiled gently at the creature. "Try and remember how we saved you," she urged the wolf.

Its eyes now fell on Caitlin. It sniffed. Glowered. Tilted its head. It pivoted back, leering again at Snow.

She waved her finger in a scolding gesture, as if to say: Don't you even think about it!

The zombie wolf gave a distinctly dismissive wave of its head that seemed to say: Disappear. Before the other wolves from hell arrive.

Everyone bolted up in unison and tiptoed toward the tunnel exit.

Amethyst unclamped the quartz prism from the candelabrum in Cindy's hand and slipped it into his vest pocket.

On the way out, Natalie scurried past the big bad zombie wolf.

Its nostrils flared as she passed. A growl grew at the rear of its throat. It curled its lips and clenched its jaw, as if trying consciously to hold its instinct to eat her at bay.

Natalie passed him so closely, she caught a hefty whiff of hot, rancid wolf breath.

Caitlin heard the yowls of the approaching wolf pack.

"Natalie, we gotta go!"

Caitlin was too afraid to look the wolf in the eye. But she forced a weak smile as she passed him, nodding just a tad, as if to bid the wolf farewell.

The Blood-Eyed canine ghoul stared back, eyes stoic. As she turned to leave, Caitlin snuck a quick look at him. She was sure she saw that beast bow his head ever so slightly, as if in gratitude.

Goose bumps covered her entire body.

"Wow, even a Blood-Eyed zombie can have a drop of compassion," Caitlin said as she kneeled at the entrance to the tunnel.

The caterpillar scuttled up alongside her and smiled. "Only because you and Snow put it there. You gave that undead creature compassion—he therefore received something that he could give back to you."

The caterpillar quickly summoned everyone around the tunnel entrance.

"Where's Cindy?" Rapunzel asked.

Caitlin glanced behind them. Cinderella had just finished stuffing her pockets with jalapeño peppers, garlic cloves, horse-radish, and wasabi roots. She joined the group at the exit.

Amethyst seemed tense. "After that rather close brush with death, a sublime revelation has come to me," he said. "You girls must work together to resolve this dire situation."

They looked at him, obviously waiting for more details.

"That's all I can tell you," he said. "You better hurry on."

Caitlin stared blankly at Amethyst.

That's it?

"Now if you'll excuse me, I have somewhere important to

be." Lord Amethyst handed a startled Caitlin a folded sheet of paper. "You will find all the answers written here, my child."

And with that Lord Amethyst Bartholomew, the royal-blue caterpillar, took a small sip of drink from a flask he pulled from another pocket and immediately shrunk back to his former three-inch length. He turned away from the tunnel entrance and scurried over to a mushroom. He sat under it, twirled his tail, and quickly spun the most enchanting cocoon Caitlin had ever seen. In a blink he was completely encased and hanging from the underside of the mushroom. A perfect disguise from the pack of wolves that were minutes away.

The Blood-Eyed Big Bad Wolf meanwhile let out a lengthy, low-pitched howl. His cry pierced the cave, traveled through the tunnel, and rang out across the land. And when that soaring howl finally died into silence, the six friends had disappeared from the home of the caterpillar, well on their way to safer ground.

CHAPTER THIRTY

THE GROUP TRAVELED A GREAT DISTANCE OVER A SWEEPING, wooded terrain in Zeno's Forest in the shortest time span imaginable. Caitlin and company had now reached the outer edge of the forest, back on the border of Wonderland, far from the wolves—for now.

Caitlin took out the paper that Amethyst had given her. She quickly unfolded it. A map.

She handed it to Rapunzel.

"According to this, the queen's castle should be just east of here." Rapunzel flipped the map over. On the back was a detailed blueprint of the castle and its surrounding area. "Now *this* could come in handy. Follow me."

The air felt wet and heavy. Clouds hung low. Caitlin could practically taste their dull, gray fluff.

After a short while, they came to a fork in the road. A large marsh lay directly in front of them. To their right was a dirt road. On the left an overgrown, cobblestone path led to an abandoned-looking castle. Pointed spires with clover-shaped finials tilted over into crumbling stone walls. Stained-glass windows lay in shards on the ground. Dead weeds and mushrooms were the gate's only apparent guards.

Cinderella lifted the corner of her skirt and twirled.

"I remember this place. It belonged to the good old Duke of Clubs. He used to throw the most outrageous parties."

Cinderella danced and dipped from side to side. Then, suddenly, she stopped. Her shoulders slumped forward and she bowed her head. Snow White pulled out a handkerchief to dab her eyes.

"The poor duke. He fell to the Blood-Eyed courageously . . . alongside our husbands."

Natalie whispered to Caitlin. "I feel kinda bad. Prince Charming and all the princes—they're all Blood-Eyed ghouls now. These girls are hurting."

Caitlin swallowed, sort of embarrassed that she hadn't thought of that herself.

Rapunzel studied the map and, without lifting her eyes from the page, said, "No time for tears." She traced a line on the map with her finger. "This road on the right is the route to the Queen of Hearts' castle."

She stood up straight, hands on her hips, and stared at the castle on her left. Then she marched over to the dancing Cinderella and plucked a few strands of hair from her head.

"Ow! Bloody hell, pretty princess!"

One corner of Snow White's mouth curled into a smile.

"Quite clever. Would you like some strands of mine as well?"

Rapunzel winked. "By the root, if you can."

She turned to Beauty. "You too. A nice clump."

Beauty scrunched her nose. "Seriously?"

Rapunzel didn't answer. She simply yanked a couple of gold locks out herself.

Beauty winced. "You're welcome. And that *hurt!*"

Rapunzel yanked a handful of strands from her own scalp.

She turned and approached Caitlin.

"Never!" Caitlin shouted, bug-eyed, as she tried to guard her head with both hands.

Rapunzel stared blankly at Caitlin. Then she picked a dried-up sugar maple leaf from a dead tree and brought it to Caitlin. She held it up to Caitlin's mouth.

"Spit."

Caitlin stared at her, open-mouthed. Rapunzel remained steadfast.

"Spit on the leaf, or I pluck a clump of hair."

Caitlin snorted and amassed a swirl of saliva in her mouth. She chucked the huge wad of phlegm all over the leaf.

"Eloquent performance," Natalie said.

Cindy ripped a few thin strips of fabric from Sleeping Beauty's cape and descended on Caitlin, using the strips to wipe perspiration from her brow and to swab out her ears.

Rapunzel took the fabric strips and rubbed Caitlin's earwax on a long branch. "Wait here," she commanded.

"Hang on," Cindy said to her.

She reached into her pocket. She pulled out four jalapeño peppers, three garlic cloves, and a wasabi root. Rapunzel grabbed the spices.

"Good thinking."

She marched toward the old castle, dragging the stick across the ground. Along the way, she dropped the strands of hair and scraps of fabric. When she got to the castle entrance she opened the large, wooden doors and disappeared inside.

"What in the world is she up to?" Caitlin asked no one in particular.

"Sly as a fox," Natalie muttered. "She's buying us time."

After a long few minutes, Rapunzel returned. A self-satisfied grin was planted on her face. "Time to get out of here!"

The girls turned to the right and started down the road in the direction of the queen's castle.

Rapunzel stopped them. "Not that way." She pointed to the marsh. "*This* way."

"I don't get it. Thought we needed to hurry?" Caitlin said.

Rapunzel waded knee-deep into the marsh. She turned and waved her arm, summoning the others. She made a wide right turn and walked about a hundred yards through the shallow water before wading back out of the marsh and onto the dirt road. The girls followed Rapunzel's path.

After twenty minutes of trekking in the stifling heat, their clothes had dried out completely.

Natalie wiped beads of perspiration from her forehead. "Are we almost there?"

"Yes," Rapunzel replied. "But keep your voice down, and be on the lookout. The queen has minions everywhere."

As if on cue, menacing black crows appeared overhead, flying in a *V* formation. The leader made a sudden nosedive. It returned to the flock and led the birds in a new formation—a figure-eight pattern close to the ground and right above the girls' heads. *There must be hundreds of them. Not exactly the warmest of welcomes.*

The dirt road ended and a cobblestone lane took its place. It wound around a mess of tangled, brown branches. As they followed it, Caitlin noticed that the branches were evenly spaced, in clumps, and that most were encrusted in dead leaves. Even more curious was that they looked like sculptures in the forms of classic shapes. One tangled clump was shaped like a perfect diamond. Another was shaped like a heart. A third was shaped like Cupid pulling back on his bow, ready to shoot his arrow.

The cobblestone lane twisted around one more bramble, and then Caitlin saw a fortress-style castle surrounded by a massive rock wall. A crimson-colored flag flapped in the wind on the highest spire.

They had arrived at their destination: the Queen of Hearts' castle.

Its gray stone towers pierced a heavy blanket of hot smog. Sunshine heated the thick soup of vapor.

"Pick up the pace," Rapunzel said. "Those crows have already signaled the wolves."

Rapunzel unfolded the map and scoped out their position.

"The front gate leads to the drawbridge," she said. "So that entrance is not an option. The queen will spot us for sure, which leaves only one way to break into this royal fortress . . . "

Caitlin's mouth fell agape. "You mean that ginormous rock wall in front of us?"

Natalie nudged her sister in the ribs. "Acrophobia. Aka, fear of heights."

The ash-gray bricks of the wall were chipped, broken, and worn, but it still stood a solid four stories high.

"Those chips will make it easier to climb," Beauty said.

Caitlin went weak in the knees.

When they reached the base of the wall, the girls cast expectant eyes upon Rapunzel. Her grin was sly. She twirled her golden braid until it formed a lasso again. She flung her rope-hair high, and it landed over the top of a bastion. She tugged on it, and it held fast.

Rapunzel began to climb the wall of rock. Her bare, spindly toes dug into crevices. Her powerful arms yanked her upward as she pulled on her own golden rope.

She stopped abruptly after a moment and looked down at the group, grimacing. "These stone chips are sharp. Careful you don't cut your feet."

Rapunzel renewed her climb, leaving a red-stained footprint on the gray wall beneath her.

Caitlin thought she heard a wolf's howl echo in the distance.

Rapunzel finally mounted the ramparts. She turned around and flung her golden braid down to Beauty.

"Your turn."

Beauty started climbing. She was quickly followed by Snow, Cindy, and then Natalie.

Caitlin bit her lower lip. "I'll stay here and be the lookout," she volunteered meekly.

Natalie threw a look at Caitlin before she took her first step. "We need you. *You're* the imperceptible one, remember?"

Cindy called down to Caitlin as quietly as she could. "Move it, sister. Those wolves are definitely back on our scent."

Caitlin glanced behind her, then back up at Natalie. Her sister waved at her to follow.

She took a deep breath and started climbing.

Slowly and carefully, the girls scaled the face of solid rock, holding on to Rapunzel's hair for dear life.

"What if we fall?" Snow cried as she passed the halfway mark.

Now she asks?

"Not to worry," Cindy said, "you're already dead."

The color drained from Caitlin's face. She didn't dare look down. She fought to keep her focus on Natalie's backside and legs, moving steadily upward above her.

Then Natalie stopped climbing.

Caitlin then made the worst possible mistake. She stole a quick look down. She saw the spot on the cobblestones below where she'd splatter if she slipped and fell. She glanced back up. Black crows were circling above them, drawing closer with each rotation. Caitlin's brow dribbled sweat, and her palms became slippery from perspiration. She tightened her grip. She recalled what Amethyst had told her: the crows sensed courage, not fear. Which meant she was now in stealth mode. This gave her a small measure of comfort. Enough to keep her climbing.

Caitlin took a deep breath and tried to focus on Natalie, who was still stalled near the top. "What's the holdup?" she asked.

"Beauty!" Rapunzel yelled. "Bad time to catch a nap!"

"Someone give her a nudge," Snow said. "We don't want her to fall."

The bell in the castle's clock tower rang out.

Beauty opened her eyes and yawned after being woken by the clanging. She glanced up at Rapunzel. "Another dream," she said. "The wolves are sprinting to the castle."

The girls hastily resumed their ascent. Upward they climbed, tired arms tugging, aching legs driving. Just when Caitlin's limbs seemed spent and ready to give out, she reached the top. She waggled over the ledge and then crouched on the ramparts with the other girls.

Directly in front of them loomed the higher levels of the castle. The windows were glassless but barred by rusted iron. Below them flowed the moat.

Rapunzel pointed to the map. "According to this, we should be able to sneak in through some unguarded windows on this level."

Cinderella skulked up to a small window. She peered inside.

She could hear a loud, booming backbeat penetrating the walls and shaking the ceiling.

Caitlin whispered to Natalie, "Sounds like the music Mom and Dad listened to when we were kids. I think this is The Who!"

"Who?" Natalie asked.

"*The* Who. It's a band."

Cinderella wiggled her butt. "Ooh! Rockin'. Sounds like a party."

Rapunzel peered through the small window. "The place is crawling with Blood-Eyed."

They took turns peeking through the window and peering down on the heads of well over fifteen hundred hard-partying zombies. The Blood-Eyed jerked, jostled, and jumped on the crowded dance floor.

If ever there was a wanton party from hell, this was it!

Natalie whipped out her camera and stood up.

"Awesome shot!" She snapped photos in a rapid-fire sequence.

"Get down!" Rapunzel said. "They'll spot us!"

Caitlin knelt, listening to the melody reverberating through the roof. The music stirred a memory as only music could. Caitlin was transported back in time; she remembered dancing around the house with her mother to oldies from the 1960s. Especially one of her mom's favorites, "She's Not There." The irony was not lost on Caitlin. She really was not there.

Caitlin had to have been nine or so at that time. Natalie six. Her mom had taught them all sorts of dances with funny names, though Caitlin couldn't recall the names at that moment. She just remembered everyone laughing and dancing in the living room.

She remembered something else. That might have been the very last time she had ever danced without being self-conscious in front of another human being. Sure, she danced alone in her bedroom, in front of the mirror. But that was the last time she had truly let go.

Caitlin glanced over at Natalie. Girl Wonder seemed transfixed by the music. Soon her eyes even began to mist over. Then Natalie abruptly scooted over to Caitlin and, for the first time ever, leaped into her sister's arms. She wrapped her legs tightly around Caitlin's waist and flung her arms around her neck. Caitlin's eyes welled up as she pulled Natalie closer. As they were embracing warmly, Caitlin suddenly felt Natalie's body stiffen.

"Desmodus rotundus!" Natalie shouted out. "The common vampire bat."

Caitlin spun around with her sister still tight in her arms. She glanced up at the sky.

She gasped.

A colony of Blood-Eyed bats was winging swiftly across the orange sky.

Natalie squeezed Caitlin tighter.

"It's twilight," Natalie said. "They're hunting for food."

What happened next happened so fast, Caitlin didn't even have time to react.

A flapping Blood-Eyed bat suddenly nosedived. It hurtled like a heat-seeking missile straight for the red chili pepper in Caitlin's arms. Before Caitlin could dodge it, the incoming winged ghoul nipped Natalie on the scalp. It broke the skin.

Oh God, no! That didn't just happen. It couldn't have.

It did.

A Blood-Eyed zombie had just bitten Natalie Fletcher.

CHAPTER THIRTY-ONE

CAITLIN SET HER SISTER DOWN IN FRONT OF HER. A TRICKLE OF blood dripped down Natalie's forehead from the wound.

Natalie's hands immediately took on a throbbing glow and sizzled with electrical currents the color of sapphires. Her body began to tremble. Her camera fell from her grip and swung like a pendulum from the strap that hung around her neck.

Her veins flashed from blue to red to orange to violet under translucent skin. The current sizzled up her arm, swam across her shoulder, and then spread out, swallowing her torso and face. It devoured Natalie Fletcher from head to toe.

Her raincoat was shredded and in tatters. Her face flickered with specks of neon that split her skin into sections.

"No! Make it stop! Make it stop! Caitlin, please, make it stop!" Natalie writhed in pain.

Caitlin's heart froze as she watched her sister's flesh separate from the bone. Layers of skin then reformed and reattached

over her cheekbones and around her eye sockets with zipper-
stitch scars where they met.

Natalie looked up at Caitlin. "What's happening to me?!"

The word fell out from Caitlin's mouth in a somber whisper,
"Zombification."

"But I don't want to turn into a ghoul!" Natalie wailed.

Caitlin grabbed her and hugged tight as she stared helplessly at the zombie princesses.

Rapunzel turned to Cinderella. "Okay, Cindy. Take your
bite."

Caitlin's eyebrows arched sharply in surprise. Cinderella's
eyes burned with hunger. Caitlin's heart skipped a beat as Cindy
seized Natalie's hand and slid it into her mouth.

Caitlin squeezed her sibling tighter. "What's going on?" she
asked, horrified.

Rapunzel ignored her. "Just a nibble, Cindy."

Chomp!

Cindy bit the tip of Natalie's thumb as Caitlin's eyes went
wide. A droplet of blood flowed. When Natalie saw her own
blood, her eyes rolled up into their sockets.

"What on earth are you doing?" Caitlin shrieked.

Rapunzel calmly rolled up her sleeve. "We're not on Earth.
What I'm doing is arranging a makeshift blood transfusion."

Rapunzel placed her wrist in front of Cindy's mouth.

"Bite, girl."

Cindy's teeth pierced her friend's pale flesh. When she
extracted her teeth, blood dribbled from Rapunzel's wrist.

"Better hurry!" Beauty cried. "If you don't inject some royal blood cells into Natalie's circulatory system now, she'll be a Blood-Eyed in minutes."

Caitlin's chest tightened.

Rapunzel extended her wrist and smeared a few droplets of blood against Natalie's reddened thumb.

Natalie broke away from Caitlin's embrace.

She snarled.

Then she grunted like the ghoulish beast she was on her way to becoming.

Saliva dripped from her teeth. Her eyes blazed pink. Like a hound from hell, she tore off on all fours along the stone ledge of the wall, then dove through the palace window.

"Party animal," Cinderella quipped. She dabbed a drop of blood from her lip with her pinkie and then licked it clean.

Rapunzel's response was a grim look of concern.

Caitlin stood motionless, tears streaming down her face.

This can't be happening.

Only a moment ago she'd held her beloved baby sister warmly in her arms.

Now her decomposing sister had just crashed a rampantly wild party crawling with savage ghouls—literally!

CHAPTER THIRTY-TWO

DEEP IN THE HEART OF ZENO'S FOREST, JACK, LIMPING AND exhausted from crawling through the glowworm tunnel, emerged into the cavernous hideout of the caterpillar. Grapevines with only a few remaining clusters hung above decapitated artichoke stems. Bean plants with but a few pods left drooped against tomato vines almost devoid of fruit. Though a few watermelons and pumpkins—both far taller than Jack—lay on the floor, it appeared that all the plants had been freshly harvested.

"This place has been picked clean," Jack declared.

Alfonzo hopped out of the tunnel and joined Jack in the cave. "Fortunately, there are still a few morsels for me."

Alfonzo scooped a baby glowworm off the wall with his tongue and swallowed it whole. "Scrumptious." His belly shone with a faint, green light. The frog looked down at his glowing gut. "And quite stylish."

Jack couldn't help but notice his own shadow, cast on the wall from the glowworms' green light. Although he was the size of a worm, his shadow was tall and curved up to the ceiling. The bone sticking out of his leg formed an unnatural-looking appendage that loomed large.

"You think the caterpillar can help me grow back to my normal size?" he asked the prince frog.

"Yes, amigo, but what is making that other shadow?"

Other shadow?

Indeed, a much larger shadow was being cast by something in the room. Jack turned. His eyes focused on a huge, limp pile of fur. The light from the glowworms shifted, and then Jack saw it: a dead zombie wolf.

Jack grimaced.

"Must have ruffled somebody's feathers," Alfonzo said.

Jack made his way over to the large mushroom that sat in the center of the cavern.

"Caterpillar?" Jack said.

No answer. The frog tried. "Lord Amethyst? It is I, Alfonzo the Frog Prince, in person and in the flesh."

Jack took out his pocketknife. He carved a hole in the side of a watermelon. With a mighty yank, he unplugged the cork of rind and began scooping out fistfuls of red, juicy melon flesh. He was in up to his shoulders when he heard a faint rustle coming from the mushroom. He rushed over, looked around, and then found where the sound was coming from: a fluffy cocoon hanging securely from the underside of the mushroom's cap. It rocked back and forth. He could see a tiny hole forming—it was being chewed from the inside.

Jack leaned in close. "Are you there, Amethyst?"

"I'll be out in a moment," replied a little mouth from inside the hole. "Some privacy, please."

While Jack waited, he got a wonderful idea. He tore a wide strip of fabric from one of the large mohair throw blankets hanging off the sofa. Then he ripped a few strips of vine from the grapes and fashioned a make-do rucksack. It would come in handy later, he knew. Then he knelt on the cool, rich soil of the cavern and started scooping up dirt. He filled the rucksack with soil. Next, he plucked the two remaining beans from the plant's stem and shoved them inside the sack as well.

He had just begun to wash his hands with watermelon juice when he heard an authoritative "Ahem."

He spun around.

The caterpillar had blossomed into a magnificent butterfly. He shimmered a deep purple, with black accents. His tremendous wingspan extended almost wall to wall.

"You're looking for Caitlin, I presume?" asked Amethyst.

"Desperately."

Jack dried his hands and motioned to the wolf. "What happened here?"

"That wolf saved us," Amethyst said, pointing to the dead Big Bad Wolf. "The other wolves were none too pleased about it. He gave his life for us. But now the murderous wolf pack is after Caitlin and the girls."

"I need to find her."

Amethyst saw the fragment of shinbone protruding from Jack's leg. "What happened there?"

"Tussle with a troll. No big deal." Jack tried to walk, but winced in pain.

"You'll not be going far on that leg, my boy."

"I've got to get to Caitlin."

"I'm aware of that."

Jack tried to walk again. A squirt of blood sprayed from the wound as he put pressure on his leg.

"Well then, I do hope you're not afraid of heights," Amethyst said as he beckoned Jack closer.

"But first, some of this." He opened a cupboard and pulled out a bottle of Scotch. He poured it over the wound. Jack grimaced and writhed in pain. Amethyst tore a strip of fabric from a sofa cushion and used it to bandage Jack's leg to stanch the bleeding.

He then reached back into the cupboard and retrieved two pieces of cake. He wrapped them in cellophane.

"Put these in your rucksack. We'll need them soon enough."

Jack did as he was told, but asked, "What's the cake for?"

Amethyst grinned. "This cake is from Wonderland. At some point, we all have to grow . . . *up*." Jack nodded.

"Climb aboard, my boy," Amethyst invited.

Jack swung the rucksack over one shoulder and climbed onto the butterfly's back. The chunky part of Amethyst's torso was a good ten times larger than Jack's whole body. *But not for long.*

Jack glanced down at his new friend Alfonzo with concern.

"Don't worry about me, amigo," Alfonzo said. "I will find you when you least expect. In the meantime—*croak*—there's lunch to be had."

Alfonzo snapped up another baby glowworm and gulped it down.

Jack winked at his friend. He swung the backpack over his shoulders and clambered onto the back of Lord Amethyst Bartholomew, the butterfly.

Amethyst spread his wings wide.

With Jack securely on board, they fluttered up through the skylight and off into the rays of the sun.

"I, Alfonzo Thadius Bertram the Second, wish you a heartfelt fare thee well, amigo," Alfonzo said. "Good luck finding the girl. Take care of that leg. And don't forget to write."

CHAPTER THIRTY-THREE

A TEARDROP SPLASHED ON THE COLD, STONE ROOFTOP OF THE QUEEN'S castle. Caitlin's eyes were already bloodshot from crying.

"We have to find a way to get my sister back." She buried her face in her hands. "I wish Jack were here. All I wanted was a night out with him and a chance to write a good article. That's why I agreed to go to the stupid cemetery in the first place. *I want my sister back!*"

Snow White put her arm around Caitlin's shoulder.

Rapunzel took her gently by the hand. "I'm not going to sugarcoat this, Caitlin. Your sister will walk as the living dead— eternally—if we don't get her to your earthly home before *our* sunrise."

Caitlin couldn't swallow.

"She needs the healing rays of *your* morning sun to cure her of the affliction."

Caitlin sobbed harder as she listened.

"The first risen sun—ours *or* yours—that touches her will determine if she becomes one of the living dead or reverts back to the living."

Just when Caitlin thought it couldn't get any worse, Cindy stepped forward.

"And we won't be able to help you if the queen raises that scepter at midnight tonight." She pointed to her eyes. Cindy fixed both hands on her hips. "The clock is ticking, pretty princesses, let's get a move on."

Caitlin felt a meltdown coming on.

She held her breath . . . long . . . longer . . . still longer . . . until her body *forced* her to exhale.

She couldn't have a panic attack now. No way. Not with Natalie's life on the line.

"How do we get inside?" she asked.

Rapunzel examined the map. "This upper level is barred off. Except for those side stairs to the castle keep in the tower. No point going to the scene of the crime."

Beauty peered over the wall and down below. "The main entrance is patrolled by castle guards."

Snow frowned. "And the Blood-Eyed will pick up our scent if we go in that way anyway."

"Ideas?" Beauty asked.

Before anyone could answer, they heard an army of boots thumping up the stone steps that led directly to their level.

"Exit time, ladies," Cindy said.

"Where to?" Beauty asked.

Rapunzel pointed. "Up those side stairs, to the castle keep. We'll hide in the herald's chamber."

"What if he's inside?" Snow asked.

"Six of us against one skinny herald, or six of us against the queen's Blood-Eyed armed guards—what do you think?"

Up the stairs they ran.

They arrived at the castle keep and quickly crept over to the herald's chamber. Snow White picked the lock. Rapunzel and Cindy led the way, tense and ready to jump the herald. The chamber was empty.

Caitlin put her hand on her chest.

Is my heart rate finally slowing down?

"He and the other ghouls must be dancing their arses off," Cindy said.

The girls tiptoed quietly to the back wall, away from the glassless window and as far from the door as possible. They lined up side by side against the cold stone, standing silent and still, waiting for the guards to pass.

THE QUEEN'S PACK OF WOLVES HAD COLD-BLOODED MURDER IN THEIR eyes. They had stalked the girls' tracks all the way to the castle. And now they howled and circled outside the castle entrance in a mad frenzy. The leader of the pack, the alpha male, reared and stood on its hind legs. The fur on his chest and paws and snout was matted with blood. He licked some blood from its snout and twitched his nose. He sniffed the air, then the ground, and followed its nose to the castle door.

Six other Blood-Eyed wolves followed hungrily as the alpha male opened the castle door and entered. It led its pack up toward the castle keep, where the scent was strongest. The wolves climbed the steps, leaving bloodstained paw prints on the stone slabs.

The wolves reached the castle keep.

Empty. Not a body in sight.

The Blood-Eyed alpha wolf sniffed. Scanned.

The carnivore was attracted to a thick wooden door. From the chamber behind the door, the stink of zombies and humans flowed—tangy to their taste buds.

The alpha male glanced back at its pack.

He flashed his fangs. Growled. He turned. He approached the door, stalking upright on two legs, his canine's eyes ablaze with red. The other wolves remained on all fours. They arched their backs, prepared to pounce, saliva drooling from their jowls.

CAITLIN HEARD THE NOISE. THEY ALL DID.

"Someone's out there," Rapunzel said.

"It's not the queen's guards," Snow said. "They must have climbed past this level. There's only one someone out there, right at the door. I can sense him edging closer."

Rapunzel tightened her hand into a fist. Cinderella rotated her foot back and forth, loosening it up.

Caitlin's eyes were glued to the door handle.

It turned.

The zombie princesses stormed the intruder. Cindy walloped him with a roundhouse kick across the jaw.

The queen's herald!

Cindy's wallop had knocked him out cold.

"Fancy footwork," Beauty said.

They propped the unconscious herald up against the wall. "He'll be napping for a few," Cindy said proudly.

"All clear out here," Caitlin said, peering out the door.

The girls snuck out.

THE ALPHA WOLF TILTED ITS HEAD, SNIFFING. IT GLARED AT A PILE of stuff lying on the floor of the abandoned castle: a mound of hair, a stick smeared with earwax, a rag soaked in saliva and sweat, and a pile of green peppers, garlic cloves, and various roots. The scent was pungent to their sensitive noses.

The wolves dove in, face-and-fangs-first, shredding everything to bits and chowed it all down.

Uncontrollable sneezing erupted from the pack. The peppers, garlic, and wasabi scalded the wolves' nostril tissues.

Tongues burned and blistered from the strong plants' searing heat, and their eyes stung like they had been staring at the sun.

The cries of the canine ghouls rang out far and wide.

The zombie wolves were off the scent.

For now.

CHAPTER THIRTY-FOUR

THE GIRLS RETURNED TO THE STONE ROOFTOP ON THE FIRST LEVEL of the castle.

Cindy, Snow, and Rapunzel peered down through the window at the sea of bobbing zombie heads cramming the dance floor of the grand ballroom.

"Even if we *could* sneak in," Rapunzel said, "how would we find Natalie among the others?"

Cinderella clucked her tongue. "She shouldn't be hard to spot in that outrageous chili pepper getup."

Snow White placed her hand on Caitlin's shoulder. "Fret not, sweet Caitlin. Your sad eyes are so red, you almost look like a Blood-Eyed yourself."

Cindy's eyes lit up. "That's it!"

"That's *what?*" said Rapunzel.

"We disguise ourselves as Blood-Eyed zombies."

Rapunzel tapped her temple. "Brilliant! Sneak past the guards in plain sight."

Snow furrowed her brow.

"What about our noble blood? The Blood-Eyed will pick up our royal scent straightaway."

Caitlin lifted her eyes, blinking away salty tears. "And what about my *human* smell? And my blue eyes?"

Rapunzel took out the map and studied it intently. She grinned. "There's a clay bank on the east side of the moat. It's connected to the bog and the wetlands surrounding the castle."

Snow bounced with excitement. "Clay! That just might work!"

Clay? Might?

Rapunzel looked up from the map. "We'll take clay from the castle moat and smear it in a thick layer over our flesh, head to toe. Like a mud bath. When it dries, it'll harden into a silvery white skin."

"That's a ridiculous idea!" Caitlin cried. "It's absurd. Disguise or no disguise, they'll smell *my* blood, sniff *my* flesh, and devour *me* limb by limb."

Snow shook her head. "No. Clay camouflages the scent of flesh *and* blood."

Rapunzel's smile was a shrewd one. "Which means, ladies, the clay will also cover our not-quite-as-dead royal aroma."

The royals exchanged gleeful grins.

A dire look overcame Caitlin. "What about our eyes?"

Rapunzel scratched her head and slowly exhaled. "That's a tricky one."

"Don't suppose we can turn on the tears and cry till our eyes turn bloodshot?" Cindy said.

"Watery tears won't cut it," Rapunzel said.

Snow's eyebrows rose. "Water! I have an idea."

She borrowed the map from Rapunzel and surveyed it.

"There are all types of aquatic plants, shrubs, and vines growing in the wetlands around the moat," Snow said. "They hardly need any sunlight. I know of one vine bursting with brilliant-red berry clusters. We can stain our eyes with red berry juice!"

Caitlin broke out in a cold sweat. "Never!" she shrieked, shielding both eyes with her hands. "That won't ever happen. Don't even think about it."

Rapunzel gave Caitlin a stern look. "Your hair also has to go."

Caitlin uncovered her eyes and stared at Rapunzel in dismay. "Huh?"

Snow caressed a handful of Caitlin's cinnamon locks. "Human hair reeks of life force. There's little chance that the clay will fully shroud it."

Cindy seized the clump of Caitlin's hair from out of Snow's hand. She sniffed it heartily. "Yeah—with this mop, the Blood-Eyed will hunt you down and spread you on a scone for high tea."

Rapunzel stepped face-to-face with Caitlin. "Look, to get to the queen, you've got to get past the Blood-Eyed. There's no choice. But don't worry, we can leave a *little* hair on your pretty head. It will just have to be drenched in clay."

Caitlin woefully bowed her head. Her shoulders slumped. Her lips quivered, and tears streamed down both cheeks.

Caitlin then slowly raised her arms. The princesses nodded in unison.

They all held hands.

And held their breaths.

And then . . . as the fiery, red-orange sun began to set behind the pink horizon, the girls leaped off the inner edge of the wall, plummeting toward the earth!

CHAPTER THIRTY-FIVE

CAITLIN AND THE ZOMBIE PRINCESSES PLUNGED INTO THE MOAT, landing with a splash. They swam to the bank. Thick deposits of white clay were caked against it. They slogged ankle-deep in the squish.

Beauty scooped up two heaping handfuls of silver-white clay and slathered Caitlin's arms and legs with it in a circular motion.

Caitlin wrinkled her nose. "It tickles."

"Smear it on thick," Rapunzel said. "Blood-Eyed ghouls possess a hyper-acute sense of smell."

Rapunzel pulled out a sharp knife and starting cutting off clumps of Caitlin's long, cinnamon-colored hair. Then Beauty shampooed the top of Caitlin's head with it too. The clay had a musty smell. Caitlin fought back a rush of tears as she rubbed clay on her shoulders, chest, and tummy. To make the ache in her heart bearable, she kept thinking about Girl Wonder. Her kid sister. Her *baby* sister. And the pink in her eyes.

"You'll look adorable in a bob," Rapunzel said in a comforting manner.

Caitlin couldn't answer. She simply gazed at her long locks floating away atop the moat water.

She was soon coated in thick, whitish, pasty clay, from head to toe.

Snow White stared impressively at Caitlin. "You look pale as a ghost."

Rapunzel then touched her forehead.

"We need to let it dry and harden."

"Why?" Caitlin asked.

"You'll see. Meanwhile, let's start on your clothes."

Rapunzel artfully sliced Caitlin's top and bottoms.

"Now that's a stunning zombie ensemble if I ever saw one—fashionably tattered and stylishly frayed," said Rapunzel with an assuring wink.

"Just another day at the clay-bank spa," Beauty said. "Too bad there's no masseuse around."

Caitlin almost, *almost*, let a hint of a smile slip out.

Snow White returned from the bog, pockets filled with glittering clusters of plump red berries. She placed her hand gently on Caitlin's shoulder.

"Look, I don't want to lie to you, Caitlin, honey," Snow said. "This is probably going to sting your eyes. I mean, *really*, really sting. But hopefully only for a few seconds. Then the pain should disappear. After that, your pupils and the whites of your eyes will be dyed a very berry red."

Caitlin sat herself on a small boulder at the edge of the

bank. She had no idea how she was going to allow burning, acidic juice to be poured into her eyes when she never even let the salami-breath eye doctor get a contact lens within an inch of her eyeball.

Natalie.

"Fine," Caitlin said. "Let's just get this over with." A flutter gnawed in her chest.

Snow sighed. "I don't have the heart to do it." She stretched out an open hand toward Rapunzel. Nestled in her palm was a batch of red berries.

Rapunzel plucked a single berry with her thumb and index finger. She held it chest high. "Head back, glasses off," she instructed Caitlin.

"No!" Caitlin's tone was more than bold.

Everyone froze.

Caitlin let out a big, long breath of resolve. Her shoulders broadened. "I need to do it myself."

Rapunzel smiled proudly. She handed the red berry to Caitlin.

"Bless her little heart," Snow said, pressing her hand on her own chest.

Caitlin took in a reasonable gulp of oxygen and then blew it out gently.

She removed her glasses. Tilted back her head. She held the red berry centimeters from her left eyeball.

She squeezed.

Squirt!

The berry burst. Pulpy, acidic juice dripped into her eye.

Snow White was altogether wrong about the stinging. It didn't really, really sting. It really, really, really, *really* stung! Caitlin's burning eye slammed shut reflexively. The pain was fierce. Blood rushed to her head and gushed to the back of her throbbing eyeball. She flapped her hands furiously, as if that action might cool and ease the stinging—which it surely did not.

After twenty heartbeats and ten tormenting seconds, though, her eye was . . .

Hmm, perfectly fine!

"That wasn't so bad, was it?" Rapunzel said.

Caitlin blinked a few times. She looked up. "Your berry-juiced eye is blazing bright red," Rapunzel said. "And the other is still sparkling blue."

Caitlin summoned up her courage, along with another big breath of air, and juiced her other eye. The stabbing sting wrapped around her eyeball, and sent shudders throughout her body. This time she flapped both her hands frantically, trying to ease the throbbing. After ten more stinging seconds, she became a perfect match to a Blood-Eyed zombie.

Except for one thing.

Snow poked her finger into some dirt. Using the rich, dark soil as eye shadow, she blackened Caitlin's eye sockets and lids. Next, she added dark shadow to her cheekbones to mimic sunken cheeks on her pale, white skin.

Rapunzel touched Caitlin's forehead. "The clay feels hard and dry now. Okay kiddo, tense your body, squeeze your facial muscles tight, and hold."

Caitlin flexed her arms, tightened her tummy, and tensed up

her legs. Then she scrunched up her face, squeezing tight until her lips, nose, eyes, and cheeks creased up like crumpled paper.

Rapunzel leaned in close to Caitlin's face, studying it intently.

"Hold it a little longer . . . hold . . . hold . . . now release!"

Crack!

A sharp crackling sound erupted as the hardened clay fractured along fault lines that branched out across her face, neck, chest, arms, and legs. Caitlin exhaled, relaxing her muscles.

"Voilà!" Rapunzel said. "A short-haired, silver-toned, Blood-Eyed zombie is born!"

Caitlin strolled to the edge of the moat and leaned over the water. She looked at herself in the clear reflection on the surface. No question. Standing there, bathed in the hues of a pale, twilight sky, Caitlin Rose looked absolutely ghoulishly cool and freaking fearsome!

"Our turn!" Cindy said with the excitement of a kid ready to jump into a pool.

Rapunzel shook her head. "There's no time for another full spa treatment. We better just dunk and roll around in the muck. We can squirt red berry juice in our eyes along the way."

It took only a few dunks in the mire of the bank to completely cloak the zombie princesses in thick sheets of clay.

"C'mon," Caitlin called with new resolve, her eyes glittering red. "Let's go get my sister!"

Caitlin prepared herself to make a running start out of the moat.

SLURP!

At first, Caitlin thought the weakness in her legs was due to the fact she'd been moving all day long. Then she heard the wet noise and felt suction. Her feet got sucked into the mud. Then her ankles. Then her calves.

This was no ordinary moat.

"What's happening?" Caitlin asked.

"Very curious," Snow said. "It's almost as if the mud is alive."

"It's trying to swallow me up," Caitlin said. "Like quicksand!"

One giant bubble rose up from the mud. Then another.

Cindy made a run for it. "Time to ditch this ditch!"

Snow shook her head. "No, Cindy. Don't! If you try to flee, the clay will—"

Sure enough, globs of clay seized Cinderella around the ankles, leaving her stuck in one spot as surely as if she were standing in a vat of superglue.

"This clay's a little overly possessive, dontcha think?" Cinderella quipped.

Caitlin felt a dreadful twinge in her chest. This was exactly like a nightmare she often had. She would be trying to run from some hairy, winged creature, but her legs moved in slow motion, as if through peanut butter. The feeling was maddening.

Rapunzel checked the map. "The moat is called the *Enchanted Clay Bank*. Now we know why."

"It's fascinating," Snow said. "You can walk on it easily, but if you try to run away, it stops you."

"It was probably meant to stop thieves or anyone trying to flee the castle," Beauty said.

An interesting thought popped into Caitlin's mind. She asked herself what Natalie would do.

Girl Wonder would approach it scientifically!

Since Natalie wasn't there, Caitlin was going to try a two-part experiment of her own.

Part One: Caitlin imagined herself escaping from this bank in a mad panic. Then she tried to lift her leg. Wet clay thickened around her, sucking her ankles deeper into the muck.

Part Two: Caitlin thought about staying put. She imagined the moat as a white, sandy beach under a warm, tropical sun where she wanted to lie for days on end. She tried lifting her leg again. The clay loosened around her legs, liquefying like water. Her foot rose easily.

End of experiment.

Caitlin grinned.

She reached for Cinderella's hand and cried out, "Pay attention, everyone! I know how to get us out of here!"

CHAPTER THIRTY-SIX

NIGHT HAD FALLEN. THE AIR WAS COMFORTABLY COOL, AND LIGHT humidity produced a balmy evening. The stars in the purply-dark sky winked a hazy red as Caitlin and the princess ghouls marched confidently toward the palace gates.

Though she was determined and brimming with resolve, Caitlin's nerves were nevertheless on edge as they approached the gates. She knew the score. If that ghoul of a front-gate guard caught the slightest whiff of her hair or blood, he'd chew her up. She'd become a Blood-Eyed ghoul, cursed to walk as the living dead forever.

She'd never see her dad again. Or Jack. And Natalie would be condemned to zombieland for all eternity.

She shoved aside her morbid thoughts and focused.

The girls approached the guard.

The uniformed ghoul wore a long, slim-fitting, black

overcoat and a tattered black top hat. A bloodstained white shirt and a thin black tie were visible under his coat.

He examined the girls one at a time, top to bottom.

His eyes met Caitlin's. Her stomach knotted. A coat of clay was all that stood between her and zombie hell. She prayed it was thick enough. The guard looked at her hair . . . checked out her clothes . . . then saluted and let them all pass.

How freaking easy was that!

A playful grin cracked the corner of Caitlin's mouth. Old Mrs. Sliwinski, the Kingshire social studies teacher, turned out to be a far better guard than this ghoul.

Caitlin stood up straight. Raised her chin. A gleam even twinkled in her red-berry-dyed eyes. The cold clay on her skin gave her more than anonymity. It gave her comfort.

Caitlin now led the way. A pack of Blood-Eyed wolves patrolled the perimeter of the palace grounds. They paid no attention to Caitlin's group. Her chest inched outward. Her footsteps became deliberate and determined.

An army of guards and bouncers lined a long, gated walkway that led to the main ballroom's entrance.

Caitlin sauntered right past the first guards outside the gate, right past the guards on the inside of the gate, right through a hallway door, and right up to the end of a huge line of partygoers who were waiting behind a bright-red velvet rope in the foyer.

Music pounded through the ballroom door up ahead. Strobe lights reflected off the windows.

Cinderella snorted. "A line? Royalty doesn't wait in lines."

She glanced around, annoyed. "Can't we find the VIP entrance or something?"

"Now's not the time to play the royal card, Cindy," Rapunzel said, rolling her eyes. "We need to blend in and not draw attention."

The girls took their places at the end of the line—and behind a snarling, frothing, wet, and pungent herd of Blood-Eyed zombie sheep. Flayed skin adorned bare patches where zipper stitches and open sores had replaced their wool. The smallest lamb, at the end of the line, turned toward Caitlin and lifted its upper lip, revealing a sharp set of pale-green fangs. The zombie-sheep breath hit her in the face like an encore performance of carnival chili after an upside-down roller coaster ride.

Caitlin felt her stomach begin to churn. The stench was unbearable.

"Fluffy!" shouted a girl's voice. "You stop that right now!"

The voice belonged to a young female ghoul who stood alongside the sheep. She wore a big, floppy hat adorned with dingy pink ribbons that matched her shredded, blousy dress. Her face bore an alarming number of zipper stitches, and even though her lips displayed no traces of residual lipstick, red beads of goo clung to the corners of her mouth.

Caitlin's temple began to pulse.

Could it be Little Bo Peep? Has she been chowing on the ribs of her own sheep?

Bo Peep pounded a long, curved staff against the floor, and the zombie sheep quickly stood at attention.

As Caitlin and company shuffled up the line to the entrance-way, the volume of the music spiked. Caitlin craned her neck to get a peek inside the party.

A throng of undead witches, pirates, princes, and a whole cast of ghoulish characters moved together in a steamy, sweaty mass. They shuffled their decaying feet in unison to a pounding rock-and-roll drumbeat.

Cinderella leaned her cheek into Caitlin's. She whispered, "Awesome taste in music."

Caitlin nodded. Say what you would about these flesh-eating ghouls—they knew how to throw a party.

And dance.

CHAPTER THIRTY-SEVEN

Rapunzel led the girls into the hot, loud, sweaty ballroom. It was bigger than a soccer stadium and packed with bodies. Caitlin clung to the perimeter while summoning the nerve to wade deeper into the seething mass of dancing dead.

A savory twinge stirred in her nostrils. The air was sweetly pungent with the scent of barbecued meats, fire-roasted vegetables, and boiled stews.

Cinderella chuckled as she elbowed Caitlin's ribs. "At least there's something to eat here—besides you."

Herds of ghouls trudged around Caitlin from all sides, their mortified arms brushing cold against her skin. A foul odor of rotting flesh seeped through floral perfumes and musk colognes. The undead were crammed in so tight that their zombie hair caressed Caitlin's cheeks and lips as the ghouls squeezed by.

Caitlin stood on her toes. She peered over the crowd of heads, trying to locate Natalie.

Impossible. Not from this vantage point.

She was going to have to venture deep into the crowd.

She stood back up on her toes, pinpointing all the exits. If her panic erupted—or if she was discovered to be a human—she wanted to know the best direction to bolt. She sighed as she realized it didn't really matter where the exits were. The humongous ballroom was a sea of swarming ghouls that she would have to swim through, so there really was no easy way out of there.

She lifted her eyes to the arched ceiling. A whole colony of bats was perched upside down on the rafters above the dance floor—the same species that bit Natalie.

Their blood-red eyes scanned the area continuously, like infrared detectors.

"What are they doing?" Caitlin asked Rapunzel.

"Keeping watch. Their built-in sonar monitors the movements of the crowd, watching out for any sort of irregular behavior. That's why it's imperative we blend in."

Caitlin jiggled her shoulders up and down, then slowly rotated her head from side to side to loosen her neck muscles.

A ghoul passed by suddenly, alarmingly close to Caitlin. He swiveled his head and made eye contact with her. She saw her first Blood-Eyed eyeball up close. Its coveting gaze turned her cold. It flitted more like a tongue, she thought, than an organ of sight. As if the pupil had taste buds. Each eye movement was like a lick of Caitlin's flesh. The ghoul glanced off in another direction and Caitlin shivered in relief. Her disguise was still working!

The majority of the undead paid her no attention, making her feel emboldened. She held her chest out confidently as they straggled onward through the crowd. The girls plodded toward a section of the ballroom where there was a bit less congestion.

Long buffet tables lined the room's perimeter, stretching wall to wall. Glass bowls overflowed with selections of raw and roasted meats from various animals. "Impressive entrees," Cindy said as her eyes hungrily scanned the serving trays. "Raw livers, gizzards, sausages, roasted pig knuckles, and sweetbreads. Nice selection."

Caitlin peeked into a serving tray. She saw something she was sure looked like blood pudding.

How weird. It feels like it has been weeks since I last saw Dad.

Platters of eyeball sushi served with a crimson dipping sauce were artfully arranged between bowls. She had never seen such a repulsively decadent display.

Centerpieces of floating crystal bowls filled with greens magically hovered in midair over the tables. Bunches of parsley, green onions, cabbages, lettuces, and greens of all sorts—and plenty of spicy hot peppers—grew out of them. Cindy stole a bite of a cucumber that dangled from its vine in one.

"How curious," Snow said, after Cindy had swallowed. "They grow with no sun."

She was right. The room's only light came from torches fitted in iron brackets on the thick gray stone walls. Their orange flames flicked like serpents' tongues and cast a fiery glow of shifting light and shadows along the walls.

Cindy spotted the hot peppers. She plucked a clump and

shoved them into her mouth, then followed them with a couple of fresh livers and a few lumps of goose fat from the buffet.

Snow White gasped. "How very unprincesslike of you."

Cinderella, still bent over the buffet table, shoveled thick sausages and eyeball sushi onto a plate. She looked up at Snow.

"Wha?" she mumbled, her mouth chock-full of goose fat. "I'm using a plate . . ."

Caitlin shook her head as she absorbed the sights. "I've never seen so many dead people in one place. How are we going to find Natalie?"

Many of the partygoers were familiar to Caitlin as characters from books she'd read as a kid. Milling about were zombified coachmen, genies, fairies, and munchkins.

Tweedledee and Tweedledum were terrorizing the dance floor with some super-loose hip-hop moves. An undead and pale Peter Pan was chatting up a Blood-Eyed, rotting Red Riding Hood.

If he weren't Blood-Eyed, Pan probably would be kind of cute . . .

But seeing both of them ghouled to the max creeped out Caitlin and made her sad. At least the royal-blooded zombies had retained a generous measure of beauty, grace, and glamour—Cindy's obscene appetite excepted.

Toward the front of the dance floor, three zombie bears and seven zombie dwarfs moshed with the Tin Woodman, the Cowardly Lion, and the Scarecrow.

Caitlin took notice of one particular girl—a gorgeous ghoul with dazzling auburn hair that flared in the torchlight—shimmying across a small platform near the dance floor. She wore a tattered, cherry-red dress with a golden-yellow sash. Her complexion was the usual zombie silver with black-rimmed eyes. She also had zipper-like stitches on her arms and legs, Caitlin noticed.

"Who's that?" she asked.

Sleeping Beauty let out a sad sigh. "That's Belle. Or should I say, that *was* Belle."

"From *Beauty and the Beast?*"

"Uh-huh. One of my dearest friends. But she doesn't remember me anymore."

"Doesn't she have royal blood?" Caitlin asked. "How did she turn?"

"Bitten," Cindy sighed, "She couldn't stand being apart from her prince. She invited the bite."

Zombie waiters stepped deftly through the crowd of revelers. Dressed in tattered tuxedos, white cloths over their arms, they carried silver trays of bronze goblets.

Cinderella looked up from her plate. "Who's a girl gotta slay to get a drink around here?"

A waiter approached Cindy and offered his tray.

Cindy's eyes lit up. "Tom? Is that you?"

The waiter's reply was a blank stare.

"Tom, the piper's son? It's me, Cindy—Cinderella. Remember?"

Waiter Tom shook his head as if he'd never seen the girl before.

"Your loss, fella," Cindy said as she plucked a goblet off the tray before he moved on.

The liquid in the cup was deep red, thick as syrup, and full to the brim. An eager Cinderella chugged it down in three straight swigs. Caitlin had to choke back a gag.

Cindy smacked her lips. "Ahh. Much better." She looked around at her friends, who were staring at her in disbelief. "What—a girl can't get thirsty?"

A catchy new song filled the ballroom. Caitlin turned to see where the music was coming from. A live band was performing on a spotlit stage adjacent to where they were standing. Feeling reassured by her disguise, Caitlin ambled closer.

Natalie loves to dance. Maybe she's nearby.

A three-man rock band of ghoul pirates jammed hard. The lead guitarist had a full black beard and wore a brass-button coat.

Blackbeard?

The bass guitar player was tall and dark-haired. A long steel sword was sheathed on his belt. His thick, long hair shimmered in the mirrored light reflected by a disco ball above the stage. He had a five-o'clock shadow and wore tight black leather pants, a puffy-sleeve shirt, and a leather vest. He was altogether . . . swashbuckling. Caitlin's eyes widened when she saw that he was plucking his guitar strings with a gleaming silver hook.

The Captain himself!

The drummer's head was wrapped in a burgundy bandana with a black skull emblazoned on the front. His wooden peg leg pounded the bass drum pedal and his long, silver drumsticks rhythmically beat the tom-toms and snare drums.

Their music seriously rocks.

And though this ghoul band was a ghastly bunch, Caitlin thought they were also kind of cool, especially—

SPLASH!

Rapunzel had sloshed a clear liquid from a goblet onto Caitlin's arm. The fluid washed away a layer of clay, exposing a patch of pink skin.

And just like that, the music stopped.

The dancing halted.

Fifteen hundred dancing-dead cannibals cocked their heads. Their hyper-acute senses had sprung to alert as they caught the sudden succulent scent.

My God! They smell my flesh!

CHAPTER THIRTY-EIGHT

THE GHOULS IN THE BALLROOM TWITCHED THEIR NOSES AS THEIR bodies writhed in hunger.

The Blood-Eyed bats on the rafters screeched high-pitched sound waves. They also detected the unfamiliar but irresistible aroma of human meat and hot blood.

Caitlin's veins iced over. She furiously smudged a gob of clay over her bare skin.

After what felt like an eternity, the aroma dissipated. The pirates started playing music and the savage partygoers began dancing again. The bat colony went quiet as they continued their upside-down watch from the rafters.

Caitlin pretended to gaze across the room with a vacant stare as she pulled Rapunzel aside.

"Why did you try to kill me?"

A zombie bumped into Caitlin. The ghoul tilted his head

and sniffed her like a dog. Caitlin growled and slogged off in another direction, Rapunzel in tow.

Rapunzel whispered, "Sorry. But you were getting too cocky. Some bats were glaring in your direction. If they sense you, you're dead meat. Literally. Your fear protects you—at least for the time being."

Rapunzel had just saved her life. Caitlin wanted to stop and hug her, but that would of course be too dangerous.

They had to locate Natalie and the queen quickly.

A commotion erupted on the dance floor between two Blood-Eyeds. Tin Woodman had picked a fight with the Scarecrow. He had him down on the floor, and was pulling straw from Scarecrow's torso with his rusty tin teeth.

The fight quickly escalated and grew more violent. An arrow of swirling, purple light suddenly pulsed from the direction of the stage. It struck Tin Woodman in the chest. He convulsed as the bolt of electricity shot through his metal frame. A faint electrical smell accompanied a white trickle of smoke that rose from the Woodman's head. When his convulsions stopped, the Tin Woodman was still. After a moment, he rose to his feet and held out his arm to assist Scarecrow, who was still on the floor, half-stuffed. They both turned toward the stage.

A shrill voice rang out and hushed the crowd. "Insolence will not be tolerated!"

Rapunzel and the princesses exchanged grim looks.

"Oh. My. Goodness," said Snow in a tense whisper. "I know that voice. It's *her.*"

Caitlin suddenly felt grossly unprepared for whatever was going to happen next.

Her eyes reluctantly searched in the direction from which the beam of light had been fired. There, standing in front of a bejeweled throne on a stage in front of the dance floor, was the Queen of Hearts. Torches blazed like hellfire on the walls of stone behind her.

The first thing that caught Caitlin's eye was the queen's bouffant, heart-shaped hairdo; it was extravagantly opulent and the color was a striking neon pink-red. Her lips were smeared with rose-colored lipstick, and her large, festooned, heart-shaped glasses reminded Caitlin of a mask worn at a masquerade ball.

And sure enough, tightly gripped in her left hand . . .

The scepter!

The glass dome on top of the royal staff enthralled Caitlin. It looked alive because it swirled with incandescent violets, blues, and purples. The whirling forces had an almost hypnotic effect on her. She felt drawn to it like a magnet. Caitlin struggled to avert her gaze.

The Queen of Hearts cackled. "The midnight hour is near! Prepare yourselves for the raising of the scepter!"

The ballroom of ghouls grunted and applauded.

Caitlin shook her head.

Cheering?

These creatures might've displayed intelligence when it came to hunting for food. However, they lacked any semblance of self-awareness. They had no idea what had happened to them.

In that regard they were mindless—mere chattels of the queen, slaves to the primal cravings of the Red Spectrum.

"Soon all the kingdoms will become united as one!" the queen declared.

They cheered louder.

"She means 'witless as one,'" Rapunzel whispered, not holding back the sarcasm.

Something compelled Caitlin to look to her left.

Her heart skipped a beat when she saw her.

My baby sister! Natalie!

She was dancing, far too seductively for a little girl, on one of the elevated platforms. Another one of those big, bad-looking zombie wolves was watching her with hungry eyes.

Caitlin felt steam rise off her chest. Her nostrils flared and her fists clenched. When Natalie started twerking, she lost it.

"Not gonna happen!"

Caitlin jolted forward, ready to pounce, her face flushed with anger. Rapunzel hooked her by the collar and held her back. "Not yet. You'll blow our cover. Stick to the plan."

Caitlin motioned toward her almost-undead sister. "What about her? She's an important part of the plan! And my life!"

"We'll take care of Natalie," Rapunzel said. Her eyes shone with assurance. "I promise."

Rapunzel turned to her friends. "Ready, girls?"

Cindy cracked her knuckles and said. "Ready. I'll meet you *upstairs.*"

Caitlin shot a reluctant glance at the lengthy dance floor

spread out in front of the stage. The zombies were partying hard, dancing in sensuous rhythm to the music.

She knew what was coming. To get close to the throne, Caitlin needed to make her way through that long and crowded dance floor.

Rapunzel nudged in beside Caitlin. She wrapped her arm around her, squeezing her gently and drawing her close.

"You'll have to blend in," Rapunzel said in a forthright manner.

Caitlin didn't answer. Didn't respond. She just listened.

"Your fear will render you invisible to the crows, bats, and ghouls. But if you *walk* across that dance floor toward the queen, you'll stand out like a hummingbird flying north for the winter. The bats' sonar will detect your irregular movement. The zombies will close in, quick. You won't stand a chance."

Caitlin remained wordless.

"Last thing," Rapunzel said as she placed two fingers under Caitlin's chin. "If those bats above the dance floor *do* attack, make two fists. Lock them tight and press them hard against your eyes." Rapunzel lifted Caitlin's chin and looked at her square on.

"They'll try to eat your eyeballs first. So you can't see where to run."

Caitlin's face twisted in disgust. She looked up to the ceiling, where the Blood-Eyed bats hung topsy-turvy from the rafters. Rapunzel wasn't trying to spook her, she knew. Those were just the facts. Caitlin, like it or not, had to deal with them.

She gazed silently at the grinding ghouls. The last time she had stood on a dance floor was last year. At her old school. When she bolted the dance, leaving Dillon Slater standing alone and dumbfounded. Thinking back to that horrid event, a new perspective surfaced.

Had Dillon Slater been, like, totally embarrassed when I ditched him? Practically the whole school witnessed the drama.

Could that be why he shouted out the callous comment about the disappearing Fletchers?

All of a sudden the music in the ballroom ended. The spotlights illuminating the stage abruptly died, and the dancing ceased.

Yes!

The wave of relief that swept over Caitlin almost made her fist pump the air. No music meant no dancing.

But her relief didn't last long. Across the ballroom, another spotlight shone on another stage, and a new rock band appeared.

This band called themselves . . . The Zombies?

This can't be!

Their guitars unleashed melodic, up-tempo chords intimately familiar to Caitlin. She pressed both her palms against her forehead, fingers apart.

It's the song! "She's Not There!"

That sixties oldie her mom played for her almost every day as they danced around the house; the same song that had brought on that first heaving wave of panic with Dillon Slater. This was madly surreal.

It's beyond fluky.

Caitlin's chest heaved as she drew in oxygen. She pushed it out boldly, determined to tackle the precarious situation with poise. She had to. For Natalie.

"Well no one told me about her, the way she lied.

Well no one told me about her, how many people cried.

But it's too late to say you're sorry.

How would I know, why should I care?

Please don't bother tryin' to find her.

She's not there."

As the ghoul band jammed, Caitlin slid onto the dance floor, pushing her fear out of her mind. After all, she was caked in clay, masked in zombie makeup, and she was sporting a new, cropped bob.

Which meant she was unrecognizable.

And no one here knew her anyway.

Caitlin was anonymous. Inconspicuous. Practically invisible. And technically, they weren't even human beings.

Hmmm.

Something somewhere inside of her let go. She found herself bending her knees up and down, up and down, over and over, swiveling right and swiveling left. Her hips began to bounce. Arms moved in a crawl stroke, backstroke, breaststroke, and suddenly, she was dancing the Swim and dancing it well. She segued into the Monkey and the Jerk as the music and memories erupted inside of her with volcanic force, and when that old familiar song hit the upbeat, catchy chorus, Caitlin Fletcher was dancing a perfect Mashed Potato . . .

> "Well let me tell you 'bout the way she looked,
>
> The way she'd act and the color of her hair.
>
> Her voice was soft and cool,
>
> Her eyes were clear and bright,
>
> But she's not there!"

Her feet swiveled inward, outward, inward, outward as she melted into the melody. She spun around and around and leaped, pumping her fists and jumping higher, until she was dancing on air—free, happy, and high as a kite can fly. Her troubles had vanished, for now.

And the whole time, she was shrewdly moving and bopping in the direction of the evil Queen of Hearts!

Caitlin grooved smoothly toward the stage where the loathsome queen stood wielding the scepter in all her treacherous glory. Monstrous beings jumped and bopped and danced the rumba all around her. Caitlin's stomach wrenched as the reality of what was about to take place struck her in the gut like a gong. She was going to confront, face-to-face, the depraved monarch of Wonderland.

Suddenly, for the first time in her life, Caitlin was not afraid of being afraid. The fluttering in her chest no longer bothered her. Instead, she used it. She welcomed her fear, full-on, as a way to avoid the crows and the ghouls all around her.

Caitlin reached the edge of the stage. She gulped. A strange, untimely thought struck her.

If I'm no longer afraid of being afraid, that would mean . . . I'm not afraid!

A flock of black crows landed around the queen.

Beady, red eyes and tar-black beaks homed in on her.

The crows cawed. And squawked. And they thrashed their black wings maniacally, outing Caitlin to the queen.

What the—

The queen's head swiveled. It tilted as she squarely fixed her gaze on Caitlin.

"It's her!" the monarch shrieked, pointing frantically.

Caitlin freaked. The crows scrambled. The queen sneered.

Then the unthinkable.

A bell clanged.

The clock was striking midnight!

Midnight?

No!

No!!

CHAPTER THIRTY-NINE

THE QUEEN'S HERALD APPEARED AT CENTER STAGE, HIS BLACK-AND-blue jaw wired shut. He rolled out a big brass gong.

Then he picked up a mallet.

God, no!

The herald took a mighty swing and hammered it.

Caitlin sobbed as the gong rang out, the booming sound reverberating right through her body and across the kingdom. She wailed, "Natalie!"

The queen laughed. She paid no further attention to Caitlin, for the midnight hour had arrived. All that was left for the Queen of Hearts was to raise her royal scepter high enough to transmit the final wave.

Caitlin clenched her teeth. Both hands tightened into fists. Nails dug into palms.

No. Freaking. Way.

Caitlin leaped onto the stage and dove toward the queen just as the malevolent monarch started to raise her scepter.

Caitlin sailed across the stage. Her fingers latched on to the scepter's shaft, but the queen shook her off and she tumbled to the floor.

The queen maintained her grip as Caitlin bounced back up, primed for battle.

Both clutched the scepter.

It swung back and forth, back and forth, in a ferocious tug-of-war.

The queen used her weight and height to overpower Caitlin. She lifted the scepter into the air to launch the final wave.

A few more inches, and we're all done for.

Caitlin pulled downward with all her might.

The scepter inched higher.

Caitlin's arm muscles strained as she cleaved on to the shaft. Both her legs dangled off the ground. She used every ounce of her body weight to push that wicked rod back down.

The scepter rose a few millimeters more.

Caitlin cupped her hand over the queen's pale hand. She dug in between the queen's knuckles, trying to pry her fingers from the shaft.

The scepter rose a tad higher.

The queen took her other hand and cupped it over Caitlin's, trying to wring her fingers off her own.

The queen hissed like a snake. Then a strange, high-pitched sound seeped out from her mouth.

At once, a vampire bat took flight.

It nosedived toward Caitlin.

She ducked, squeezing her eyes tightly shut, and all the while clinging to the shaft with both hands.

Caitlin felt a strange stinging sensation on her forehead.

The abominable bat had bitten her when it swooped by.

The scepter rose again as the queen shouted, "It's done!"

A hot, electrostatic buzz shivered through Caitlin's body. Her eyes swam with bright-red tears. Red berry juice leaked from her eyes and rolled down her cheeks like running mascara. The hardened clay over Caitlin's body broke apart, shattered into a million soft, powdery flakes, and fell clean off her body. She felt vulnerable. Defenseless. Naked. Her eyeballs began to glow hot pink. Her warm, flesh-toned skin began to cool and decolorize.

Still clutching the queen's hand and scepter, Caitlin body-slammed her hard. She followed that punishing body-check with another and another, all the while battling to pry the queen's waxen fingers from the shaft.

She slammed the queen one more time with her full weight, putting extra hip force into the wallop.

The queen's grip broke for a split second, and she briefly lost hold of the scepter.

Caitlin snatched it.

She took three running steps and leaped off the stage. She landed upright on the dance floor, scepter in hand. Caitlin clutched the scepter firmly, but delicately.

Now what do I do with it?

The queen fell to her knees, writhing about and screaming.

Caitlin had to help Natalie first. She breathed hard as she

scanned the hall. The little zombie chili pepper was still danc-ing, eyes closed, on the platform.

In one swift move, Sleeping Beauty and Snow White swooped in and hoisted Natalie by her underarms.

Thank God!

The Queen of Hearts found her footing on the stage, assisted by the three members of the zombie pirate band—Blackbeard, Captain Hook, and Long John Silver.

The queen's arms flailed in anger. She pointed in Caitlin's general direction. "Off with her head! And bring it back on a platter—along with the scepter!"

The words paralyzed Caitlin.

Blackbeard and Long John drew black daggers. Captain Hook unveiled a polished silver scythe that had been affixed to his left arm. The gleam in their eyes told her that they were intent on cold-blooded butchery. Torchlight glimmered off their blades.

"Cut her down by the legs!" the queen called out to Blackbeard and Long John. "And you, Hook, you take her head."

Caitlin looked up, her eyes like searchlights. Rapunzel and Cindy stood high up on some wooden scaffolding above the stage. Rapunzel was anchoring a long braid of hair to a rafter.

Blackbeard cocked his arm, taking aim.

Caitlin turned and ran.

The pirate flung his dagger. It sliced through the air.

Swoosh.

A stabbing pain shot through Caitlin's body.

She wailed.

Then she collapsed on the dance floor.

Silent and motionless.

CHAPTER FORTY

CAITLIN'S BREATH CAME IN GASPS AS SHE LAY FACEDOWN, IMMOBILE ON the ballroom floor. The pain was coming from her right thigh. She rolled slowly and gently onto her left side, wincing from the pain but keeping that scepter tightly gripped in her hand.

She snuck a glance back.

Captain Hook was cleaning his curved blade with a hanky while nodding to Long John Silver.

The peg-legged swashbuckler raised his dagger.

Aimed it—right at Caitlin!

She knew this was going to be a slaughter.

"Hurry," Rapunzel shrieked at Cinderella. Cindy then leaped from the rafters, swinging on a braided vine like a flying trapeze artist.

She kicked the black dagger from the pirate's hand as she swung by. Then she walloped each buccaneer in the head with her heel as she swung back, knocking them cold.

Caitlin exhaled in relief.

Rapunzel slid down from the rafters and dashed toward her.

Cindy released her hold on the braid and dropped to the stage. There was cold steel in her eyes.

She leaned over the pirates, examining each one to make sure he was out. Blackbeard seized her by the ankle as she stood next to him.

"That foot is spoken for," Cinderella said, firing a pulverizing front kick to his ugly, scarred face.

Lights out.

The clawed paw from a snarling zombie cat snatched Cinderella by her other foot. The feline twisted it hard, and Cindy winced as she fell on her back.

Three gruesome pigs dove in, their pale hooves clawing into Cinderella's flesh. She shook them off. With her free leg, she delivered another walloping roundhouse kick to the side of the first pig. "Get back, Baby Back!"

Whuuummppp!

She slammed the second pig's head sideways with a crushing crescent kick. Sweat, saliva, and zombie slop sprayed in all directions.

The third pig leaped onto her leg and clung tight.

Cinderella delivered a backhand and shook the sow loose.

She took a step back and wound up.

Two rapid-fire hammer kicks slammed the sow's head right and left!

Another splatter of zombie slop gushed out. The ghastly pig was out cold.

Rapunzel reached Caitlin.

"There's a dagger in my leg," Caitlin said.

"Don't move." Rapunzel replied.

Rapunzel inspected the wound.

"Good news—the blade entered cleanly. No blood to attract these cannibals. Bad news—when I pull the bloody blade out, you'll be live bait. We'll have to run. You strong enough?"

Caitlin tilted her head toward Rapunzel.

"I think so. I'm a fast limper."

Rapunzel gently patted her on the head. "That's my girl."

With a delicate touch, she began to slide the knife smoothly out of Caitlin's leg.

Caitlin winced at the sound of wet suction and slurp. Then it was out.

The blade dripped human blood. Fifteen hundred zombies jerked their heads, sniffing the fresh *food* like savage hounds. They drooled.

Rapunzel stood. She climbed on top of a table. Then she flung the bloody dagger far across the ballroom, over the heads of the crowd, and onto the stage. A mass of grunting ghouls began moving in that direction.

Rapunzel tore a long strip from a white tablecloth and knelt down by Caitlin.

"I bought us about twenty seconds. Hold still."

She ripped a hole in Caitlin's jeans, exposing a deep gash. She wrapped a bandage tight around the leg.

"You okay?"

Caitlin nodded. Rapunzel helped her to her feet.

"How do you feel?"

"Dizzy. But not weak."

"Pays to have a bit of zombie in the bloodstream."

Caitlin lifted her eyes toward the stage. "Look!"

The Queen of Hearts was back on her feet, her face red and hard.

"This isn't over!" she shouted.

Cinderella got in the queen's face. "Pity the fool who tries to stand in our way."

Cinderella then did a double reverse flip, landed on her feet, and somersaulted off the stage. She plowed through the incoming crowd of zombies still searching for the bloodied dagger.

Caitlin examined her forearms and hands while she held the scepter. Her skin had bled white. Hairline fractures were forming on her flesh.

"I need a blood transfusion!" Caitlin pleaded.

Rapunzel sighed. "Too late. For all of us. The queen raised the scepter. The Green Spectrum is dying."

"But it's not dead yet!" Caitlin cried out. "Amethyst said we have till sunrise."

Rapunzel's right eyebrow sharpened. She picked a cocktail fork off a table. She pricked the tip of her thumb, drawing blood. Caitlin took the fork and did the same.

They swabbed bloody thumbs. Rapunzel said, "Blood sisters."

The Queen of Hearts bellowed with an operatic shrill, "Trance interruptus!"

Fifteen hundred ruby-eyed zombies froze.

"After them!"

Fifteen hundred heads swiveled in Caitlin's direction. All eyes burned fire. Not one, not two . . . but every single ghoul in the ballroom lunged at once.

"Run, Caitlin!" Rapunzel screamed. "Run!"

CHAPTER FORTY-ONE

Caitlin's legs pumped with fury as she rocketed toward the exit. She glanced up at a corner of the ceiling.

One, two, thr—forget it!

She rocketed out of the ballroom, racing to stay ahead of the undead. The girls followed close behind, restraining the struggling Natalie as they fled.

The chili pepper faced backward. Snow and Beauty immobilized her arms and sandwiched her thrashing torso between theirs. They held her off the ground as her legs kicked wildly.

Their footsteps echoed with each slap on the stone floor as they hustled down the corridor.

Seven filthy zombie dwarfs were already after them. Along with a bloodthirsty Hansel and a ghoulish Gretel. Belle was right behind. She let out an ear-piercing war cry.

"Oooh-owowowow!"

Caitlin ignored the scream as she scrambled full throttle, like a young doe fleeing a hungry lion.

"We need to get out of this castle, fast."

"But how?" Snow asked, panting. "There's a ghoul guarding every exit."

"We need to surprise them," Rapunzel said.

"I have an idea!" Caitlin shouted. "When we reach the door, bend over. Ready . . ."

The guard was poised. He held his staff crossed over the doorway, barring their exit. The girls reached the threshold.

"Now!" Caitlin screamed.

They crouched and bent forward, sending the maniacally kicking legs of the flailing Natalie into the guard's jaw and knocking him out cold.

They exploded out the castle door and fled into the moonless night. The air was thick and humid. Low-hanging black clouds looked like clumps of black coal set against a dark, deep-purple sky.

Cawing crows dipped beneath the cloud cover, giving chase like feathered beasts from hell. Then the clouds began to release black rain.

"Careful you don't slip," Rapunzel warned as they high-tailed it across the wet rear lawn.

Rapunzel turned to Natalie and then back to Caitlin. "We must get you and Natalie home before sunrise."

"Unless we can shut down the scepter," Beauty shouted from the rear.

Caitlin had no clue how to do that, and they had no time to stop and figure it out.

They raced across the rotted lawn. It dead-ended at a wide, ominous-looking maze of tall, dark-green hedges encrusted with moldy leaves. They rose twelve feet high above the mud-soaked ground.

"We can't go in there!" Beauty shouted, blinking hard as raindrops splashed her eyes.

Cindy threw up her hands. "The maze is too wide to go around."

The drum of galloping feet grew louder.

"There has to be a way out on the other side," Rapunzel said.

"Yeah, but we might get stuck in that snarl for hours—maybe days," Beauty cried. "Caitlin and Natalie will miss the portal."

The relentless cadence of running feet drew closer.

Caitlin's expression hardened. She wiped rain from her face with a forearm. "No choice. Let's go."

She ducked into the maze. The rest followed.

"Hang on tight to that scepter," Rapunzel warned. They glided around a corner, hydroplaning on the mud as they raced into the complex tangle of hedges.

"Oh my goodness," said Snow, "it's not what I expected."

Cindy's eyes sprung wide open.

This was no ordinary maze. It appeared to be some sort of bizarre . . . closet? *The queen's closet?*

"She's a borderline loon," Cindy said. "And quite the hoarder."

Along the insides of the hedges hung closet bars five rods

high, overflowing with gowns, shirts, skirts, pants, blouses, coats, and capes. Packed boxes and trunks stuffed with all kinds of merchandise lined the dirt at ground level.

"That loon looted the Kingdom," Rapunzel said.

Snow White placed her hand on the nearest hedge and closed her eyes, concentrating. "We should head south. It's our best way out of here."

They veered around a sharp bend, and found themselves surrounded by twelve-foot-high shelves. The shelves were stocked with a selection of hats and handbags—enough to fill the best Parisian department store.

Natalie squirmed to break free. She kept screaming one word over and over again: "Hungry!"

Caitlin felt a twinge in her heart. She missed Girl Wonder's copious vocabulary.

The girls banked another corner.

They ran flat into a wall of shoes that climbed up to the sky. There were purple, pointy princess heels; raw-silk pumps; leopard-print wooden mules; gold ballet flats; pointe shoes; black, strappy sandals; ankle-strap, six-inch wedges; snakeskin stilettos; velvet-bowed peep-toes; corkies; and even flip-flops.

"Cindy, stop staring!" Beauty yelled as she and Snow struggled to contain Natalie. "A little help over here, huh?"

Caitlin spotted the raging flesh-eaters charging after them from the far end of the shoe corridor. They were in hot pursuit with one single-minded purpose. Dinner!

A man in aged leather and dyed-green wool now led the hunt. He wore a chaperon hat and had a quiver strapped to his back.

Robin Hood?

He pulled out a wooden bow. Then a polished tin arrow. He handed the arrow to a strange-looking fellow galloping beside him, who sported a bow tie and a silk high hat.

The Hatter!

Mad as a hatter he must've been, because he suddenly stabbed himself in the gut with the tin arrow. He yanked it back out without breaking stride and returned it to red-eyed Robin Hood. The glistening arrowhead was smeared in hot blood.

Contaminated blood!

Robin Hood took aim.

These fiends are utterly evil!

Rapunzel clutched Caitlin tight under her arm.

"Ouch—you're bruising me!" Caitlin cried.

The legendary outlaw drew back the bowstring.

Rapunzel catapulted Caitlin directly in front of her with a swing of her arm. "You don't want that infected glob of blood inside of you."

Right!

Caitlin crouched slightly as she hurtled along the path using Rapunzel as cover. "But what about you?"

Robin Hood fired. The arrow shot like a bullet, cutting raindrops in half midair.

Caitlin heard a swoosh. Rapunzel's hands gripped her shoulders and shoved her to the left.

Blood sprayed both girls' cheeks when the arrow whizzed by, barely missing them.

"Wash the blood off!" Rapunzel screamed.

Caitlin swung her hand in the air to catch some drops of rain. She splashed it on her face.

Caitlin glanced back. The zombie archer was aiming a second arrow. He pulled back. This time, though, his target was not Rapunzel and Caitlin.

Swoosh!

The arrow closed in on Natalie, who was dangling between Snow and Beauty.

A strike won't turn her eyes red. It will kill her!

Cinderella dove in front of the projectile just before it sliced into the back of Natalie's neck.

Cindy went down.

Everyone skidded to a stop.

Blood bubbled from the wound in Cindy's shoulder. The arrow had pierced her flesh.

Her crown had also fallen from her head.

Caitlin ran over to her.

"Stay back," Cindy growled as she groveled along the dirt. The whites of her eyes glazed over with blood. Her silver-tone skin cracked like ice. Then her face contorted as if some dark, primal force had taken possession of her.

"Leave me!" Cindy snarled. "And run!"

Her voice had changed and its new tone chilled Caitlin.

Rapunzel suppressed her sorrow as she seized Caitlin's wrist. "We gotta leave. Or the Cinderella that we love will have died in vain."

The horde of zombies was moving in.

The rain was beginning to taper off.

Caitlin's lower lip trembled. She stared helplessly at Cindy. *She literally saved Natalie's life.*

Caitlin wanted to thank her, but the words froze in her throat.

Rapunzel pulled her back. Caitlin was numb inside as she and the girls took flight again.

They galloped onward. Tears had begun to water Snow White's eyes. Beauty's face was waxen and sullen.

"I never foresaw this happening to her," Beauty mourned. "I could've prevented it."

Rapunzel suddenly slammed on the brakes.

The rest of them screeched to a standstill, churning up a spray of mud.

They had reached a dead end.

There was no other place to go.

CHAPTER FORTY-TWO

A HUGE ZOMBIE WEREWOLF STOOD OVER CINDERELLA AS THE throng of ghouls crowded around.

"Another Big Bad Wolf?" Caitlin asked in shock.

"That first one hunted Little Red Riding Hood," Beauty said. "This one stalks the Three Little Pigs."

"Pray that Cindy is a full-fledged Blood-Eyed now," Rapunzel said as she peered back.

Caitlin's brow creased in confusion.

"If she hasn't turned yet," Rapunzel continued, "they'll eat her alive."

Caitlin's emotions seesawed as she saw a fiery red glow emerge from Cinderella's eyes. She rose from the dirt and fell in behind the wolf.

Caitlin pressed her fist hard against her mouth as she fought back grief. Cindy was now one of *them*. Caitlin couldn't allow herself to imagine Natalie turning completely.

The Blood-Eyed wolf proceeded to take a slow, heaving breath.

"What's he doing?" Caitlin asked.

The wolf exhaled. He drew in a second, deeper breath.

"I think that first one was a huff," said Beauty. "Which means this one's the puff . . . "

The wolf unleashed a gale-force gust of breath, deep from his gut. He blew forth a violent windstorm of spit, saliva, chewed food, and bile.

Rapunzel grimaced and ducked. "Brace yourselves!"

They were walloped by a wet, foul wind that sent them tumbling to the ground and that showered them in a froth of slobber.

Caitlin and the girls picked themselves up and wiped off the phlegm and mucus from their hair, faces, and clothes. Beauty and Snow struggled to restrain Natalie.

The wolf, a decomposing Pinocchio, drooling dwarfs, and a savage gang of other ghouls were closing in for the final kill.

At first, the Blood-Eyed advanced toward them in a cruel, merciless, unhurried manner.

A moment later, their ruby eyes brightened and they broke out in a run.

Caitlin's blood ran cold. She tried to mount a wall. "Let's climb these hedges! Or maybe we could—"

Before she finished, another gust of wind nearly knocked her over. But this one didn't come from the lungs of the wolf.

"You lovely ladies need a lift?"

Caitlin looked up.

IT'S JACK! JACK!

Her heart swelled.

He was airborne, riding some kind of giant . . . insect?!

Its colossal, flapping wings were producing these new wind gusts.

How'd he get into this world? How'd he find me? And where did he get that mammoth purple moth?

"Grab on," Jack shouted, "before you're dinner for dwarfs."

The purple insect swooped down, and Jack scooped up Caitlin.

Caitlin tucked the scepter under one arm and grabbed on to Jack's forearm with the other.

"What about Natalie?" Caitlin screamed.

He lifted her up as the butterfly ascended into the sky.

"She's next."

Caitlin swung her legs around and straddled the torso of the winged insect, settling in behind Jack. She wrapped one arm around his waist and held the scepter in the other.

"Hold tight," he said.

She turned her head to the side and pressed her cheek against his warm back to shield her from the winds. It felt nice—so nice she forgot about her fear of flying.

Until the humongous butterfly turned sharply at a steep angle. They were making a rapid descent. The contents of Caitlin's stomach leaped into her chest as the aeronautically talented insect swooped back down toward the girls on the ground.

The insect hovered low, like a rescue helicopter, waiting for Jack to retrieve the rest of the girls.

The Blood-Eyed ghouls were closing in.

"Leg it, ladies!" Jack said. "The wolves are at the door."

Snow White grabbed on to Caitlin's ankles, Rapunzel held fast to Snow's calf, and Sleeping Beauty grabbed on to one of Rapunzel's feet with one hand. Beauty's other hand secured Natalie by her underarm. Natalie hung between them, suspended by her arms, thrashing.

"Food!" Natalie grunted.

Half a heartbeat later, the wolf clawed at Beauty's dangling ankle. He missed, narrowly.

And with a heavy flap, the purple moth or butterfly—or whatever it was—lugged the girls over the tall hedge and to safety.

CHAPTER FORTY-THREE

CAITLIN HELD JACK TIGHT, HER RIGHT CHEEK PRESSED AGAINST HIS warm back. At this awkward, painful moment, an untimely thought came from out of nowhere.

Imagine if Piper and her coven could see me straddling an over-sized, winged insect with one arm around Jack.

"Where we headed?" Caitlin asked Jack.

"Back to the village. To the portal."

"We gotta make it there before sunrise. Hurry!" Rapunzel shouted from below.

The butterfly panted. "I'm afraid our passenger load has surpassed my limit. I might have fractured a wing. I need to set you down before we tumble out of the sky."

I know that voice.

"Uh-oh!" Rapunzel's shouted.

The butterfly banked left and began his descent out of the dark night sky.

Of course! That voice belongs to the caterpillar! Lord Amethyst Bartholomew!

The last time Caitlin had seen him, they were tiptoeing as fast as they could away from the Big Bad Wolf. Amethyst had spun himself into a cocoon—he had obviously completed his metamorphosis. The bug had impeccable timing when it came to rescuing them from that maze. But even with his help, they were still on the verge of missing the portal.

Caitlin's ears suddenly plugged up as Amethyst quickened his descent. She squeezed Jack's waist tighter as the drop in altitude steepened.

A moment later the girls, still clinging to one another's legs beneath the butterfly, gently touched down upon the grainy sands of a dune.

Jack grimaced as he helped Caitlin dismount from Amethyst's torso.

The balmy night air smelled of salt and sea. A beaming crescent moon and blinking stars lit a plum-black sky.

Caitlin opened her jaw to pop her eardrums. "Where are we?"

"Castle Beach," Amethyst said. "I'm afraid we're still hours away from the village."

"Let's run," Caitlin said.

Amethyst shook his head. "I'm afraid you won't be able to walk, either."

"I don't understa—"

Caitlin saw Jack limping. Then she saw *why* he was limping, and her mouth fell open.

"Oh my God, there's a bone sticking out of your leg!"

"I'm fine."

"Jack, what happened to you?" Caitlin cried.

"I'll explain later."

"Hey, take a look," Rapunzel said. She was pointing to a single-mast sloop boat, bearing a black skull-and-crossbones flag, bobbing in the moonlight just offshore.

A pirate ship—and it looked abandoned. It reminded Caitlin of a ghost ship.

A seagull cawed softly from somewhere out to sea.

There was a distant roll of thunder.

"Is that a storm coming?" Jack asked.

"Skies are clear," Snow replied, scanning the horizon.

Amethyst frowned. "That's not impending weather you hear. It's the rumbling of fifteen hundred Blood-Eyed running after us."

"Don't they ever stop?" Caitlin said.

Jack took hold of her hand.

A frothy wave lapped up at their toes. Amethyst fluttered upward to avoid getting wet. "I've sent out a distress signal. Alerted some friends to our situation," he said.

Caitlin looked out upon the water. The light of the moon was like warm, golden syrup on the sea. It reminded her of summer camping trips the Fletchers had taken in the Adirondacks. To Lake Saranac. She could almost smell the pine trees. And the scent of a campfire, with its delightful pops and crackles of burning wood.

Her mom used to spray her with insect repellent to keep the

mosquitoes at bay. She remembered being frightened of bees and wasps.

Caitlin glanced over at Natalie, who was still being restrained by Snow and Beauty.

"May I ask you something?" Caitlin said to Amethyst.

"Of course, my child."

"Natalie and I were both infected. She's pink-eyed and out of control. I'm not. Why?"

"Adolescence, my dear. Her will is not fully formed."

"But she's brilliant."

"Intelligence has nothing to do with will. Evil people can be brilliant—some are even mad geniuses—but their will is too weak to repel the Red Spectrum."

Caitlin suddenly spotted something moving in the water. It splashed to and fro, glistening on the ocean's surface.

"What was that?"

"Ooh! Fish," gurgled Natalie. "Hungry for fish taco!"

That was the first full sentence Natalie had spoken since the bite.

"I beg to differ; that is no ordinary fish," Amethyst said. "It should be our friend, who has come to assist."

A purple tail shimmered in the moonlight. Then a mermaid popped up out of the water and waved.

Caitlin's face lit up.

It was really *her*.

The Little Mermaid.

She dove back into the sea and resurfaced a few moments later, closer to shore. She had huge, deep-set eyes and a lovely, warm smile. Her bikini top was made of two ribbed scallop shells that were coral pink, and they matched a pink starfish comb in her hair. Her flowing strawberry-blonde locks cascaded down her back, twinkling the same way the moon glowed on the waves.

And she too was partially zombified.

"Come down to the shoreline," the Little Mermaid called to them. "I'll return shortly with help. You should be safe here until I return. However, under no circumstances are you to leave the shoreline. It can get rather dangerous and spooky around these parts at night."

And with that, the Little Mermaid dove under the sea. Her purple tail flapped in the air before disappearing beneath the surface.

Caitlin turned to Jack. "How did you find us?"

"A good friend led me to the caterpillar."

"How's your leg?"

"Hurts like hell."

Caitlin felt like crying.

Except for that distant thunder of stomping feet, everything was calm and quiet. *Maybe a bit too quiet.*

Caitlin glanced over at her friends, Snow and Beauty. Neither had spoken Cindy's name since she turned. But she could see the pain etched on their faces. Rapunzel remained resolute. She was being strong for the group.

Caitlin suddenly heard the churning of waves. A clang of metal and the creaking of wood followed.

She cast her eyes just off the shoreline.

The pirate ship was suddenly turning in the sea, its bow spreading the black moonlit waters.

The vessel angled directly toward them.

"We've got trouble," Rapunzel said as she paced the shore-line. She stopped and turned to Caitlin. "Hide that blasted scepter! It's glowing like a lighthouse. And be gentle with it!"

Caitlin carefully flipped it upside down and buried the dome under the sand. Blue glimmers leaked up through the grains.

"No one's on board that boat!" Jack said, staring intently at the ship. "How could that be?"

Snow White licked a finger and raised it in the air.

"Not a puff of wind for the sails to catch either."

"Then who's sailing the ship?" Beauty asked. "And *how* is it sailing?"

This was beyond creepy. It *was* a ghost ship, carried by a ghost wind, with no living or even living-dead crew aboard. The ship was steering itself, and somehow sailing on a wind-less sea.

"I say we leave before our ship comes in," Jack said.

Lord Amethyst abruptly flitted back into the skies.

"He's bailing!" Caitlin cried.

"Maybe we should too," said Beauty.

Caitlin seriously considered it. The dead were already hunting her down; now a ghost ship was coming for her.

"We stay put," Rapunzel said. "Direct orders from the Little Mermaid. We don't know what's out there in the dark."

"We don't know what deviant force is sailing that boat

either," Beauty said. "At least with the undead, you see their dead, red eyes coming for you."

Amethyst swooped down to the shoreline, a hopeful smile on his face. "She's almost here," he said.

In unison, the group replied, "Who?"

A head splashed out of the dark waters. "Me!"

The Little Mermaid waved. "Almost there," she said, breathing heavily.

She dove back under the sea and flapped her fin above the surface. A thick, yellow braided rope was tied around it in a bowline knot.

"She's towing the pirate ship to shore," Jack said.

By herself?

Somehow, the Little Mermaid tugged the boat to the beach and docked it at the shoreline. She came ashore as her fins . . . transformed into actual feet!

She carried two wooden branches. She approached Jack. "I need to set that bone."

Jack nodded and laid himself on the sandy beach. The Little Mermaid kneeled down beside him. With hands that moved as skillfully as any orthopedic doctor's, she unwrapped the makeshift bandage on Jack's leg. Then she snapped the bone back into place. Jack recoiled in pain and sweat beaded on his brow. She sprinkled some kind of medicinal aquatic plant juice over the wound and slid an exotic-looking herb into his mouth.

"Pain killer and antiseptic," she said. "Chew."

The Little Mermaid made two splints out of the branches

as Jack consumed the medicine. She pulled out some strips of seaweed that were tucked into her waist. She placed the splints on either side of Jack's leg, then wound the seaweed around the splint, creating a new makeshift bandage-cast.

"What kind of medicine is this?" Jack asked with a grin.

She helped Jack stand up. Then she gestured toward the pirate ship and said to the group, "We have a long way to go. We need to leave now."

"But how can you possibly tow such a large ship by yourself?" Caitlin asked. "Especially when we're all on board?"

Little Mermaid gave a wry smile and pointed out to sea.

Dozens of mermaid tails suddenly splashed through the surface of the ocean.

Caitlin shook her head. "There must be a hundred mermaids out there."

"Actually, there's one hundred and thirty-seven," Little Mermaid replied. "Now please hurry."

CAITLIN COULDN'T BELIEVE IT. SHE WAS NOW ABOARD A GENUINE pirate ship, sailing upon a moonlit sea, and Jack was kindly keeping her warm with his arm around her. She was over the moon—and under it!

She was glad Jack was feeling better. The salty night air stroked her face as she looked around the boat. Everyone had found a corner to snuggle up in and steal a nap.

Even Natalie. Amethyst perched at the end of the bow, napping under the starlight. Only the Little Mermaid remained awake. She swam beneath the water, tugging the vessel to its final destination.

The skull-and-crossbones flag flapped and flashed in the night's wind, reflecting slivers of autumn moonlight.

"Who would've believed this whole scene?" Jack said softly. "It feels like months ago that we were chatting at our lockers in school. But it was only yesterday. Or was it this morning?"

Caitlin chuckled. "I've lost track of time." She nuzzled her head against Jack's shoulder as she gazed out at the starlit sea. "Thank you, Jack."

"For what?"

"For being a good friend. For never judging me." She chuckled. "Especially now—with my pale face, cracking skin, and oh-so-not-flattering hairdo."

He winked at her.

"I hope you know I didn't send that text. Telling you to meet me at Mount Cemetery instead of the dance."

"What do you mean?"

"Piper sent it. She had my phone. I would never let you go to that place alone."

Caitlin smiled. "I've always admired how you stand up for kids at school. You're a special person, Jack. I mean that. And you came all this way to help me. You risked your life for some ordinary new kid at school."

Jack held her closer. "You're far from ordinary, Caitlin." Caitlin glanced up and met his gaze. There was moonlight in his eyes.

"I can tell you quite honestly that you're positively one of prettiest girls I've ever known. And quirky as hell."

Caitlin smiled wider and brighter than the moon. Except for those small pecks she offered during a game of spin the bottle, Caitlin had never really kissed a boy before. But tonight it seemed she would. Jack leaned in. Their lips tenderly touched in a lingering embrace.

"I hope that was okay," Jack said softly. "I should have asked permission."

"Permission granted," Caitlin said, smiling. "What I mean is, it was okay." She blinked. "Wait, I didn't mean that the kiss was *just* okay, as in it was nothing special; the kiss, was, um, well . . . it was great! I meant that it was okay for you to kiss me."

He smiled. Caitlin let out a leisurely breath. She was feeling good for the first time in a long time. She couldn't believe she'd had the guts to duke it out with the queen. Or to do all the other crazy things she had done.

Especially dance.

Especially open up to Jack right now and share her feelings.

"You know why I want to get home before sunrise?" Caitlin asked Jack.

"Tell me."

"Because if I become a mindless ghoul, I'll forget who you are. Belle forgot Sleeping Beauty, her best friend. I don't want that to happen to me. I don't want to forget this moment."

Something compelled Caitlin to sit up and look to the back of the boat just then. There was Natalie, still and silent, as if asleep. But her eyes were open, like she was in a trance. She was staring at the scepter next to Caitlin. She was clearly mesmerized by the whirlpool of light swirling in the glass dome.

Jack pulled Caitlin back around as he glanced out to sea. "Did you notice?"

"What?"

"Listen."

The night had turned peaceful and quiet. The only sounds were waves breaking beneath the bow and stern.

"No thunder," Jack said. "We must be getting farther away from those ungodly savages."

It hurt Caitlin to think of Cindy as some kind of ungodly savage. And the thought of herself and Natalie falling into the same ghoulish state unnerved her to no end.

The good feelings were suddenly gone. "I don't want to turn into one of *them*, Jack."

He looked at his watch. He then cast his eyes toward the eastern horizon.

"I'm afraid that doesn't give us much time. It's almost sunrise."

CHAPTER FORTY-FOUR

THE LITTLE MERMAID PULLED THE PIRATE SHIP ALONGSIDE A ROCK-strewn beach. She docked the boat to a large pier made of piled stone bound by wire mesh.

Caitlin grabbed the scepter. She and Jack disembarked from the vessel and helped the zombie girls—who were struggling to subdue pink-eyed Natalie—off the boat.

Her sister was still held spellbound by the scepter. Natalie's gaze followed its iridescent, swirling blues and purples. She looked like a cat enthralled by floating lint.

They marched hurriedly up the pier, Caitlin limping and Jack hobbling, as quickly as their pain would allow.

"Have you figured out what to do with the scepter?" Amethyst abruptly asked Caitlin.

"No clue," she said, "but at least it seems to be taming the beast in my kid sister."

"You need to somehow deactivate it before sunrise. There's

no other who can liberate the kingdoms from this horrid affliction."

Rapunzel, Snow, and Beauty were suddenly looking at her with desperately hopeful eyes. She bit the tip of her thumbnail. Caitlin knew what they were thinking.

Lord Amethyst added. "And we must also get you home before sunrise."

"You'd better hurry it along," the Little Mermaid said. "Dawn will soon be here."

Rapunzel smiled gratefully at the Little Mermaid. "We owe you, my dear friend. Big time."

"I'll be watching over you from the sea," she sang as the girls and Jack hobbled toward the village where Caitlin's adventure had first begun. The Little Mermaid dunked under the waves and disappeared into the sea with a final farewell flap of her purple fin.

"Look," Snow White said, pointing as they approached the outskirts of the village. A narrow beam of light shone down from the sky—right into the roofless barn.

"The wormhole!" Rapunzel said.

The girls raced up to the barn, skidded to a dusty stop in the dirt outside it, threw open the double doors . . . and the whole barn collapsed.

"Subtle," Jack quipped as he hobbled up from behind.

"At least the portal is intact," Snow said. "But why is it moving higher and higher into the sky?"

Rapunzel pointed upward as her mouth curved into a frown. "It's not moving. It's *closing*."

The entrance looked like a floating sphere. It hovered a good fifty meters high in the night sky. Worse still, the black sky was already turning pink on the eastern horizon.

Caitlin cast a hard glance at the brightening sky. Then she looked back at the portal.

"How do we get up there?"

Beauty and Snow looked at one another and shrugged.

Caitlin turned to Rapunzel. "How did you first get up the wormhole?"

"By my hair. But even my long locks won't reach that high. And Amethyst's wing is fractured."

"No problem," Jack said with a rascally gleam in his eye. He reached into his rucksack and produced two beans—he had picked them off the stem of the bean plant back at Amethyst's cavern.

"I knew these bad boys would come in handy."

Jack inspected the beans carefully. Then his shoulders slumped.

"Oh no! They're damaged. They're useless."

Caitlin reached into the pocket of her jeans and pulled out the garbanzo beans she had found in her closet.

Except now they had turned into shiny, opalescent beans.

"Found them this morning. Or yesterday. Or whenever."

Jack's body sprung to alert. He selected one bean and placed it on the ground beneath the wormhole. Then he scooped out a handful of rich, black soil from the rucksack.

"What's that?" Caitlin asked.

"Dirt from Zeno's Forest."

He flipped his hand over and clumps of moist, black soil fell atop the bean. Jack patted it into a soft mound.

"If Zeno's Forest can transport someone long distances uncommonly fast, the soil should prompt a slow-germinating plant to grow rather quickly. If given the intent."

Caitlin smiled hopefully.

"Besides," Jack said, "if we can't bring the bean to the forest, why not bring the forest to the bean?"

They stared at the mound of dirt. Nothing was happening.

Snow pulled out her bota bag and splashed water on the soil.

Not a moment later, a tiny sprout curled and poked up from the dirt. It immediately began to thicken and expand and twist and climb skyward. The beauty of the unnatural sight took Caitlin's breath away. It was as if she were watching time-lapse photography happen with her very eyes.

Rapunzel broke into a smile. "It's working!"

In the distance, Caitlin heard the approaching thunder of stampeding feet. She looked back and cupped her hand over her mouth. Over the horizon, a cloud of dust whirled, and a sliver of orange sky was creeping up behind it. From that dust emerged the headlong rush of raging, living-dead cannibals. Like a herd of snorting buffalo, they charged toward the village.

"They're relentless," Caitlin muttered, shaking her head. "Why don't they just stop chasing us? The queen isn't controlling them anymore."

"Maybe because you have the scepter," Rapunzel said.

Natalie lunged at her, grunting, "Hungry!"

Snow and Beauty tightened their restraints.

Beauty gestured toward Natalie. "Any minute now, we'll have a legion of these to contend with."

"We can't fight off a thousand ghouls," Rapunzel said.

Caitlin stamped her foot as she inspected the scepter. "There's no On-Off switch on this thing," she said.

"Try something—*anything*," Rapunzel said.

Caitlin's hand trembled as she examined the scepter from top to bottom.

"Impossible!" she grunted. "There's no way to get inside of it." She looked at Rapunzel. "Can you try?"

"Only a human hand can wield the scepter."

The rim of the sun dawned on the horizon.

Amethyst flitted over to Caitlin. "Time is running out, young lady. Do you see the scepter?"

That's an odd question.

"Of course I see the scepter."

"But do you *see* the scepter?"

She shook her head. Blinked.

Amethyst gazed into her eyes.

"Do you recognize it?"

Caitlin stared intently. "Not really."

Caitlin felt the heaviness of everyone's eyes upon her.

What is Amethyst seeing that I'm not?

Caitlin checked her arms, hands. The zombie affliction advanced rapidly as the sun crept higher. Her arms were pale as a pearl and her skin was cracking like eggshells. She could tell the rims of her eyes were blackening. Caitlin was quickly becoming the authentic version of her clay-bank zombie disguise.

She glanced toward the eastern sky. The sun was a quarter risen already.

"It's time to let go, Caitlin," Amethyst said.

Her neck stiffened.

"Let go? Let go of *what*?"

Amethyst unfolded his vast wings. "The magic."

She swallowed hard.

"There is no magic, my dear young lady. There's nothing supernatural out there in the moonlit mist that will protect you. No spells. No sorcery."

Her legs felt heavy.

"What is there, then?"

"There's Caitlin." Amethyst flapped his bright-purple wings and rose in the air. "And within Caitlin is her will to choose the Red or Violet Spectrum and in turn, to choose the kind of world she wants to inhabit. But when you wait for magic to conjure up the world you seek, you hand all that power away."

An uncontrollable rush of tears rolled down her cheeks as she looked at the scepter once more.

Something indescribable startled her.

It was as if a shuttered window had opened somewhere inside of her. Her sky-blue eyes grew bright and wide like a June sunrise. A realization stuck, and it was unmistakable. A flash of brilliant clarity, a crystal-clear, razor-sharp image, and it suddenly shined in her mind's eye.

Caitlin *saw* the scepter.

For what it really is.

Then a memory.

Of what it *was*.

All dots connected—clean, crisp.

The scepter was *her* magic wand!

Or as Natalie called it, "that dumb lucky charm." Caitlin had bought it to help her cope with her fears and to avoid the devastating truth she could not face.

Somehow the magic wand had wound up here. And it had been blown up to life-size. She had just been too afraid earlier to recognize it. Her fear had gotten in the way yet again.

Since she was a child, she had put all of her hope and faith in a worthless ornament. It became her crutch and an excuse to deny heartrending truth.

Rapunzel interrupted her thoughts, pointing frantically toward the horizon. "The sun is three-quarters high, Caitlin."

Amethyst whispered in her ear. "The sun always shines, Caitlin; even when clouds obscure it. Instead of chasing the light, find the clouds hiding it."

The herd of Blood-Eyed zombies began flooding the streets of the village.

Caitlin drew a deep breath.

The eyes of Amethyst, Jack, and the zombie princesses suddenly glazed the color of pink as the sun rose higher on the horizon. They were turning.

Caitlin hadn't been able to figure out how she had managed to overcome all the frightening obstacles she had encountered in this strange universe. Before this day, she'd always been paralyzed by such daunting fears.

Now she knew.

The color spectrum.

It shined red, constantly urging her to occupy herself with herself, to worry about her own fears and anxiety. But it shimmered violet when she repelled the red and got busy assisting others.

The *clouds* weren't her fears.

The *clouds* were her obsessive concern for herself. When she went to the aid of others, and felt *their* pain, her debilitating fears dissipated.

Which is exactly what she needed to do now. The time had come to free her new friends and her sister from this cruel affliction.

With all eyes on her, Caitlin walked gallantly over to a large granite boulder that lay in the center of the town square.

She gripped the glowing scepter with both hands.

She lifted her arms high, as if preparing to swing a sledgehammer . . .

And then Caitlin Fletcher smashed the top of the scepter down hard on the rock with all her might.

The glass dome shattered.

The ground thundered and quaked.

Swirling sparkles of energetic color twinkled and sparked with electricity. Luminous streaks of swirling light spun up to the sun like a swarm of colorful fireflies.

The Blood-Eyed zombies stopped in their tracks.

They looked up. "Oooh."

A rainbow surged through the sky. The biggest, widest rainbow that Caitlin, or anyone else for that matter, had ever seen.

The zombies stared, their drooling mouths agape. "Aaah."

This rainbow did not beckon just out of reach, high up in a distant sky, but instead came raining down all over them, like crystal-covered gumdrops of color from the sky.

The air cooled and filled with luminous mists of yellow, orange, green, blue, indigo, and violet. The colors fell upon the people and creatures and plants and flowers.

Leaves filled with green and stretched their fresh faces toward the revitalized sun. Flowers stood erect.

Blades of withered brown grass were immediately renewed with life and waved bright green.

Black autumn foliage found its true colors of red, pink, yellow, purple, and brown.

One by one, the gleaming, blood-red eyes of the zombies faded. Eye colors began to transmute to sapphire blues and emerald greens and golden browns and lavender purples. Caitlin had never seen such exotic eye colors before . . . except in fairy tales.

And though all the ghouls' flesh remained pale, they all reclaimed their internal beauty and grace, which shined luminously through their zombified exteriors.

Natalie was not going to find her light here, though, Caitlin knew. The sisters required direct sunlight from their own world to heal.

Instinctively, Natalie scrambled like a monkey up the ever-thickening beanstalk that had grown well up past the portal. Caitlin was overjoyed that her sister was on her way home. But Caitlin knew it wasn't time for her to return just yet. The truth was still waiting for her.

She smiled warmly at Amethyst. Then Jack. She broke down crying when her eyes found Rapunzel. And Snow. And Beauty. They all wept.

When Caitlin had finally recognized the scepter, a truth had surfaced. The one that had devastated a vulnerable, inconsolable young girl.

Was she ready to confront it?

She wasn't. But Caitlin had found new courage when she helped others overcome their own pain. Her sibling. Her new friends. And so now she would help one more person . . .

"Where is she?" Caitlin asked as she turned to Amethyst.

He spread his wings. With his left, he pointed *behind* Caitlin.

She turned.

Everything seemed out of focus. Blurred. Caitlin rubbed her eyes. Out of the shapeless blur emerged a razor-sharp . . . Queen of Hearts!

She walked toward Caitlin as if in slow motion. Her arms were poised to strike, fingers fixed like claws. "You shattered my scepter!"

"Yes. But it was always *mine*."

"Who. Are. You?"

Caitlin laughed and cried at the same time. Her heart pounded as stinging tears fell from her eyes. "Take off your red glasses," Caitlin said. "And come see who I am."

The queen laughed incredulously. "No need, for I can sense you. You are rebellious. And obviously dangerous."

She's sensing me through those enchanted glasses! She's perceiving the opposite!

Caitlin suddenly realized what she had to do. She searched deep for a place untouched and raw. As fragile as a dry, crisp leaf. A dim flame of violet-blue suddenly flared in scintillating brilliance inside her.

And then Caitlin harnessed all of that emotion and yelled.

"I hate you! Do you hear me? I *hate* you. I don't ever want to see you again. Ever! You are dead to me!"

A tear rolled out from under the red glasses of the queen.

My God! It's working!

The queen raised her right arm to her face. With two fingers she removed the cursed red glasses, unmasking her face.

The queen let out an anguished scream that cut through Caitlin and resounded through the kingdom.

The queen recoiled.

She clutched her face and shielded her eyes.

Caitlin composed herself.

"Mom . . . Mommy . . . It's me. Look . . . Please, look!"

Evelyn Fletcher froze.

Her hands came away from her face. But her eyes remained tightly closed. She seemed almost frightened to turn toward the voice . . . but she did.

Her head tilted to one side. Her eyes opened slowly. She squinted, as though the brightness of truth had touched her eyes and brought with it a great pain. She blinked like a newborn infant seeing the world for the very first time. As if seeing the world right-side up and true.

Her green eyes found Caitlin. Evelyn Fletcher was a strikingly beautiful woman, despite her current heart-shaped hairdo.

Wisps of color continued to descend from the rainbow, showering the world with light. Life returned to her mother's eyes. So did a gleaming spark of awareness and the luminous light of love stolen from her by the enchanted eyeglasses.

"Oh my goodness . . . dear God . . . Caitlin . . . my precious Caitlin . . ."

Caitlin Rose Fletcher rushed into her mother's arms. Evelyn Fletcher seized her daughter. They squeezed and hugged one another tightly and deeply as they sobbed and wept uncontrollably. Her mother then leaned back to behold her daughter, tenderly brushing away the wet from her cheeks, caressing her forehead, laughing, crying, and again pulling Caitlin close—so very close. Caitlin prayed that all of this was real.

Amethyst pulled a hanky from a pouch. He dabbed his misty eyes and said, "Sorry to break up this long-overdue reunion, but the portal is almost closed."

Caitlin squeezed her mom. "What happened to you?"

Evelyn Fletcher spoke through her sobs and laughter. "I remember that you bought the wand. To help you cope with your fears. It hurt me deeply to see you suffer. We were in London. On your birthday. I went to visit the grave of your grandfather—to ask for his help. I brought the wand. I also stopped at the grave of Lewis Carroll."

"You mean Charles Dodgson."

Evelyn Fletcher laughed through her tears. "Yes, I mean Charles Dodgson. Honey, I read you *Alice's Adventures in Wonderland* every night. You couldn't get enough of it. I asked him for help as well, to give you the strength and creativity and conviction to overcome your challenges without having to rely on a toy wand. A strong wind came and knocked the wand from my hand. It landed on top of his grave." Evelyn Fletcher shook her head. "And that's all I can remember. I feel as though I've been sleeping for a lifetime."

Amethyst landed beside Caitlin. "Your mother was taken by a dark and dangerous being, Caitlin. He came through the portal to your world and brought your mother here. He knew all about the Spectrum. How to manipulate the colors. But he needed the wand, for it had become infused with the power of human imagination. Your imagination. He wasn't human and could not unleash its power. So he blinded Evelyn Fletcher, erasing her memory by employing the dark arts. Those dreadful glasses made her see the world in reverse. Light became dark—and so did her heart. He used her and the wand to try to destroy the kingdoms of our world. He abducted the real Queen of Hearts and put your mother in her place. Which is why I sent the princesses after you. And they, in turn, sent Jack to find you."

Caitlin's heart skipped. "Jack?"

"Jack is from our world. You know, Jack Spriggins . . . and the beanstalk?"

She turned to Jack. He was wiping off his copper-colored suntan.

Makeup?

Jack was unnaturally pale. His eyes were rimmed in shadowy darkness.

"You're from here?" she asked, her eyebrows arced like bows.

"Born and bred."

Her fingers grazed her lips as a gleam of awareness dawned in her eyes.

"Those were *your* beans on my window ledge. It was *you* inside my room."

He nodded. "I came to find you, after you moved to London. I couldn't stay in my world during sunrise—or I'd become a Blood-Eyed. I went back and forth each night, using the different portals."

"How did you get up that hole? And climb the ten stories to my apartment?"

"I'm pretty good at scaling great heights," he said with a smile. "Using beans and soil, of course."

Caitlin, near speechlessness, wasn't sure if she wanted to laugh or cry. All those sightings in all those graveyards around the world . . . it had been Jack every time, traveling through the wormholes.

An ache rose inside of her. She feared the answer to her next question. "Will you be at school tomorrow?"

He bowed his head. When he shook it, her heart broke.

"Caitlin, you need to get back home—fast," Jack warned as he glanced back up and nodded at the eastern sky.

Caitlin couldn't even begin to imagine how much she'd miss him.

Evelyn Fletcher took her daughter by the hand.

"Caitlin, honey. I cannot come back either."

Caitlin's face reddened. "No!" she shouted. "The scepter is destroyed. The light and courage and the Green Spectrum! Everything's been restored! You can come home, Mom!"

Amethyst wrapped a silky wing around her. "Destroying the scepter eradicated the affliction of the Blood-Eyed. For that we are all grateful to you, young lady. But there was great damage done to our atmosphere by the scepter. Some of the Green Spectrum reaches us again, but much is still filtered out. Thus, a lot of work must still be done. Until we figure this all out, we will remain in this condition. Your mother as well. She's been here, under our sun, for many years. Your sun will no longer heal her."

Caitlin crossed her arms. "So that's it?" she said to her mom. "I lose you again?"

Evelyn Fletcher knelt before her daughter. She placed her hands firmly upon her shoulders. She held her close and whispered, "You will never lose me, Caity-kins. We will work to fix what's broken. We will."

Jack urgently strode over to Caitlin and took her hand. "You gotta go. The portal is almost closed."

She pulled her hand back. "I'm staying!" Caitlin commanded, as though she were a queen.

Evelyn Fletcher stood back up. "Caitlin Rose Fletcher, you march up that beanstalk *this instant*. And you help your sister and your father, and you play my records and go to school dances and live your life to the absolute fullest, young lady! This will all work out in the end."

Caitlin couldn't believe how beautiful her mother was.

Fifteen hundred zombies broke out in applause and soft song. Caitlin choked up. Their sweet-sounding hymn filled her with inexpressible emotion.

Suddenly, from out of the crowd came someone that brightened Caitlin's heart. She was blonde, with zombie-pale skin, and she was dressed in a tattered blue-and-pink gown.

Cinderella!

She approached Caitlin and smiled warmly.

"You reshaped an entire universe, Caitlin. Saved countless lives."

"But everyone is still zombified."

Rapunzel lifted Caitlin's chin with her finger. "Only on the outside."

"You mean, like you?"

Rapunzel's face was angelic, with a gleam in her eye that bespoke deep wisdom. She winked. "Like us."

Snow White tapped Caitlin on the shoulder. "Because of you, we have an abundance of beauty and compassion in our hearts."

"And we managed to remain abundantly beautiful on the exterior as well," Cindy added, batting her eyelashes.

Amethyst rolled his eyes. "Evidently we're not short on self-admiration, either."

Jack stepped forward and dragged Caitlin by the arm over to the beanstalk.

Her mother came to her one more time, holding Caitlin's face gently and firmly in her delicate hands. She planted a kiss on her forehead. "Make me proud, my darling daughter."

And with that, Evelyn Fletcher stood back and waved.

Rapunzel came forth and kissed Caitlin on the cheek. "I have to say goodbye." Caitlin wrapped her arms around Rapunzel in a warm embrace. Her face pressed against Rapunzel's golden hair. It smelled of milky coconut and was soft as feathers. Caitlin wouldn't let her go. She firmed up her grip with her fingers.

"You're the older sister I always dreamed I had. Please look after my mom," she whispered in Rapunzel's ear.

Rapunzel broke away, crying. She offered a final fond wave and disappeared into a lush, green forest nearby.

"How's the gluten-free pizza in your neck of the woods?" Cinderella asked as she kissed Caitlin's cheeks one at a time.

Caitlin chuckled. "Order one sometime. I'll deliver it with extra hot peppers."

Cindy smiled warmly and winked. "Be sure to give Natalie a hug from *moi.*" She waved farewell as she danced toward the crowd of zombies. She snuggled up to one particular young man who was most attractive and handsome even through his zombification. He was attired in tattered royal raiment. Cinderella interlocked her arm with his.

Prince Charming nodded gratefully at Caitlin.

Snow White came forward with open arms.

"I am honored to know you, Caitlin."

Sleeping Beauty had fallen asleep. Caitlin gave her a goodnight kiss on her cheek and affectionately stroked her hair.

Caitlin's bottom lip quivered when she turned to Jack, who was now tugging on her arm to hurry her along.

"I thought you had to stay here?"

"I said I *lived* here. Doesn't mean I don't travel to other places. I climb beanstalks and battle giants, remember? And your world is a giant mess. Besides, you literally saved me from living dead forever after. And you saved my world. The least I can do is escort you back to your world. If you'll permit me."

Caitlin felt a ray of sun brighten her heart. "Such a gentleman."

Jack winked. "You good to go?"

"Good to go."

She gave one last look around. Lord Amethyst Bartholomew flitted over and wrapped his wings around her.

She whispered, "Did this really happen?"

Amethyst's antennae stiffened.

"Did it happen?" He waved an antenna and said, "Don't answer, young lady, it was a rhetorical question. But now that we're on the subject, what do *you* think?"

"Well, you really meant to say do I *know* it really happened, not do I *think* it happened." Caitlin raised a finger and continued. "But don't answer, Lord Amethyst Bartholomew—that was a statement, not a question!" They both smiled.

Jack started climbing. Caitlin followed. She turned back and blew a kiss to her mom. She held her gaze a moment longer, smiled, and then continued to climb.

Amethyst's voice echoed up the light shaft as she and Jack traveled at the speed of sound, courtesy of the rich, black soil of Zeno's Forest. "It's not the people looking at you on the dance floor that frightened you. It's that you cared what they thought. Repel the red and let go. Then, my dear, you'll always dance unbothered and free . . . like a clay-covered, short-haired zombie."

CHAPTER FORTY-FIVE

SHE WOKE AS IF SHE HAD BEEN SLEEPING WITH A HIGH FEVER. HER chest was sweaty, her bones lethargic, and her legs heavy as iron. The fragrant scent of moist grass and fresh dirt filled her nostrils as she blinked her eyes open. Cool night air brushed against her cheeks.

Caitlin twisted her torso, extended her limbs, and yawned a prodigious yawn. She savored the pleasurable sensation of stretching her body and muscles into wakefulness.

She was lying next to the headstone of Charles Dodgson, aka Lewis Carroll. A sea of stars winked at her through the dark, purple sky above. The moon hung like a narrow lantern, spilling slivers of light.

There was no rainfall, but the grass felt damp. She had hardened mud on her arm. She sat up. The feverish feeling suddenly passed. Now she felt oddly refreshed.

Caitlin looked around. Right. Left. Mount Cemetery was empty except for a scattering of trees and staggered rows of graves that stretched into darkness.

She hopped to her feet and brushed away blades of grass, autumn leaves, and soil.

Caitlin spotted her digital tablet lying by the foot of Dodgson's grave. She picked it up and touched the screen. How long had she slept?

The date and time glowed. She gasped.

Ten minutes?

How could that be possible? That intensely vivid dream felt like it had lasted for days. And it had seemed so achingly real. Caitlin could not begin to imagine how her subconscious fueled such a profoundly weird experience. Part of her felt as though she had just climbed out of a high-efficiency, top-load washing machine. All the soot, soil, and splotches had been wrung out of her.

The sorrow, too.

She slipped her phone into her pocket. And then Caitlin Fletcher began a long-overdue walk through Mount Cemetery.

Somehow she knew which grassy hill to climb, which shadowy trees to pass, where to turn right and where to turn left.

She stopped in front of a particular plot of headstones.

She released a big breath. The pressure had all but dissipated from her neck and shoulders.

Caitlin had finally come face-to-face with the grave. She was ready to confront the *incident*. The truth. She stared at it solemnly. The date inscribed on it was the same as Caitlin's tenth birthday. And now it stood before her under a thick blanket of stars.

E<small>VELYN</small> F<small>LETCHER</small>
B<small>ELOVED</small> W<small>IFE</small>, L<small>OVING</small> M<small>OTHER</small>
W<small>HO WILL</small> <small>FOREVER</small> <small>LIVE IN OUR</small> H<small>EARTS</small>

My mom—the Queen of Hearts.

Caitlin smiled on the outside and wept inwardly. The psyche had a funny way of repairing broken hearts.

Caitlin began rocking side to side as she gazed at the marker.

She had been too grief-stricken to say good-bye last year when her mom was finally declared dead after having been missing for three years. Caitlin had refused to accept her mom's disappearance. And then she buried the painful truth about her passing when it surfaced last year and the grave marker went up across from her grandpa's.

Caitlin never attended the funeral in Guildford. But she was here tonight to say her good-byes.

"I love you, Mom. And one day I promise to read stories to my children, just like you did for me. I'll teach them the dances you taught me, and introduce them to your favorite music . . . " Caitlin sniffled as she whispered. "They'll learn all about their lovely grandma."

In the distance behind her, Caitlin heard the crumpling of leaves and the steady snap of breaking twigs.

She waited for the footsteps to find her.

As Caitlin continued to gaze at the marker, a wry voice called out from behind the headstone of her grandfather's grave, directly behind her.

"Hey, Caity-pie!" Natalie shouted. "Told ya you weren't adventurous."

"Yeah, yeah," Caitlin said.

"Did I fall asleep?" Natalie asked. "How long were we here? I had the most oddball dreams. There was a kaleidoscope of imagery that symbolically suggested a subconscious—"

"Will you shut up!"

Caitlin turned to face Natalie. Her sister's eyes were bloodshot. Her face slightly pale.

Suddenly, Girl Wonder's mouth fell open.

"Caitlin, what on earth happened to you?" Natalie was staring at her all bug-eyed.

"What do you mean?"

Natalie pointed. "Your hair. It's gone. You cut it all off! And you're wearing zombie makeup!"

Huh?!

Caitlin reached for her long locks. They weren't there!

Strangely, Caitlin Fletcher did not feel compelled to panic. Nor did she feel frightened or shocked or confused. Rather, a heartening smile touched her lips, followed by a whimsical giggle.

This actually made perfectly ridiculous sense to her.

"Don't you remember the ghouls?" Caitlin asked Natalie. "Snow White, Rapunzel . . . You *must* remember Cinderella."

It wasn't often that Natalie wore a dumbfounded look on her face.

Caitlin was delighted the pink was gone from Natalie's eyes. Perhaps the sunlight reflecting off the moon had already begun to heal her. The pain in Caitlin's leg had already dissolved, she noticed.

Caitlin's thoughts were interrupted by the buzz of her mobile.

"Caitlin, where *are* you?"

Harold Fletcher's words came through quickly when she answered her phone. His voice was higher pitched than normal.

"Your sister's not here and I—"

"It's okay, Dad; she's with me."

"Natalie's with you at the dance?"

"I'm not at the dance—yet."

"Where are you?"

"I went to visit mom first."

There was a long silence.

Caitlin could hear her dad breathing. It sounded like his breath was quavering. She thought perhaps she heard a snuffle.

Caitlin so badly wanted to hug her father right now. He had *never* been in denial about her mom. He had simply been patient with his daughter.

He cleared his throat. "Honey . . . I waited so long for you, to . . . to let go. For this to happen, for you to be able to say good-bye to her. Please listen, please listen . . . I am so, so very proud of you."

"I know you are, Dad. And thank you."

"How did you even get there so late at night, and how are you getting back? Should I come get you?"

"We took the train. And you don't have to come get me. We'll take the train back. I'm also here with Jack."

Where the heck was "that boy Jack"?

"I love you, Caitlin. Do you hear me?"

"I know, Dad. Love you too."

"Okay, honey. I'll see you both at home after the dance. Nine thirty, right?"

"You said ten, remember?"

"Okay, but not a minute later!"

"Thanks, Papa Bear."

She disconnected.

"There you are!" a familiar voice said from behind Caitlin. "I looked all over this graveyard for you."

Natalie was now pointing behind her. "When did *he* get here?"

Caitlin's face widened into a broad smile.

"Jack?"

She turned to greet him, breathless and bright-eyed. A sliver of pale moonlight fell upon Jack's face. He was slightly scarred and silver-toned, making for one good-looking zombie knight. His grin was infectious. "Thought I wouldn't show up?"

Caitlin beamed. "You always show up, Jack."

"Hey, Romeo and Ghouliet," Natalie said with a confused look on her face, "Can we search for an all-night diner? A traditional English one. I have this sudden weird craving for blood pudding." Her face scrunched up even more. "I think I can totally smell the leftover blood pudding in our fridge from here. How freaky."

She was serious.

"Jack, she's serious."

"Don't worry," he whispered. "Those urges will pass at sunrise."

Jack brushed dirt off his tunic.

"Hey, what time is it?" Jack asked Caitlin.

"Three minutes after eight."

Jack took out his chain-mail cowl from his tunic and slipped it over his head. He stood in front of Caitlin and formally offered his hand. "May I escort m'lady to the Kingshire Masquerade Ball? There's still time to make it."

Caitlin took his hand and curtsied. "Why, of course . . . Sir Jack the zombie knight! As long as you don't mind this one tagging along." She nodded toward Natalie, who took off and was soon halfway down the path.

"Meet you at the front gate," Natalie's voice echoed. "I want to snap a few more shots of the front of this place before we head out."

Caitlin and Jack began to make their way along the road leading out of Mount Cemetery. The stars above twinkled like diamonds. The air was sweet and fresh from the evening's rainfall.

"How long can you hang out *here*?" Caitlin said.

"Until after we win first prize for best zombie costumes at the masquerade ball."

"No. Seriously."

"I'll head home after the dance."

"You mean like *home* home, down *there*?" Caitlin pointed

to the ground. "And what happens when you're not at school tomorrow?"

"The principal will be receiving a note from my parents, telling him that we moved to Scotland."

"Scotland?"

"What's wrong with Scotland? J. M. Barrie's buried there."

"The author of *Peter Pan*? Very cool. Hey, do you know him?"

"J. M. Barrie?"

She rolled her eyes. "No, silly. Do you know Peter Pan?"

"Know him? I had a run-in with him before all of this dodgy zombie business happened. We're combative rivals."

Jack casually rested his hands in his pockets as he strode along. He had a slight limp in his step, she noticed. "But he's a good mate. Why, do you fancy *him* now?"

Caitlin stopped in her tracks. "You're jealous!"

"Of him? Not one bit." Jack made an unruffled face. "Pan's too young for you anyhow."

They continued to stroll. Natalie's voice rang out. "Forget blood pudding. Let's do beef kabobs and hummus!"

Caitlin made eyes at Jack. "So, what do I tell my dad when I come home looking like a short-haired zombie?"

"Remind him that it's Halloween."

Caitlin smiled mischievously. "Do you really think we can win best costume?"

He held her hand as a thin cloud passed in front of the crescent moon. A soft, piney wind blew. "Look at us. How could we lose? But that's not the real prize I fancy."

Caitlin mocked a British accent. "Which prize *do* you fancy, Sir Jack Spriggins?""

"Best dancers at the ball, m'lady!"

Natalie Fletcher took off again just as they caught up to her. She ran to the other side of the road, straight across from the Mount Cemetery entrance.

She aimed her camera at her sister.

Jack took out a gift-wrapped package and presented it to Caitlin. She smiled appreciatively. And then, with playful eyes, she unwrapped the box to find a dainty bottle of perfume called Elisabethan Rose.

"Happy Birthday, Caitlin Rose Fletcher," Jack said.

She swooned.

Natalie's camera flashed.

Caitlin smiled. This was the perfect scene for the last photo taken at Guildford's Mount Cemetery. Caitlin and Jack sharing a hug by a wrought-iron gate beneath an autumn moon as a lone crow cawed faintly in the night.

EPILOGUE

CAITLIN AND JACK TIED FOR THIRD PLACE FOR BEST ZOMBIE COStume. At first, Caitlin felt robbed. But she quickly concluded it was a fair-minded decision. After all, technically speaking, she and Jack weren't really wearing makeup or costumes. They were the real deal.

They didn't get a trophy for the best couple's dance, either. They were, in fact, expelled from the competition. As adept as Jack was at fighting trolls, leaf surfing, and piloting winged insects, as a dancer sporting a leg splint he was as clumsy as a drunken dog on a trampoline.

He stomped on two people's toes and bounced one poor couple into the punch bowl, making quite the splashing mess.

There was a silver lining for Caitlin. Caitlin Rose Fletcher had danced at the All Hallows Eve Masquerade Ball—without a mask and without a panic attack.

Who needs a trophy?

When the Kingshire All Hallows Eve Masquerade Ball had ended, she and Jack wandered out to the parking lot.

Jack gave Caitlin a warm hug and a kiss goodnight.

"Promise to see me again? Like on a date?" Caitlin asked.

"Only totally."

Natalie burst out of the building with her mouth full. "Eew. Gross, guys. Is it time to go home yet?"

It was.

Caitlin and Natalie Fletcher snuck in past their snoring dad just before 10 p.m.

Caitlin snuggled into her warm bed and opened her laptop. She started writing her column for unexplainednews.com.

Before long a slow yawn came, as did the heavy eyelids and, in the middle of typing a sentence, Caitlin fell into a deep sleep.

Something woke her an hour later.

Her laptop was in sleep mode and resting on her chest. She grabbed it and leaned over to put it on her nightstand. The lit screen cast a soft glow in her bedroom.

That's when Caitlin saw the girl.

Her blood ran cold.

The girl stood motionless by her bedside.

Caitlin had to cup her own mouth with her hand to stop from screaming.

The girl was dressed in a tattered, pale-blue dress with puffed sleeves and a white pinafore. Her stockings were striped. Caitlin sighed in relief.

Alice. From Wonderland.

Zombified and pretty as a peach.

"You forgot about me," Alice said.

A heavy wave of tiredness suddenly came over Caitlin. She had to fight to keep her eyes open. "What are you doing here?"

"He abducted us."

Caitlin yawned. "Who?"

"The Lord of the Curtain."

She yawned again.

"The *who* of the *what?*"

"The Lord of the Curtain. The one who took your mother. The one they call the Enchanter."

"Can you e-mail me the rest of this story?"

Caitlin flopped her head onto her pillow.

Alice grabbed hold of Caitlin's foot and shook it.

"Go away . . . I'm trying to sleep," Caitlin mumbled.

Alice continued. "After you destroyed the scepter, we were still held captive in his lair. Peter Pan came to rescue us and helped us escape. Now the Lord of the Curtain is upset."

"Tell him to take a pill and chill. I'm going back to bed." She pulled a pillow over her head.

Alice wagged a finger. "Caitlin, listen to me. This is not someone anyone would want to upset. Do you know Captain Hook?"

"Not personally."

"And the Wicked Witch of the West? Plus the Wicked Queen and the evil stepsisters and the Red Queen and Long John Silver and all evil-minded monsters who seek to destroy and frighten and bring darkness to the world?"

"Like my English lit teacher?"

"Caitlin Rose Fletcher, your mother is the one who sent me to call on you."

That jolted Caitlin out of her slumber. She sat up in her bed. "Okay. I'm listening."

"The Lord of the Curtain is the one who gave the Wicked Witch of the West and all the immoral, cutthroat villains their power. He is the inciter of their dark ways. A maker of monsters. He's not the bringer of darkness or the cause of the cold that comes from the dead." Alice's face grew grim. "He *is* the darkness. He *is* the cold."

The temperature in the room dropped.

"We need your help," Alice said.

Caitlin's voice softened. "Look, Alice. I just got home. I have a test in algebra on Tuesday, and I plan to start dance classes two nights a week. I'm really trying to change my life. When do you need me to go back?"

"You don't have to go back."

"Oh. Okay. Why not?"

"He's coming here. To your world."

The room was so cold now that Caitlin's breath turned to fog. She pulled her comforter closer.

"When?"

Alice took out a pocket watch. *White Rabbit* was engraved on its backside.

Alice checked the current time. 2:37 a.m.

"About an hour ago."

THE END

EXPLORE THE WORLD OF OUAZ

www.onceuponazombie.com

www.caitlinfletcher.com

www.facebook.com/onceuponazombie

@onceuponazombie

www.unexplainablenews.com

WATCH FOR THE SEQUEL

ONCE UPON A ZOMBIE

BOOK TWO

COMING SOON

TO YOUR FAVORITE BOOKSTORES